W9-BYQ-647

A Fatal
Finale

A Fatal Finale

Kathleen Marple Kalb

KENSINGTON BOOKS
www.kensingtonbooks.com

KENSINGTON BOOKS are published by

Kensington Publishing Corp.
119 West 40th Street
New York, NY 10018

Copyright © 2020 by Kathleen Marple Kalb

All Kensington titles, imprints, and distributed lines are available at special quantity discounts for bulk purchases for sales promotion, premiums, fund-raising, educational, or institutional use. Special book excerpts or customized printings can also be created to fit specific needs. For details, write or phone the office of the Kensington Special Sales Manager: Attn. Special Sales Department. Kensington Publishing Corp, 119 West 40th Street, New York, NY 10018. Phone: 1-800-221-2647.

Library of Congress Card Catalogue Number: 2019953659

Kensington and the K logo Reg. U.S. Pat. & TM Off.

ISBN-13: 978-1-4967-2723-7
ISBN-10: 1-4967-2723-1
First Kensington Hardcover Edition: May 2020

ISBN-13: 978-1-4967-2729-9 (ebook)
ISBN-10: 1-4967-2729-0 (ebook)

10 9 8 7 6 5 4 3 2 1

Printed in the United States of America

Acknowledgments

It still feels like a miracle that we made it here.

This all starts with my agent Eric Myers, and my editor, John Scognamiglio. Thank you for giving Ella, and me, a chance. Much appreciation to the team at Kensington for getting Ella ready for showtime.

Special thanks to Ben Mevorach, my boss at 1010 WINS, for years of support and understanding, and to my mentor Mark Mason for the break that made everything else possible.

I don't have enough words for my weekend WINS family. You saved me in every possible way, from beta reads to endless discussions of plot points, to simply talking me down. It took a lot more than 22 minutes, but you gave me the world.

Deepest and most personal thanks to Dr. Andrew Zelenetz and the staff at Memorial Sloan Kettering Westchester, and Dr. Annapoorna Kini and the staff at Mount Sinai's Cardiac Lab, for making sure my husband is here for this day . . . and for their kindness to the crazy lady with the laptop.

Similar gratitude to my eye surgeon, Dr. Aron Rose; it helps to be able to see the screen!

Yes, 2018 really was *that* year. Surviving was enough, but we were blessed with so much more.

Which brings me to my family. To my mother, who believed—my husband, who *knew*—and my son, who bought the first copy . . . none of it happens without you.

With love, awe and appreciation,
Kathleen Marple Kalb

Chapter 1

She Was Her Man

Juliets are more trouble than they're worth. We have never yet hired one who did not bring some spectacular disaster down upon the company, and quite often herself. Every time, Tommy does his best to choose the soprano who seems sane, quiet and smart enough not to waste the opportunity, and, still, something goes terribly wrong. Our first eloped with the tenor in Chicago. The second took sacred vows at a convent in Boston. And then there was the third Juliet. It's enough to make a Romeo wonder—and certainly enough to make a diva take other operas on the circuit.

This time, New Haven was the last stop on the tour, leaving us just a short train ride from home in New York and my next bookings in the City. We'd sold out Poli's Wonderland for the run, even though we had played it just two years before, admittedly with a different repertoire. The Bellini *I Capuleti e i Montecchi* is always a winner, and there are still plenty of people willing to plunk down good cash money to see trouser diva Ella Shane in her most famous role. And I'm quite happy to oblige them. I didn't grow up with nearly enough to afford pretensions.

Besides, I like Romeo. While I'm nearly twice his age now, the score is wonderful and the role, of course, is a great deal of fun for me, and, better, for the audience. Yes, I know that there's the whole frisson of an attractive adult woman in doublet and hose making operatic love to the soprano, but I am not responsible for what people think in the dark of the theater. I know who I am, and am not, and I love putting on a good show.

That icy night in February 1899, I was just hoping that my latest Juliet would behave herself in the final duet. Miss Violette Saint Claire (who almost certainly was not born with that name, not that Ellen O'Shaughnessy can throw stones) had been doing her level lightweight best to overshadow me. First, I had gently pointed out that the audience gets a better show if we all work together. When that proved fruitless, I had Tommy rather less kindly remind her that the marquee says "Ella Shane Opera Company," and when it says "Violette Saint Claire," she can chew all the scenery she likes.

In the wings, preparing to walk out into the footlights, I was trying to think about the music and my technique, and not her escalating overacting. For Heaven's sake, I thought irritably, it is almost the twentieth century. We do not need the florid nonsense that people used to find acceptable in the 1830s.

I am, naturally, well aware of the irony of an opera singer complaining about overacting. But as Tommy's been known to say, I know it when I see it. And indeed I saw it that night, as Violette sang her little heart out, climbing all over me, and making sure the audience got a much better look at her sweet, heart-shaped face than mine. Too bad this one didn't run off with the tenor.

Not that I was worried about the competition; while she was undeniably lovely, with black hair, pale blue eyes and perfect white skin, I'm not exactly unappealing myself.

Tall, of course, with greenish-blue eyes and, thank you, naturally blond hair with a reddish cast, all perfectly set off by my midnight-blue costume. Though, when the curtain is down, I'm more likely to be smiling, or laughing at Tommy's latest joke, than cultivating the soulful look you might have seen in my *cartes de visite*.

At least it was quiet at the moment. After the intermission, there'd been some kind of donnybrook among the young stagehands. It had happened before, though not in usually professional New Haven. This scuffle wasn't especially serious, unlike the incident in Cleveland where one hand tossed another right into the orchestra pit, ruining the rehearsal, the timpani and his career in the performing arts.

Tonight, though, all I'd heard was a treble voice yelling, "Take yer hands off me, ye *nathrach*. I'm done wi' ye!" and some running footsteps.

If it had gone any further than that, I'd have had to ask Tommy to have a word, which I absolutely did not want to do. From the accent, the boy was fresh off the boat, probably from Scotland, and he almost certainly could not afford to lose his livelihood.

In any case, I had other concerns just then. Beyond the warring stagehands, the aggressively lovely Miss Violette would still be in need of correction later tonight, and I owed the audience my best in the final scene.

Whoever might be the fairest of them all, real talent beats overwrought hopeful every time. I finished my final aria and expired, satisfied to hear that moment of absolute silence from the audience that means they're truly moved.

As Violette took her turn, I watched her through my eyelashes, suddenly realizing she looked really sick. Jealousy's an ugly thing, I reflected, only slightly uncharitably, as she collapsed on me with a strangled cry, without finishing her final notes. How very unprofessional, I thought, remembering the many times I'd pushed through all manner of unpleasantness.

She didn't move during the last few moments of the show, but thanks to the heavy costumes we all wear, I did not realize she wasn't breathing until the curtain was falling.

"Tommy!" I yelled, thoroughly inelegantly, as I tried to climb out from under her and see what I could do to help.

Tommy Hurley, my cousin, manager, best friend, and rock, ran over from the wings, his usually cool blue-green eyes wide with concern. "What happened?"

"There's something very wrong with Violette."

It was one of my more magnificent understatements.

Chapter 2

In Which We Meet the Wicked Duke

Late April, in Washington Square

"Come on, Tommy. At least try to parry," I urged, swiping my foil. Really, I should stop practicing my fencing with him, but I didn't have anyone else at the minute, and it's like dancing—you have to stay sharp. I usually alternate days between the two, and, no, I don't even attempt dancing with Toms.

"I'm trying, Heller." He rarely calls me by anything but the childhood nickname, earned during any number of street scuffles. "Too bad you don't box."

"Sorry, Champ"—I pointed, jokingly, to my face—"can't afford to risk my lovely visage."

Tommy laughed. He really had briefly been a top fighter, until he decided that no amount of violence would make him the man he wasn't, and didn't want to be, and turned his management skills from his career to mine. He'd gotten out soon enough that he still had the muscles and dangerous air, but no noticeable damage to his sharp Celtic features. "Hard to hit the high notes with a bloody nose."

"Too true." I moved back into position. "All right, just try to keep up."

" 'Try to keep up'!" squawked another voice from the rafters as Montezuma swept down toward us.

I like to think of the studio as my domain, but in truth, it belongs to Montezuma, my Amazon parrot. He requires space to fly, and enjoys singing along when I vocalize. Tommy and his sports writer friends are also fond of Montezuma, and, unfortunately, they've taught him a few colorful turns of phrase.

Montezuma came with the town house, a condition of sale from the importer who'd owned it, and had given him run of the attic, which the bird kept, once it became the studio. I call him "my" parrot, even though one doesn't really own such an amazing creature, because he's attached himself to me. Montezuma flew just over our heads, took a perch at a window and started preening his vivid green feathers with his bright blue beak, enjoying the spring breeze as much as we were.

"There's someone here to see you, miss," Rosa, the housemaid, called, running in ahead of a very tall, dark stranger.

"Oh?" I stepped away from Tommy, still holding my foil.

"He says he's a duke or something." Her big brown eyes were wide with excitement.

"Everybody's got a confidence game." Tommy chuckled as the man walked in.

"Not a confidence game at all, my good man. I am Gilbert Saint Aubyn, Duke of Leith."

"Of course, you are," I replied, taking a good look at him. Whoever he was, he was certainly a positive addition to the rehearsal studio. He was several inches over my height, with nearly black hair, ice-blue eyes and enough time on him to make him interesting. Not ostentatiously dressed—a neat black coat over a dark gray day suit, a plain black fedora in his hand—so he might just be something real, and not a swell. But probably just another opera fancier, if at least a creative and nice-looking one, so I decided we'll give him a minute or two.

"Are you Miss Shane?"

"None other." I held out my hand to shake, but he didn't take it. I remembered that British aristocrats are very uncomfortable with the new American ways. The accent seemed right, too; I'd spent enough time singing for my elegant supper in London to recognize the vowels, and pick up a faint trace of somewhere else in the consonants. I put my hand in my pocket, and did my best not to giggle as I realized he was trying very, very hard not to look below my face.

He would not have seen much if he had; I was wearing one of Tommy's discarded shirts loosely tucked into a pair of dark blue cotton cavalry twill breeches so old I didn't remember where I'd acquired them. With, of course, the light, but modest, underpinnings any proper lady would wear with such.

"Good. I am trying to gather information on the fate of a young lady. You would have known her as Violette Saint Claire."

The giggle strangled in my throat. Poor, dead Juliet. The New Haven coroner had ruled it accidental, for the sake of her family, if they were ever found, but since it was real poison in the prop vial that only she touched, we all knew what it really was. "Oh, dear. I'm terribly sorry. Was she a relative?"

"A cousin. I am the head of the family, of course, so I am taking charge of finding out what happened to her." A muscle flicked in his jaw, and the skin around his eyes tightened a little, the way it does when people are trying not to show too much emotion.

"Well, Your Grace, I don't know how much you know."

"I have already seen the report from New Haven. I want to know what she was doing with you *theater people*."

Tommy's eyes narrowed at the last two words, pronounced in a tone redolent with disdain, and the unmistakable suggestion of all manner of impropriety.

I offered a cool response as my sympathy for the Duke of Something died an early death. "'Theater people'?" I repeated.

"She was a gently-brought-up young lady who did not belong in that world."

Well, aren't you the precious one. I took a breath, and tried to tamp down my Irish temper. I explain—if not excuse—my next action as an effort to do something other than slap the judgmental scowl off his face. I grabbed Tommy's foil. "How's your fencing?"

"What?"

"My practice time is limited, and we *theater people* have to stay sharp to earn our keep. I'll talk to you while we spar."

Gilbert Saint Aubyn's stern face softened a bit. "All right."

He doffed his immaculately tailored coat and suit jacket, with a black armband still on the sleeve, no doubt for poor Violette or whatever her name really was. I had no compunction about taking a good look at him, and was not disappointed with what I saw. I may be a proper maiden lady, but I do appreciate the well-assembled male form, especially in a nicely fitted gray waistcoat, neat white shirt and dark trousers. I tossed him the foil, and he dropped it.

"Good thing we're fencing and not playing baseball," I observed, carefully not snickering, in case it was a feint.

Saint Aubyn, who would have been the late, lamented himself if this had been an actual duel, gave me a wry, and rather appealing, shrug. "I have not been on the field of honor in a while."

"Well, let's see what you've still got. *En garde.*"

I started on the attack. At first, he was very cautious, clearly uncomfortable with the idea of fencing with a woman. But he quickly realized I was much better than he was expecting, and began matching my parry and thrust. He was far more skilled than you'd have expected from that awkward start, but still nowhere near my level. Thankfully (and entirely uncharacteristically), Montezuma observed all of this without providing commentary. I knew it was just a matter of time.

"What was her real name?" I asked. Still better than fencing with Tommy, who was not always able to hang on to the sword for more than a few minutes.

"Lady Frances Saint Aubyn. Daughter of one of my uncles."

I let him back me up a bit before I went on the attack again. "She was a very well-trained operatic soprano." And a rotten little show-off, but we don't need to go into that.

"A lifetime of singing lessons wasted," he replied as I forced him back across the studio. "It is supposed to be merely a ladylike accomplishment."

"Clearly, she didn't see it that way." Parry.

"Clearly." Thrust.

"Singing opera is an honorable profession."

"Maybe for a woman who has to earn her way in the world." He nodded as he attacked. "I will give you that."

"Generous of you." I met the attack and very nearly twisted the foil out of his hand.

"Well done. I probably deserved that." He smiled faintly

as he backed up and regrouped, then started toward me again. "She ran off two years ago. We got a letter from the coroner of New Haven. I gather you did not know she had a family."

"No. The last I heard, the authorities were still trying to identify her." I let him back me up a bit, before launching a new attack. "I am sorry we didn't know. I would have notified you myself."

His eyes met mine, cold blue. "Really?"

"Really. I run a respectable company, and I take care of my employees."

"Not so well, it seems."

"That's hardly fair." Thrust. Attack. "I am sorry about what she did, but we had no indication she was desperate."

"No?"

"The role was a big break for her. She certainly seemed happy about it. And before you ask, we protect our in-génues."

"Oh?"

"In every city we stay, they are placed at respectable women's hotels. And I personally make sure there is no fraternizing." Since I lost a Juliet to a tenor, but that's none of his business.

For a few moments, there was nothing but the sound of steel on steel. I clearly had the better of him, but he wasn't bad.

"You fence well, Miss Shane."

"You also, Your Grace."

"I note that you are familiar with the forms."

"I am an opera singer with a certain following." I smiled as I backed him off. "I have been a few places and met a few people."

Out of the corner of my eye, I saw Tommy grinning at that one.

"I don't doubt it." Saint Aubyn's eyes sparkled. "Might

we continue this discussion at some other time, perhaps dinner, without weapons?"

At that, I took a good hard look at him over the swords. "I am fond of tea at the Waldorf. I do not go out to dinner with men outside my family."

His brows flicked up and he almost missed the parry. "What?"

"I told you, I am a respectable maiden lady and an artist, not a chorus girl."

Tommy was laughing, but hiding it well. Of course, I hadn't said anything untrue; clearly, the Duke of Wherever didn't understand.

"Oh."

I had him almost in the corner now. "It is not my fault that you can't tell a soprano from a soubrette."

He half-smiled at that, and backed up, giving me a chance to corner him. "Actually, mezzo, no? Most trouser roles aren't soprano."

"I'll give *you* that."

"Well played." He tried one more attack, but I'd already backed him up too far to recover.

"Draw?" I offered in the interest of diplomacy.

"Draw. Nicely done."

We bowed.

"Try to keep up!" Montezuma pronounced from above.

Saint Aubyn laughed, completely changing his rather severe features. "Amazon parrot?"

"Montezuma is a very bad boy."

"'Montezuma'? My mother's is called Robert Burns. She's taught him some Gaelic."

My turn to laugh.

"He also sings 'Sweet Afton,' naturally, usually when Mother is pouring tea."

We nodded together as I put down my foil, and he tossed his back to Tommy, who caught it with a laugh.

Gilbert Saint Aubyn put his jacket on and favored me with a full, amazing smile. "This was not the conversation I was expecting, Miss Shane."

"Perhaps you need to adjust your expectations."

"With the new century coming, I suppose I might." He nodded to me. "Tea tomorrow?"

"Certainly."

"I will look forward to it. And not, I suspect, merely for the information I may gather."

He bowed to Tommy and me, bid us a gracious "good day" and walked out.

Tommy grinned at me as he left. "There goes trouble."

"That is a fine figure of a man," I admitted. "Even if he is an English stick."

"*'English stick'!*" crowed Montezuma.

I glared at him.

"Love the birdie!" he called, cocking his head and giving me the closest thing to an adorable smile that a creature with a blue beak can manage. Like any other male of my acquaintance, he had to have the last word.

Chapter 3

Dinner en Famille in
Washington Square

That evening, Tommy and I were alone for dinner, and so, for that matter, was Montezuma, since he was happily devouring seeds and carrots in the studio, as he did at most mealtimes. While Montezuma wasn't welcome in the dining room, we would have happily shared our table with Rosa, our housemaid; Anna and Louis Abramovitz, my costumer and accompanist—and their adorable small son, nicknamed "the Morsel"; or even Mrs. Grazich, the cook, for that matter, but they were all at their respective homes (in Mrs. Grazich's case, probably unwilling to break protocol by eating upstairs). Though we shared the comfortable and respectable town house in Washington Square these days, we both remembered far less happy bed and board down in the tenements of the Lower East Side.

Tommy's mother, my aunt Ellen, took me in when I was barely eight, after my mother finally succumbed to the consumption she'd been fighting, as long as I could remember, and went to join my father. All I had of my father was his name, and my mother's stories of the beautiful redheaded Irishman she fell in love with while standing in line at immigration. An outbreak of typhoid carried him off, just about a year after they had married over the objections of almost all of their world. He'd lived to see me, and hold me, and that was about all. It was enough for her.

I had more of her, including the Sabbath candlesticks that my aunt had amazingly allowed me to light every Friday night, even though she made it clear to the rest of her very Catholic brood that it wasn't something for them, and I still went to Mass to keep up appearances. By then, I knew enough about the world to be grateful for her understanding, and hope that whoever was in charge of the next world, they were kind enough to let my mother and father be together.

I'd always had an ear for music, singing while I worked, which was mostly helping Aunt Ellen clean houses for what we'd have called "our betters." I was ten when I happened to be dusting a piano one day at a lady's house when she heard me, and sat down at the bench.

"Sing for me, child. I've never heard anything like that."

The lady turned out to be the "respectable" sister of Madame Suzanne Lentini. Yes, that Lentini. Within a month after that day, I was dusting Lentini's piano in return for singing lessons. At first, I was just a pet, like a lapdog with an unusually good party trick. But I turned out to be a coloratura mezzo instead of a soprano like her, and so no threat as a protégée. Even better, I shot up to my full height early. Lentini and her manager, Art Fritzel, realized a tall girl with a big voice and the scrappy attitude to carry off a boy's role could be a sensation. And indeed I was.

A word here about "trouser roles," with an apology for the inevitable indelicacy. A couple of hundred years ago, there were a good number of castrati, men who'd been, well, un-manned, to keep their voices high. In our modern age, thankfully, we do not believe in such barbarism. But there were a good number of heroic roles written for these unfortunates, and someone has to sing them. Which brings us to me, a woman who has the vocal range to sing the part well, and the acting ability to perform believably enough.

I don't doubt that some people, men, in the audience are more interested in the frisson of an attractive woman in trousers, especially since there is no other respectable circumstance where a man might see a woman's legs in public. But this is opera, not the dance hall, and I am responsible only for my art, not what people think. Anna always makes my costumes with modesty in mind, and I am very careful to avoid vulgarity in my movements, so, really, any ill you may see is entirely in your own mind.

Lentini was my first Juliet, when I was still Romeo's age. I spent the next several years playing the opera houses in the City, occasionally going on the road with Lentini, including an amazing London run, and even a few solo bookings.

Everything changed when Lentini and Fritzel decided it was time to retire together to the Amalfi Coast, an absolute lightning bolt to anyone used to watching the regal diva and her small, scruffy manager argue about quite literally everything. Tommy had just defended his title with an impressive win, but I knew he was wretchedly unhappy, despite it all. I had several offers from companies in the City and elsewhere, but none felt right. I wasn't at all sure what I would do with myself without my mentors, until I met up with Tommy after a sparring session one afternoon, and it all suddenly fit together. He had an old trainer who served as his official manager, but he did most of his own bookings, logistics and other things, being the smart Irishman on the make that he is.

We were walking back to the small, but comfortable,

house where we'd ensconced Aunt Ellen and the younger ones (Uncle Fred was gone by then) when I looked hard at him.

"You're not happy."

"I'm a champion. Nobody will ever call me a 'sissy' again. What's not to be happy?"

That was true, as far as it went. He had spent a couple of terrible years on the wrong end of street scuffles before he grew seven inches in six months and started boxing. The tenement toughs sensed something different about him, whether it was his kindness to me, his open love of books and music or his unwillingness to join their attacks on easy targets. And it was true; he wasn't like the neighborhood brutes, and that was not a bad thing.

It was not until I was older, with a little more knowledge of the world, that I understood it was more than that. Many large Irish families have a brother who doesn't marry, and they quietly accept him as just not the marrying kind. Most of the time, people are glad of a single brother or uncle to live with an elderly parent, or take an interest in the care and education of a special niece or nephew. Aunt Ellen's brother Joe, her favorite after my father, cared for their widowed mother for many years, and always watched over the two cousins who were his godchildren.

Playground taunts like "sissy" might be muttered in an especially nasty family fight, but, usually, everyone manages happily enough, unless private matters somehow become public, and no one wants that. Better not to ask a question you don't want answered. The brother who doesn't marry is family and we love him, and that is always the most important thing.

For our part, Aunt Ellen and I knew Tommy would never bring home a wife, and were actually rather glad we would not have to share him with any other woman.

"Toms, I know you." I'd slipped my hand in his as I'd done as a little girl relying on her older cousin for protection. *"You'd be happier doing something else."*

"I'm not fit for much, Heller."

"Pish. You've fought your way to the top, and you manage your career brilliantly."

"'Manage'?" He smiled down at me, understanding immediately. *"Are you thinking about what happens now that Lentini and her little friend are leaving for Amalfi?"*

I shrugged. *"With a good manager, I could have a great solo career."*

"Turn my skills from pugilism to art?"

"Something like that. It might be fun. It would certainly be safer."

"All right, Heller. Let me think about it."

He hadn't needed much time to think at all. He retired before his next title bout—a very good thing, since the man he would have fought killed his opponent—and devoted his energies to the Ella Shane Opera Company tours and my solo engagements. And these days, if anyone uses words like "sissy" around Tommy, I slug 'em.

Well, I would, if I had to. Tommy was right. No one would believe "the Champ" and those slurs belong in the same sentence, much less dare use them in his presence. People either assume he chose to take care of me and Aunt Ellen instead of marrying, or that some unknown girl broke his heart. Good enough outside the family.

"Penny for your thoughts, Heller," he said as he tucked into a generous portion of Mrs. Grazich's shepherd's pie.

"Ancient history." I took a bite of my own. She is a magnificent cook. Nobody wants a Romeo who looks like Brünnhilde, but I eat very lightly the rest of the day, not to mention taking fencing and dance practice almost daily, so

I permit myself a fairly substantial dinner. "Ah, there's very little better than a good shepherd's pie."

"Good Shepherd?" Tommy chuckled. "Well, the pie is divine."

"Father Michael would absolutely approve." And would probably be over to enjoy some of Mrs. G's excellent cookery before the end of the week. That would send Mrs. G into raptures, since she loves cooking for the priest, and considers him a good influence. She watches over us like a lioness, though she's not nearly old enough to be the parent of grown-ups, and she's still quite pretty, with a sweet smile and a crown of braided blond hair.

"Yes, the good father." He smiled at the mention of his best friend as he sipped some lemonade; we don't usually have wine at dinner because we often have engagements or performances after—we are NOT one of those sanctimonious temperance houses. "Well, speaking of the excellent works of the Lord, what are you going to do about the Duke of Whatever?"

"First I am going to check his bona fides as much as I can. Then I am going to see what we have in our files about poor little Violette. And then, I am going to get a good night's sleep before I meet him for tea."

"I don't know what our files will have other than what Henry gave us about her. We really didn't know her very well." Tommy toyed with his fork as he thought for a moment. Henry Gosling is our booking agent, and he held the first audition for sopranos, sending us the three best. "Why don't I drop by Henry's office tomorrow while you're sipping the convivial beverage with His Grace?"

I chuckled, as he'd intended. We both read far too much and collect precious expressions. "Assuming, of course, that he is indeed His Grace."

"I didn't notice anything off. Upper-crust vowels and diction, very good but not flashy clothes, slightly antique manners?"

"All true. But there was a trace of somewhere else in the accent. Not much, just enough to make me wonder." I shrugged. "Probably nothing."

"Never hurts to be on your guard."

"Isn't that the truth!" I put down my fork. "We can settle the question of the duke right now." I got up and walked to one of the big bookshelves. The town house isn't large enough for a separate library, and since we are both ferocious bookworms, there are volumes everywhere. "We can at least find out if there is such a person, even if not that it's him."

My *Debrett's Peerage* was actually a bit dusty now, dating back to my first trip to London. I've been educating myself since my two spotty years of primary school, but I was absolutely not going to get caught short in England. So I'd read everything I could find about the empire on which the sun never sets, including buying a number of reference works like *Debrett's* and several etiquette manuals. I opened it and flipped through.

"So? Is he on the up?"

"Well." I scanned the page. "There is indeed a Dukedom of Leith—border lord, up near Scotland, which would explain the accent—and the current incumbent does, in fact, answer to Gilbert Saint Aubyn."

"All right, then."

I tapped the entry. "Age is right—midforties. Could be him."

"And?" Tommy asked archly.

"What?"

"Come on. It's not the aristocratic studbook for nothing. Is he free?"

"It doesn't matter. Even if he were, he wouldn't come

calling here. He would consider me a bit of fluff to be enjoyed and cast aside . . . and I'm damn sure not that."

Tommy smiled at my (not *entirely* unusual) profanity and shook his head. "Fifty years ago, maybe. He sure didn't look at you like you were a bit of fluff. World is changing, Heller."

"Not fast enough, Toms." I read the listing. "But, at least as of this edition, yes. Widowed—wife Millicent died more than ten years ago. Two sons, the traditional 'heir and spare.' Both adults now."

"What about our little Violette? Marriageable daughters are listed somewhere in there, too."

It took a little time to sift through the apparently rather prolific Saint Aubyns, but I found her, exactly where the duke said she would be. "Yes. Her too."

"So either he's on the up, or there's a person who's impersonating the Duke of Leith."

"Looks it. Now that I've made sure the people and dates are right, and we have an explanation for that accent, I'm willing to give it some credence."

"Heller, every man in the world is not one of your vile backstage admirers. Tommy shook his head. "I wonder if you'd be so cautious if he were some ugly old curio instead of a rather decent duelist in his prime."

"Not that good a duelist. I gave him the draw."

He grinned. "And if he's a very nice duke, perhaps you'll give him the time of day, too."

I tossed my napkin at him. "Enough. We have much to do before we sleep."

Sleep, however, eluded me for much of the night. I kept waking up back on that stage in New Haven, with a girl I realized I'd never known at all, wondering if I could somehow have changed the outcome.

Chapter 4

A Proper Cup of Tea

A lady who makes her living in a perhaps unladylike way must be especially vigilant as to her behavior. Particularly, when the lady in question practices a profession perilously close to that of the chorus girl, the preferred companion of many a gentleman of the world. So I err very much on the side of propriety at all times. Hence, the tea at the Waldorf.

It is true, as far as it goes, that I do not go out to dinner with men outside my family circle, if ever, and that I have absolutely no intention of becoming some swell's pet singer. As a blunt Lower East Side girl, I might observe—of course, to myself alone—that I'm nobody's whore. For public consumption, I put it more delicately, if equally emphatically: I am married to my art.

But at least part of that is because my art is probably the only suitable match for me. I am, unfortunately, reasonably sure that there's not the man living who would be a true companion. Quite honestly, I have no desire to trifle with anything less. Anyone who would be worthy would not be put off by my religion or my difficult childhood, but he *would* likely have a problem with my devotion to my career. So I poured my energy and love into my work, family and friends—and if on occasion I wished I did not sleep alone in my lovely brass bed, well, that was my business.

I spent that Thursday morning in vocal and other exercises, doing all the necessary work a disciplined singer must do to maintain the instrument and a healthy body to house it. In addition to being good for the physical health, it was excellent for burning off whatever weird shadows had been chasing me in the night.

Tommy took himself off to see Henry Gosling at about the same time as I left for tea, and we planned to sift through our findings at dinnertime. I had a treat in mind for myself after tea, a trip to my current lending library, not so far away. I had my book bag with me as I headed in, and a lesser personage might have raised eyebrows, but the staff knew me, and my reading habits. All I got from the girl who checked my coat and heavy bag was a smile and a few questions about which Shakespeare history play she might want to read next. The world is full of self-educated people, and the best of us try to help each other when we can.

I studied myself in the ladies' retiring room before heading in; it would not do to appear as anything less than Ella Shane, "the Diva," here, and especially not with the Duke of Whatever. Some society writer might spot us and remark on it, and I did not want the lead line to be a comment on my looks. Unless . . . it was a good one. It might just be, I reflected as I fluffed up the eggshell lace trim on the top of my lilac dress, a light wool suited to the changeable spring weather, with the slimmer sleeves that were the mode now. The hat was a matching confection of ribbons and lace, quite the thing of the moment. I made sure it was pinned at the perfect angle, of course, and that my hair was firmly in place in its soft knot.

My only ornament was my silver charm bracelet; while

many divas invest their earnings in jewels, or acquire them by less respectable means, I've never bothered with that. I enjoy looking at the gemstones and jewelry in the museums, but have no need for baubles of my own. Besides, I'd rather have my money invested in the town house, and Aunt Ellen's little brownstone, and a few other properties Tommy and I have bought over the years, than sitting on my fingers.

But I do enjoy having mementoes of the roles I've played, and various special milestones with close friends, as well as a sweet little watch, on my wrist. It's not what one would call serious jewelry, of course, but it's mine, and I love it.

As for the face, I did not "paint" off stage, as narrow-minded people are still wont to refer to the cosmetic arts, since I have clear fair skin (showing very few signs of age, thank you!) and naturally dark and thick brows and lashes. However, I did use a bit of rose petal salve on my lips, purely to protect them from the elements. All in all, fit for a king, never mind a Wicked Duke.

Saint Aubyn had already procured a table, a pot of tea and a tray of dainties, as protocol demanded. He did not, however, stand when I walked into the large, bright tearoom, a major breach of etiquette I would have found quite offensive, except that I quickly realized what the problem was. The duke didn't recognize me in feminine attire. I walked over to the table and simply stopped.

He stared for a moment. And then: "Miss Shane? You look quite different in your clothes." He realized what he'd said as soon as the words came out. I didn't know dukes could blush. "Um, that is, you look . . ."

I probably should have been insulted, but his embarrassment was truly hilarious—and also rather adorable. I laughed. "Well, then."

Saint Aubyn stood and very deliberately occupied himself with the gentlemanly business of getting the lady seated and settled, doing his best to pretend the earlier moment simply hadn't happened. It still took a fair amount of time for the blush to dissipate, but as much as I wanted to giggle at his discomfiture, I didn't.

"Shall I pour?" I asked, turning over my own teacup, and smiling at him over the porcelain bowl of oxeye daisies and pinks in the center of the table.

"Please," he said, composing himself into proper form.

Once the tea was poured, and the sandwich plate passed, he gave me a sheepish little shrug. "I apologize. I suppose I am a bit off balance."

"Understandable, considering the gravity of your errand."

"That, and this city of yours."

"Oh?"

"Since my arrival, I've been accosted by a pickpocket and almost run over by a hansom cab." He shook his head. "I assume neither was intended as a personal attack, but . . ."

"When you are new to the City, it can seem as if it is coming after you." I took it for nothing more than the new arrival's reaction, since there was no reason to suspect anything else.

"Quite right. At any rate, shall we begin again?"

"Certainly."

"Thank you, Miss Shane."

"My pleasure."

"I think it is, at that." His eyes twinkled. "You are looking quite lovely this afternoon."

"Thank you, Your Grace. It is finally warm enough to begin wearing the spring fashions."

"Is spring always so sullen in New York?"

"Depends on the day. I have never been in London in spring. Is it rainy?"

"It is always rainy in London." He smiled, and it really

was endearing. "We live for the rare sunny days, which are glorious, indeed."

"At least here, that first warm, sunny day makes one feel like they've come back to life after a long hibernation."

"Apt observation." Gilbert Saint Aubyn looked closely at me.

"I doubt I'm the first person to make it. Donne and Shakespeare both had some very moving passages on spring and rebirth." I did not betray my enjoyment at throwing what the baseball players would undoubtedly call a "trick pitch" as I added, "And probably Milton did, too, though I'm not as fond of him."

Saint Aubyn's pale blue eyes widened, and he smiled appreciatively. "He did. And I don't much like him, either. I only read him when the dons made me."

"*Paradise Lost* was just too heavy, and too religious for my taste." I'd given up about halfway through, despite my best intentions.

"I agree. I much preferred the more secular works, and especially Shakespeare's histories, with all that fighting and blood and intrigue."

"I prefer the comedies. All manner of adventures—and a happy ending, but only after everyone works for it."

He smiled. "Very American attitude, that."

"What?"

"That one must work for everything."

"That's life for most of us, Your Grace." I shrugged. "We don't get anything we don't work for, and sometimes fight for."

"Well, surely, occasionally one simply gets a gift from life."

"Maybe in your castle. Not often in the tenements of the Lower East Side."

"I didn't grow up in a castle, Miss Shane," he said quietly, toying with his teacup. "My family lived in a perfectly acceptable, but not fancy, town house in York. Thanks to any number of complications in the family tree, and several relations who obligingly died in various outbreaks and minor skirmishes, I inherited the title when I was twenty-five."

"Oh."

"So kindly don't assume that I'm some sort of cartoon aristocrat."

"Fair enough."

"As it happens, I find the whole system silly and outdated. And I'd happily let the castle crumble to rot as it wants to if I couldn't hear several hundred years' worth of ancestors' screams every time I think about it."

I smiled at him. "Well, so much for all the ink spilled on Wicked Dukes and Princes Charming."

"I don't have time to be wicked." He said it with such a beleaguered expression that I almost believed it. "But I should like to think I can be charming, when I want to be."

Those amazing silver-blue eyes were close on my face as he spoke, and I noticed that he had long, thick black lashes, to boot. I felt a truly impressive blush creeping over my cheekbones.

"So," he said finally, "you clearly know your Renaissance poets. Is that part of the curriculum on the Lower East Side?"

"No. I learned to read and cipher at the public school. After that, I was on my own. Thankfully, the City has many good lending libraries."

Gilbert Saint Aubyn gazed at me for a very long moment. "You are not what I was expecting."

"Sorry to disappoint you. It's a big city. I'm sure you can find some empty-headed chorus girls to share dinner with you, if that's what you'd like."

"Not at all." He shook his head. "I have no need or desire for chorus girls. I merely meant that when I found out

that Frances had joined an opera company, I had a particular picture of a touring diva and you are not it."

"You were expecting an aging, heavily-painted harridan
who led her company through the shadier parts of the
world? I can't deny such people exist. But I am not one of
them."

"No, you are not. You're quite an impressive lady. And
I have not even heard you sing."

"That's easily remedied," I said quickly, keeping things
moving to avoid drowning in those eyes. "I have an engagement early next week. A benefit performance, as it
happens, for a girls' school in my neighborhood."

"What are you singing?"

"An aria from *Xerxes*. It's an old, rarely done, Handel
piece with a marvelous lead role. Tommy teasingly calls it
my *General Shane Show*. I may take it on the road next
time."

"No more Romeo?"

"Not on the circuit. In May, a few weeks from now, I'm
doing the Balcony Scene with my favorite singing partner
at another benefit. But I won't be touring with *Capuleti*
next time."

"Does this have anything to do with Frances?"

"Perhaps." I looked at my teacup. "And I'm not sure I
want to die for love, night after night again, for a while."

"Oh."

I glanced up just at that second, and our eyes held. Too
long. "At any rate," I finally said briskly, "what can I tell
you about her, and her time with us?"

"Were there any signs of trouble?"

"None that we saw. She seemed to be very happy with
the role, which you may know is a real showcase for a
young soprano."

"Was she doing well?"

"Very well. New Haven was the last stop. Reviews were

good, and she would definitely have been able to parlay this into bigger things."

"Such as?"

"Probably the next step for her would have been a contract with a company in Boston or Philadelphia, some kind of regional operation that would cast her in several roles over a season and give her a chance to grow as an artist." I sipped my tea, and decided to permit myself one cucumber sandwich. "I don't doubt her booking agent would have been working on it."

"Would you be kind enough to find out for me?"

"Certainly." Tommy, of course, was doing just that even as we spoke.

"So, then, all rosy future for singing?"

"Singing isn't an easy career, you know. There are good runs, and setbacks, but, overall, things looked promising for her."

"So if not the work, then what?"

I shook my head. He was asking the question families like his had asked since time immemorial, and I had no good answers. Sometimes we don't know who is broken, or how, until it is too late. "I honestly don't know, and I'm terribly sorry about that."

He absorbed that in silence for a moment, swirling the tea in his cup contemplatively, if not with perfect manners. "Was there a young man?"

"Not that I knew about." I shook my head. "And I would have known. Even though she was not the confiding sort, there are very few secrets in a company."

"Apparently, she kept a very important one." The ice blue eyes burned into mine.

"Yes, by holding everyone at arm's length." I shook my head. "To the best of my knowledge, no one knew her well at all."

"But definitely no young man."

"It's probably the one thing I can say with absolute confidence." Whatever my personal views on road romances, I will never find myself in Chicago without a Juliet again. "There were—there always are—a few single men in the company, but this tour's bunch seemed far more interested in the pleasures of the road than in poaching in the dressing rooms."

One of his perfect black eyebrows flicked up.

"I am not aware of these pleasures in any kind of detail, Your Grace, only of their existence," I said rather stiffly. "But the young men tend to come in one of two types—those who partake, and those who don't. The ones who don't are the ones who concern me more, because they may be casting eyes on someone inside the company."

"I see." Saint Aubyn almost smiled. "You'd rather they were . . . partaking outside?"

I gave him a hard look. "I am a respectable maiden lady, but I am aware that young men have a great deal of energy, and most of them have to burn it off somehow."

"Perhaps they might stay in the boardinghouse reading their Bibles at night?"

I laughed. I had to. "You are teasing me."

"I am." He gave in to his smile. "You are just discussing this with such adorable maiden-lady seriousness."

"Oh." *Adorable? What?*

"Do you have any idea what this energy is and what they do with it?"

I scowled at him. "Only insofar as I know I do not want it anywhere near my sopranos."

"That's quite fair. And I appreciate your keeping this *energy* away from Frances. But I have heard that some young ladies actively seek it out."

"I am happy to say your cousin was not one of them," I assured him. "In our off-hours, she was learning new roles with my accompanist, or working on her German with the costumer."

"The costumer?"

"Anna Abramovitz, who, as it happens, is married to my accompanist, Louis Abramovitz. They're a lovely couple, with a sweet young son."

He nodded. "So no time for . . . partaking?"

I returned the nod quite firmly. "None."

"Well, that is some small consolation." He looked down into his tea again. "I can tell her mother that she was virtuous."

"Indeed you can."

"Thank you for that, Miss Shane." His eyes held mine very steadily. "It will matter a great deal."

"Anything I can do to ease a mother's heart. I do not wish that pain on anyone."

"Too true." He looked at his cup again. "It is a relief that it was ruled an accident. Otherwise, I would have had to fight the vicar . . ."

"No." I was honestly shocked. Surely, they didn't still deny suicides proper burial. "So narrow-minded, even in our day?"

"Rules are rules, Miss Shane. Aren't you Catholics just as—"

"I'm not a Catholic." I spoke before I thought.

"Oh?"

"At least not entirely."

He waited.

My faith is my own, and I don't talk about it with most people. But I also don't hide it. The way to defeat prejudice is to look it in the eye and take it on. Although I really hoped I would not see any here. "My mother was Jewish."

"So you are . . ." He watched me with curiosity, not disgust or anything else.

"Both."

"Is that even possible?" It was merely an honest question.

"I light candles on Fridays and go to Mass with Tommy."

"And when you pray, if you pray, to whom do you pray?"

"Don't we all pray to the same God?" I shrugged. "We may pray or worship differently, but there's surely only one Deity listening."

"That's what I hear." Saint Aubyn nodded. "I knew a few Jewish clerks when I was reading law. One was, and still is, a friend."

"Really." So much for the prejudiced upper crust.

"Yes. But Joshua is, what do you say, devout?"

"Observant."

"Right." He smiled. "A much better man than me."

"Not for us to judge," I reminded him.

"True. Judging others never ends well."

"I've never known it to."

We were silent for a moment, before he spoke again.

"I wonder if I could prevail upon you to do me another great favor?"

"If I can."

"Would you help me to look through Frances's things? I collected a trunk from the coroner, and you might know better than I what her possessions would mean."

"All right," I said slowly, trying to figure out how this might happen. Obviously, I would not go to his hotel to look through the items, but I also couldn't ask him to drag it to my house.

"Tell me when, and I'll have it sent to your home so we can look through it there."

I smiled a little.

"I would never expect a lady to come to my lodgings, even on an errand of mercy. You're already going beyond the call of friendship. I would not ask you to imperil your reputation as well."

"Very perceptive of you."

Saint Aubyn returned my smile. "I trained as a barrister. Observation was a key part of the art."

"I'm sure." I put down my cup. "Soon I must be going. I need to get more library books before I go home, since I am very busy for the next few days."

"Library books?" He gave me a puzzled glance.

"Well, yes. I developed a fondness for the lending library as a girl and I see no reason to change now. And it would be absolutely ruinous to buy everything I want to read."

"Quite practical." He nodded. "Thank you for joining me."

"It was my pleasure."

Gilbert Saint Aubyn favored me with a longer and warmer smile. "Mine as well."

Protocol would have normally required the gentleman to escort me to a hansom cab, but since I was walking on to the library, we exchanged bows and farewells in the lobby and took off in our separate directions.

Just as well; I was preoccupied by the thought of poor Frances, so far from home and trying to get a foothold in an uncertain new world. I admit I had not had a lot of sympathy for her at the time. Quite honestly, I have little tolerance for show-offs and I likely would not have hired her if I had known how bad it was. But she was just a girl, in her first big role, and trying desperately to be the woman she wanted to be, not the woman she'd been told she should be.

I could understand that. And perhaps if she'd felt able to confide in me . . .

Not, as I'd told Saint Aubyn, that she would have. And not, considering her background, that she'd have believed much of anything a self-made and self-educated Lower East Sider would have had to offer, in any case. I remembered the disdainful look she gave me more than once when I tried to offer some useful advice, and my irritation. Still, I was the adult. I should have seen the struggling girl, not just the annoying upstart.

I also should have seen the person who almost shoved me into the path of a grocery wagon.

By the time I realized what was happening, I was already off balance, and halfway off the curb. All of that swashbuckling has its uses, though. I managed to catch myself on a lamppost and just barely avoided the hooves. The muddy wheel, though, came close enough to brush the hem of my skirt, and I banged one ankle on the curb.

"Miss!" A gentleman offered me a hand. "Are you all right?"

"I'm fine." I stepped back onto the sidewalk and straightened my hat, biting back a most unladylike curse at the pain in my ankle. "Thank you kindly."

He bowed. "A pleasure to help a lady. What happened?"

"I don't know. One moment I was in the crowd at the corner, and the next . . ." I remembered what felt almost like a shove, but in a crush, contact is not necessarily deliberate. "Did you see anything?"

"All I saw was the people moving forward and you stumbling." My helper, a distinguished-looking fellow of a certain age, gave me a hard look. "Should we call the police?"

"Certainly not. It was just an accident. Part of city life."

"All right."

"Thank you for your help."

"A chance to assist a pretty lady is a much happier part of city life." He smiled and tipped his bowler. "Good day."

"Good day."

Chapter 5

In Which the Priest Stays to Dinner

When I returned from the library, thankfully little the worse for wear, and fortified with a new biography of poor Anne Boleyn, a fascinating illustrated volume on court dress at Versailles, and a promising-looking novel, though I usually find fiction disappointing, I heard voices in the drawing room.

I walked in, to see Tommy and a man in a cassock sitting at the checkerboard and arguing amiably. They looked like opposite sides of the same coin, both very large, with strong Irish features. Tommy had curly, dark auburn hair, and wore a neat, light gray tweed suit; the priest was in black, a few strands of his blond hair spilling over his face as he studied the board.

"Gentlemen, I can hear you in the street," I said teasingly, placing my book bag on the occasional table.

"Well, if he'd just king me—" Tommy started.

"And if he'd just play by the rules," his companion cut in.

" 'King me'!" called Montezuma from his perch on a bookshelf. He was also very fond of Father Michael.

"Argue all you like, boys, just don't scare the neighbors," I told them loftily, taking out the book on Anne Boleyn and walking toward the chaise. "Good to see you, Father Michael. I hope you're staying for dinner."

"Good to see you, too, Miss Ella. Tom already invited me, and Mrs. Grazich is in a flurry."

"I don't doubt it."

Mrs. G, also a devout Catholic, takes very seriously the idea of having the priest to dinner. Since Father Michael Riley is a close friend of ours, it happens frequently, but it is never routine for her. We sometimes joke that we invite the good father over in order to get a decent meal, but, of course, Mrs. G is incapable of cooking a bad one.

Tommy helps Father Michael with some of the older boys in the Holy Innocents Parish School when he's in town—somehow, the Champ telling them to do their homework carries a lot more weight than their teachers—and Father Michael often comes over to visit.

Tommy still goes to Mass as regularly as he can, and I often attend as well. Sometimes we go with Aunt Ellen and the youngest cousins, and enjoy the happy family moment. That's far more important to me than any religious celebration.

Toms is practically the only one who sees me light candles in my mother's small pewter sticks every Friday night, more in memory of her than in honor of the God she worshiped. I don't see the point in choosing one over the other. God made me and knows who and what I am, and He'll sort it out when the time comes.

In the meantime, Father Michael is wonderful company, in the best Irish tradition, and smart and open-minded, besides. So he's always welcome at the town house.

Needless to say, I was not going to mention my misadventure at the curb, lest I bring down the full force of Irish male protectiveness upon my head. The less of that, the better, thank you.

While the boys finished their game, I called to Montezuma, and he flew over to rest on my finger.

"Love the birdie," I said, stroking his silky head.

" 'Love the birdie,' " he chuckled back.

I started for the studio, since we did not need Montezuma providing commentary at the table, or throwing in on either side of Tommy and the father's latest play-argument.

"Sing with birdie," he demanded.

Montezuma loves to vocalize with me, so I just lightly sang a few scales and he followed along as we climbed the stairs. It reminded me of the first time I'd met him. After our initial tour brought in more money than we'd imagined possible, we'd bought the place from an old importer. He was retiring to live with his daughter, and she had absolutely refused to take "that horrid bird."

The old man had warned me that Montezuma took a long time to warm up to strangers. So I wasn't expecting much when I walked into the attic. A screech from the rafters had greeted me, and a scraggly-looking ball of green feathers glared down at me.

"Hello, birdie," I'd said, putting down a bowl of the seeds we'd been told he favored. "Nice to meet you."

Montezuma had made a horrible noise and stayed where he was. I decided I had nothing to lose by trying to charm him, so I started singing, just a gentle Irish lullaby I'd sung to my little cousins years ago. After a few stanzas, the bird started singing along, and after another chorus, he flew down from his perch. I held out my hand and he landed there. I stroked his scruffy feathers, and after I finished the lullaby, I said, "Love the birdie," over and over, to reassure him.

Eventually he hopped down and went to eat, and when Tommy came up to see how the introductions were proceeding, we were friends for life. He'd met Tommy during the sale talks, and like all small, vulnerable creatures, he trusted Tommy immediately.

Now, smiling at the memory, I got Montezuma settled with seeds and carrots, made sure there were no mud marks from my brush with the grocery wagon, and went to join the other humans at the table.

Mrs. G was clearly feeling spring-y that night. Dinner was salmon, new potatoes and peas, with a fluffy chocolate mousse for dessert. It was all probably a little too dainty for the boys, who are happiest demolishing a nice beef stew or some such, but I was delighted.

Tommy and I had much information to share from our respective busy days, but first we had to bring Father Michael up to date. He was intrigued by the advent of the Wicked Duke, amused by Toms's account of the duel and quite saddened by the fate of Lady Frances.

"So it was ruled accidental," the priest said, looking down at his plate.

"Yes," I said. "But it's hard to imagine it was anything other than—"

"Leave her to God, then, Miss Ella."

"What do you mean?"

"It gives your man, the duke, no comfort to know that she drank that poison."

"No."

"And you won't find any answers that help him or the rest of her family."

"Probably not."

"Then probably best to just leave it and ask no more. If the coroner was kind enough to leave the door open for an accident, we should, too."

"I would like to do just that. I don't think Gilbert Saint Aubyn can."

"It is terribly hard for a family." Father Michael nodded. "I guess what I would say to both of you is that you should be kind, and look to giving her family comfort, however you can."

"We can't change the outcome," I said. "They already know the worst."

"Which is why the best you can do is gently urge them to remember her as she was and be grateful for the time they had with her."

Tommy nodded ruefully. "You've seen this before, Father."

"Sadly, quite a lot." He thought about it. "It might also be good for him to know that she was doing well in her work, and that she was very gifted."

I nodded. "That we can do."

"Leave out the part about showing off, Heller."

"Probably." I took a sip of my mineral water. "All right, what did you learn from Henry?"

"Just what you thought. He wasn't able to verify the credits in Canada and Chicago."

"So she just appeared out of nowhere."

"Basically. Henry didn't mind . . . much." Tommy shrugged. "He hates lying as much as we do, but there's lying and then there's stretching the truth to get an audition. She was very good, and he was negotiating a contract for the next season in Philadelphia. Four roles, all good ones, and a real start."

"She knew that?"

"Absolutely. He said she was thrilled, and looking forward to it."

"As she should have been. If she did well there, she would have been properly launched." Better than that, I thought. Probably within a season of a New York debut.

"Which makes you wonder, doesn't it?" Father Michael asked, looking closely at me.

"Not just me." I put down my fork, my appetite ebbing

in the face of such serious matters. "I suspect it will raise more questions than it answers."

"It's too late to leave well enough alone, isn't it?" the priest asked.

"I think it was too late the moment Gilbert Saint Aubyn walked into our house," Tommy observed. "He doesn't seem the sort of man to give up or accept a comforting lie."

"What sort of man is he?"

"Well"—Tommy grinned at me—"for that, you should probably ask Heller."

"So?" Father Michael's brown eyes twinkled. "That sort of man?"

"He is a fine figure of a man," I admitted. "He is also a British aristocrat who will soon be an ocean away."

"But," said the priest as he took another portion of potatoes, "he's on our side of the pond at the moment."

Chapter 6

A Night with the Ink-Stained Wretches

After Father Michael headed home to the Holy Innocents Rectory, Tommy and I decided we needed an evening outing, mostly for social reasons, though it was entirely possible that we might glean a little useful information, too.

Well after the late-spring sunset, I loaded up a basket with Mrs. G's hermits, and we walked over to the *Beacon*'s news office, where several good friends would be happy to see us, and probably, in all honesty, happier for the cookies. There was no rush; it was a morning paper, and there'd be no point in turning up early, since our friends probably would not be there. But we didn't want to go in too late; in the last hours before the presses roll, friendship falls before the demands of the editor and typesetter. Late evening, before it was really nighttime, was the sweet spot.

As I pinned on my hat, a darling midnight-blue velvet broad-brim with a big bow, and grabbed my coat, also midnight blue, Tommy checked himself in the hall mirror, too. Like me, he's painfully proper as to dress—our shared legacy of growing up struggling and poor—and he made sure the brim of his dark gray trilby was at precisely the right angle.

I picked up the basket and took Tommy's arm as we stepped out. Considering where we were going, several crucial blocks away from our comfortable neighborhood, it wasn't a matter of form, but security. Almost no one would dare to dice with someone as large and dangerous-looking as Tommy, or the lady on his arm, no matter how prosperous we appear. Any of the various ruffians who didn't recognize Tommy as the retired champ, and surprisingly many did—he's a hero in certain circles—would take one look and seek easier pickings.

The *Beacon*'s office was in full swing when we arrived. Tommy has known several of the sports writers for years, and I became friends with one of the other reporters after we worked on a settlement house benefit, so we're usually welcome, especially since we always bring treats, and are smart enough to disappear if it's a busy news night.

The first person I saw was Yardley Stern, the *Beacon*'s top sports writer and a good friend of Tommy's. I suspect he also has a very mild crush on me, but he's never acted on it, so we can pretend it does not exist, which I vastly prefer. He looked up from his typewriter and smiled. "The Champ and the Diva."

I waved the basket. "And Mrs. G's hermits."

Yardley's brown eyes lit up. He's a grown man, of course, but he has a scrawny, half-starved look like a tenement kid, even though he actually had an *almost*-comfortable upbringing. These days, the hungry look probably comes from too much coffee and not enough sleep, but he does sometimes forget to eat when he's busy. Tommy and I have been known to drag him home on occasion to let Mrs. G do her magic. "Why don't I just take these?"

"Best not be hoarding, Yardley." My friend Hetty

MacNaughten appeared behind him. She looked tired, too, with circles under her eyes visible even behind her wire-rimmed glasses, and several strands of her red hair straggling out of its knot. There was an ink stain on the cuff of her plain white shirtwaist, and the bow of her little black tie was undone, clear signs that she was in the midst of battle.

"There's plenty for everyone," I said with a sharp look at Yardley.

He lifted the lid of the basket and offered it to Hetty with a bow. "First dibs for the lovely lady."

"Thank you, kind sir." She took the cookie with a wry little glare. The two of them sometimes fight like cats and dogs, especially when he treats her like a woman and not just another reporter. It's not really his fault; Yardley's mother, like most, taught him to treat ladies with respect, but not how to treat them as colleagues.

Yardley took his own cookie and then put the basket out on a shelf by the mailboxes, the spot for dainties to share. "Hey, boys," he called to his fellow writers, "the Champ and his coz brought cookies!"

At least at the sports desk, I'm just the cousin. I assumed that the music critic might see it the other way. I didn't see anyone else I wanted to greet among the boys; their editor, Preston Dare, is a close friend and informal uncle to both Tommy and me, but he was nowhere in evidence. Probably covering a boxing match, though Toms would observe that it's just as likely he might be chasing barmaids or shopgirls. Preston would never discuss such things with me. However, I have never seen him treat a woman with anything less than absolute respect, so the barmaids, if barmaids there were, were no doubt in safe company.

Hetty took my arm and pulled me toward her little corner. She's one of only two women reporters, and spends most of her time doing ladylike features for the "women's page." She'd really like to be covering Tammany Hall, or the latest juicy murder, but like most of the rest of the world, newspaper editors have a particular idea of what women can and cannot do. And there's no such thing as a trouser diva in news, so she can't even dress up and swing a sword once in a while.

"So what is it today, Mrs. Astor's latest costume ball?"

She scowled. "So much worse. The new spring hats."

"Ugh."

"Ugh, indeed. However, I have also convinced Morrison to let me do a feature on lady baseball fans a week from Saturday."

"So you'll be able to go out in the yard with Yardley?" I asked impishly.

She smacked me with yesterday's edition as I laughed. "Never mind that. I'm also going to work in an account of the game, so Morrison can see that I can write sports."

"Good for you." I smiled.

"And, yes, Yardley has agreed to escort me."

"Good for you both."

Hetty gave me a dirty look over her glasses. "You wouldn't like me matchmaking for you."

"You know I'm not matchmaking." I put my hands up. "I just like watching you two argue."

"Probably need to find someone for you to argue with."

"I get plenty of arguing with Tommy," I reminded her. "And I'm not in town long enough for anything else."

"True enough. You're doing the big settlement house benefit in a couple weeks, though, right?"

"Of course. Marie and I are putting on the Balcony Scene." Marie de l'Artois, my closest friend in the opera world, does not tour because she won't leave her children, but she's the best Juliet (other than Lentini) there is.

"Excellent. So she's back to singing?"

"She was vocalizing three days after Joseph was born, but didn't want to appear in public until she trimmed down a bit. It's apparently harder to get back into shape after the third one."

Hetty looked significantly at me over her glasses. "You told her to go see Dr. Silver?"

"I didn't have to. She asked me. All taken care of."

My doctor, Edith Silver, very quietly helps married ladies limit their families. Hetty and I, and a number of other progressive-minded women, do what we can to support her. For me, that mostly means slipping an extra check in with payment for my occasional visits for throat trouble. We've all seen women we loved worn out—and sometimes dead—from too much childbearing. While none of us are willing to make a public matter of it, we're glad to help where we can.

Hetty nodded. "It'll be good to see her on the stage again."

"I'll be glad to sing with her. I've missed her."

"I'm just amazed that her husband allows her to keep singing."

"She wouldn't have married anyone who didn't."

"True. When will men learn that our careers don't stop at the altar?"

I shook my head. "I don't think our new century will be enough to change that."

"Anyhow, are you two just here to say hello, or is something going on?"

"Well, now that you mention it," I said. "I'm wondering if you might be able to ask your music critic to check a few things for me."

"About what?"

"Remember poor little Violette Saint Claire?"

"The Juliet who keeled over in New Haven?"

I nodded. "Yes. Troubled girl. There's some question about where she really came from."

Hetty's eyes gleamed. "Do I hear a story here?"

"Not just yet, but there might be a corker somewhere down the line." I'd given Hetty a couple of suitably mournful and complimentary quotes about the late Miss Saint Claire for a short piece when it happened, but she didn't get much play with it. True, there wasn't a great deal to the story then, and that was also the week that a spectacular divorce trial began. Throw in a connection to a Wicked Duke (they're always wicked in the papers!) and that might change.

"Good enough for me. What do you need?"

"Anything you can find. She claimed to have sung with a couple of Canadian companies, as well as one in Chicago, but now I wonder."

Hetty nodded. "Might be better for you—and Tommy—to offer Stradivarius a cup of coffee."

I picked up something in her expression. We'd never talked about the paper's music critic, Anthony Stratford, inevitably known around the newspaper as "Stradivarius."

"Wandering eyes?"

"Wandering *hands*." She sighed irritably. "I don't think he'd dare try it with a diva, especially one whose cousin is a retired champ. But me?"

I remembered an artistic director who'd chased me around a piano in my early days. I'd been terrified and unsure of what I could, or even should, do to protect myself. Lentini happened to walk in just as he'd backed me into a corner, and read him the riot act in English and Italian, punctuated by the waving of a stiletto and an offer to train him to sing castrati roles. After that, I had a stiletto of my own, and Lentini's express orders not to be afraid to use it. It was in my vanity drawer these days, since Tommy did a more than adequate job of defending my virtue—but I never forgot that day. I nodded to Hetty. "Tommy and I will have a cup with him."

She smiled. "That should be safe."

"Does Tommy need to have a word as well?"

She shook her head. "No. I make sure I'm never alone with him."

"Fair enough." I left it, but not happily.

"Would the autopsy report help you?" Hetty offered. "I imagine Dr. Silver would be willing to look it over and offer any insight she could."

"That's a very good idea." I nodded, even as I inwardly recoiled a little from the grisly thought.

"I have a copy in my files. I'll find it and bring it over."

"Meet me in the park tomorrow, and we'll go for a velocipede ride and head home for a late breakfast."

She grinned. "Absolutely. I've missed our rides."

I grinned right back. "Me too."

We may be well-behaved maiden ladies on land, but when we get on our velocipedes, we are hellion tomboys, and Heaven help the man fool enough to cross our path. I do not generally give ground to the fossils carping about the New Woman, but, yes, we are quite a dangerous species when we are on wheels.

"It's finally warm enough for a really good spin," she said. "And the City's cleaned up the park for the season."

"Yes. The best way to welcome spring."

She held up a copy of her latest article. "Not a lovely new hat?"

"I might wear it," I admitted, "but I surely wouldn't expect a professional to write about it."

We shook our heads together, knowing the problem. Her editor doesn't see a professional. He just sees a woman.

"Ladies?" Yardley appeared at Hetty's desk with a cookie in hand. "Just wanted to make sure that Miss MacNaughten gets her share before the locusts descend."

She took the cookie and exchanged a grin with him. "Very kind."

"I have to be nice to my new reporting partner." He turned to me. "Did Hetty tell you I am taking her out to the ball game a week from Saturday?"

"That's not quite how she told it, but yes."

Yardley smiled. "Maybe you and the Champ need to take up baseball."

"I'm done with sports, Yards," Tommy said with a laugh as he walked over from one of the other writers. "I'm a music fancier now."

They laughed together. "Whatever you say."

"But we will be coming to the ball game," I promised. "We wouldn't miss this."

Tommy shrugged. "I could miss the Giants any day."

"Couldn't we all?" Yardley sighed. "The only good thing is that they're not the Cleveland Spiders."

"No one," Hetty observed with a wry smile, "is as miserable as the Cleveland Spiders. No one goes to their games, even in Cleveland."

"And in Cleveland, trust me, there is precious little to do." That much I knew. We'd had a terrific run there a few years before—except, of course, for the unfortunate flight of the stagehand—and I strongly suspected it had as much to do with the cultural hunger of the residents as the excellence of our show.

"Very nice audiences, though," Tommy reproved me. "They were happy and grateful."

"You're right about that." I shrugged. "In any case, we'll happily tag along to the Polo Grounds."

"I don't know about 'happily,'" Tommy said, "but we will tag along."

"Excellent." Hetty beamed at us both, and then caught sight of the clock. Her brow crinkled.

"We should be going." I straightened my hat. "You two have a paper to put to bed, and I need my beauty rest."

Yardley laughed. "*You* don't need it, and sleeping for a week won't help him."

"Probably true." I nodded. "But we will leave you to your work."

We paused at Anthony Stratford's desk and left a message asking him to meet us for coffee at his convenience. He was out at some performance or other, to be expected for a music critic, if annoying to us.

"Hopefully, we can get a little insight on Violette," Tommy said as we walked out into the street, quiet outside despite the hum of presses inside. "At any rate, Henry is finding us some new sopranos."

"Probably need a new system for protecting them, too," I observed gloomily.

"From what, Heller? Themselves? Life?"

"I should have done better." I took Tommy's arm as we turned onto the dim lane that would take us back toward Washington Square. Thinking about Frances had left me unsettled, and I wondered what else was lurking out there in the dark.

"You always think you can do better." He smiled down at me. "Let's go home and see if there's anything left in the cookie jar."

"Can't do better than that."

Chapter 7

The Daring Young Ladies on their Flying Machines

The next morning, Friday, just happened to bring that first perfect spring day where everyone wants to be outside enjoying the air and the blossoming flowers, and the sight of everyone else doing the same. Velocipede fanatics that we are, we would have been out on our machines even if it had been a gray day, but it was a true treat to be out this time.

Hetty took the envelope out of her basket when she pulled up beside me in Washington Square Park, and I secured it in mine.

"I included a copy of my notes and the original article, in case it might help." She shook her head, her serious expression entirely unsuited to the adorable straw cycling hat that completed her dark gray cotton drill sports costume.

"Thanks." I gave my own hat a pat to make sure it was still firmly in place. My costume is midnight-blue broadcloth, which goes better with my coloring. "I'm going to see Dr. Silver later."

Hetty nodded.

"In the meantime . . ."

We grinned.

"Sometimes a lady needs a little speed." She settled her feet on the pedals.

"More than a little."

We took off through the paths of the park at a brisk—but not dangerous—pace. We were not the only lady cyclists enjoying the spring day, and we exchanged waves and greetings with the others, most of whom we knew only by sight, but not name. Not that it mattered—we're all members of a happy sisterhood. Cycling is freeing and healthy, and gives ladies a safe and respectable way to burn off excess energy and emotion. What could be better?

Most passersby smiled at us, and little boys and girls waved, even though these days velocipedes aren't really new and exciting. Every once in a while, an older man or woman would glare. The men annoyed me, but I felt just a little sorry for the women. Their generation didn't have any similar joys, and they no doubt missed out. It's also not fair to say that all of the older generation disapproves of ladies on velocipedes. We always see several stately gents tipping their hats, and on occasion, grandmothers even cheer us on. Some of them even have white temperance ribbons on their lapels. Not surprising, really, since none other than our great heroine, Susan B. Anthony, has said that she stands and rejoices at the sight of a woman on a wheel.

As we skirted the large open area near the fountain, I noticed a familiar-looking gentleman sitting on a bench, reading some large tome. Surely not, I thought. He should be at his fancy hotel chasing chorus girls or whatever dukes do. But, no, it was. Gilbert Saint Aubyn looked up from his reading, tipped his hat and favored Hetty and me with a smile.

"Who is that?" she asked as we waved. "Best-looking stage-door Romeo I've seen in a while."

"A relative of poor Violette's," I said with perfect truth. "It turns out she was British."

"They do grow them fine over there." Hetty looked hard at me. "You're going to tell me more about this, at some point."

"When I can."

"Fair enough."

I took a quick glance back as we passed, to see Saint Aubyn watching us go, still smiling, if a little more reflectively.

We giggled like schoolgirls and sped up a bit.

"Speed Demons!" yelled a male voice as our path brought us closer to the sidewalk. "What is this world coming to!"

Yardley and Tommy were standing on the corner just outside the park, laughing. Trust the boys.

We threaded our way over to the gate and dismounted.

"Hello, gentlemen." I bowed and joined the laughter.

"Hello, ladies." Yardley swept us both a bow, and took an appreciative glance at our sports costumes, which, while quite modest, did indeed reveal a good bit of stockinged ankle.

Hetty's cheeks were pink, and it wasn't just the ride. "Hello, Yards, Tommy."

"We're heading back to the house for a late breakfast," Tommy said. "Join us?"

"Wonderful idea," I agreed.

"I'm tellin' ya, Jackie, that's Ella Shane!" a little voice piped up behind us.

"Shut up, Betsy!" snarled another childish treble.

We turned, to see a girl and boy, perhaps ten and eight, in clean, but not expensive, play clothes. She was holding a book, and he had a ball.

"Hello." I held out my hand to the girl, who had the skinny, awkward look that some do in the years before adolescence. "You're right. I'm Ella."

She shot a triumphant grin at her younger brother and took my hand. "Betsy Martin. We live over on Jane Street."

"Why, we're practically neighbors." I smiled down at her as we shook. "Nice to meet you."

"Hey, you're the Champ!" Jackie stared up at Tommy, who grinned and shook hands, too.

Hetty and Yardley took all of this with the equanimity of friends who've seen it many times before.

"Sign my card? It's my favorite bookmark." Betsy studied me for a moment, clearly comparing me to the Romeo *carte de visite* she'd pulled from the book. I knew they'd been sold at the stationer's in the neighborhood a year or so ago, and suspected that her admiration for me had little to do with singing and a great deal to do with my being a woman who got to run around in men's clothes with a sword.

"I don't carry a pencil in my sports costume—" I started.

"But I do." Hetty, the prepared reporter, pulled hers out of her pocket and handed it to me.

"Never leaves home without one," Yardley said, laughing at her.

"The better to fend off the riffraff," she shot back with a trace of a smile.

"What are you reading?" I asked as I signed, ignoring the usual sparring.

"*The Story of Queen Victoria*. I like queens."

"Me too." I finished the card (*To Betsy, with best wishes – keep reading!*) and handed it over.

Betsy beamed. Jackie, who had been happily staring at Tommy all this time, now looked at me, too.

"You're all right for a singer," the boy said.

"She's the ultimate, you drip!" Betsy snapped back, punching his arm.

"It's been a pleasure meeting you," I said, bowing to the kids.

"For me as well," Tommy added, with an equally elegant bow.

They bowed back, a tribute to their mother's excellent training, and then ran off.

"Now," Tommy said, watching them go with a laugh, "shall we see what Mrs. G hath wrought?"

As we walked home, Tommy pulled me aside. "I am only the messenger. Do not blame me."

"What?" I suspected what was coming; he'd been over to see Aunt Ellen and the cousins the previous day, and Aunt Ellen worries.

"Mother had a dream."

She also believes she has second sight. She doesn't, because there is no such thing, but even in our modern age, there are things we cannot explain, and every once in a while she does sense something.

"She wants me to tell you that a tall, dark man is going to cause you trouble."

"We can only hope."

Tommy and I chuckled together. "You know she's just being protective, Heller."

"Of course, and I love her for it. Will we see her at Mass on Sunday?"

"She's helping at a First Communion breakfast this week, so likely next week."

"I'll soothe her down then, if she needs it. In the meantime, let's see about baked goods."

"Baked *very* goods."

Mrs. G does not hold with the newfangled concept of the "brunch," a sort of late breakfast or early lunch meal that people sometimes consume on weekends or after a late night. If you are not at the table at what she considers an appropriate time for breakfast, you will not be getting any.

Except that she can't really hold that line in a household where the denizens are often out until the wee hours of the morning doing our work. And so we have reached a compromise whereby, if she knows there was a show, or if she does not see us at the proper time, she leaves out fruit and some kind of tasty baked good and we forage for ourselves. Since Hetty and Yardley are also often up, putting the paper to bed, they appear on occasion as well.

Today it was a crumb-topped coffee cake, beloved of all New Yorkers, and a strawberry-rhubarb compote. The very first strawberries of the season are starting to appear in the markets, but they're far too dear for us right now, so Mrs. G combined last summer's strawberry jam with the more reasonable fresh rhubarb for a sweet-tart taste of the season.

Hetty and I were far more interested in the fruit than the men were. In the presence of cake, any kind of cake, all men turn into happy little seven-year-old boys. But grown-up boys don't have to worry about their mamas monitoring their cake consumption, so they eat their fill, and then some. Their first pieces were gone before Hetty and I even got our fruit and sat down. It was entirely possible that there would be little or no cake left by the time Hetty and I finished our nice cut-glass bowls of fruit. Fine by me, but I felt bad for Hetty, and shot Yardley a glare as he cut his second piece.

He had the good grace to blush. "Oh . . . you ladies haven't had your first piece yet."

I just smiled. "Make sure Hetty gets one."

"Surely, you can spare a crumb for us poor maidens." The poor maiden in question scowled at Yardley.

"Wouldn't want you to get cranky from hunger." Yardley returned a teasing smile as he chivalrously cut a generous slice and handed it to her with a bow.

"Very kind." Hetty picked up her fork and tucked in.

She doesn't have to worry about fitting into breeches.

Probably not much consolation for writing about hats, though.

"And you?" Yardley asked.

"Just leave me a sliver." The boys aren't the only ones who can't resist cake.

Yardley added a bit more to his plate and Tommy scooped up another piece, while I refilled our cups, and we were all finally settled.

"A satisfying velocipede ride, ladies?" Yardley tried for polite conversation.

"There is no such thing as an *un*satisfying velocipede ride," Hetty said with a grin.

"Well, if you wrecked . . ." Yardley teased.

"Never going to happen with us," I assured him. "Perhaps with lesser riders."

Tommy just laughed. He knew about the time, soon after I bought my cycle, when I fell off and scraped myself badly. I'd spent the better part of a week trying not to limp on stage, or wince when my breeches rubbed against a raw knee.

"So, who was that gentleman who tipped his cap?" Yardley asked. "Another of your admirers, Miss Ella?"

I should have known he'd see that. *Here be dragons.* "Close enough."

Hetty glanced at me and let it pass.

"So tell us about the baseball game." Tommy must have really wanted to change topic. He is probably the only man in New York who is not a passionate baseball fancier – and the game was more than a week away still. Even Father Michael follows the unfortunate Giants. Not just men: my singing partner Marie and her family, as proud Brooklynites, are fans of the Superbas, who had at least a reasonable chance of a championship.

"Well, I'm writing an article about lady baseball fanciers."

"Of which there are many." I smiled. Even I have been known to join Hetty for a Giants game on occasion. "It is a relatively genteel game, compared to some of men's contests."

"Yes, and played by men in such sharp clothes." A wicked gleam came into my reporter friend's eye.

"And such strong men," I added, playing along. "Mostly, very tall and muscular."

Yardley scowled at his crumb cake. "If you like sturdy, empty-headed brutes, ladies. Baseball players aren't known for their intelligence."

Hetty and I shared a tiny grin as Yardley warmed to his subject. He continued: "It's not like the sweet science of boxing, after all, with the history of gentleman champs. Baseball is just a bunch of boys swinging a stick at a ball. I can't imagine why it's caught on."

"I agree with you," Tommy said, even as he cut his eyes to us. "I can't imagine it'll stay around for long."

"Preston would disagree," I pointed out, invoking Yardley's editor, Preston Dare, who was an eloquent chronicler of baseball.

Tommy laughed. "Preston just left for a road trip with the Superbas. By the time he gets back, he will be ready to take up boxing himself."

"I don't know." Yardley suddenly had a naughty little smile. "Preston is awfully fond of the pleasures of the road."

Tommy shot him a glare. Hetty and I exchanged glances and very carefully didn't acknowledge. Obviously, we are both aware of the existence of the pleasures of the road, if not the exact details of the said pleasures, but it would not do for the menfolk to discuss them in our presence.

"In the meantime," Hetty said, firmly changing topic, "this story gives me a chance to write some sports and impress *my* editor."

"Absolutely," I agreed.

"Her editor is already impressed," Yardley said coolly. "The problem is, he doesn't know what to do with a terrific writer in a skirt."

Hetty sighed. "Also true."

"And far too common." I shook my head. "Men don't know what to do with smart and competent women."

"Most men, Heller. Perhaps they'll learn in our new century."

Hetty and I laughed.

Yardley and Tommy did, too.

I reached for the coffeepot. "We won't solve the problems of the world today, but at least there's good coffee."

"Some days, that's all we get." Hetty held out her cup.

Chapter 8

In Which Dr. Silver Offers
a Second Opinion

Dr. Edith Silver's clinic is a reasonable walk from the town house, unless one is suffering from a nasty throat infection, in which case one will do well to wrap up and take a hansom cab. But in good health on a relatively nice spring day, there was no excuse not to walk, and many good reasons, in fact, to get some air.

After Hetty and Yardley headed off to prepare for the night at the *Beacon,* arguing about something to do with baseball and hats, or possibly baseball hats, I changed into respectable clothes for my own grimmer errand, permitting myself a somewhat fanciful hat piled with mauve flowers to balance out the dull plaid day dress.

One of the amazing things about New York is how close the rich and poor, ruffian and respectable, live. Our town house is in Washington Square, a good, but not overly tony, neighborhood favored by artists and writers, among others. Fifth Avenue and some of the homes of the Four Hundred are but a short walk away, across Washington Square Park.

Many of the wealthiest are moving farther uptown, all

the way to the northern end of Fifth, on Central Park, but there are still plenty of grand homes down our way. The Ladies' Mile, home of the finest stores, is also less than a dozen blocks north, well within a reasonable walk. It's not unusual for me to step into one of my favorite shopping palaces past a shiny carriage with a footman handing down some society mama and her flock of misses.

It's all miles and a lifetime away from the Lower East Side, where Tommy and I grew up, in conditions ranging from desperate poverty to making ends meet with luck and a daily struggle. And while you won't find beggars in the fanciest real estate on Fifth Avenue, because the rich have them moved along, just about anywhere else in the city, a bedraggled hungry child, a limping old woman or a man who lost his legs in the Civil War might ask you for a penny. I always give, unless the unfortunate truly scares me, because I know how lucky I am. I should add here that I also do my best to help orphanages, the settlement house, and other places, in the hope that someday people won't have to beg.

As a grocery wagon veered close to the curb while I waited to cross, I shook my head at the idea that Saint Aubyn and I had both come perilously close to disaster within a day this week. A less than amusing coincidence, but, truly, something that could happen to anyone at any time in the City.

Dr. Silver's clinic is on the bottom floor of her town house, which is still in the Village. But since she's known to treat charity cases when she can, all manner of people straggle in. On this particular afternoon, the waiting room was not yet full. I knew that would change, and quickly, as the day wore into night. The only other person there was a very young mother with a coughing baby. The cough, mercifully, wasn't the strangling hack of diphtheria or the bark of whooping cough, so it was possible that the poor little kiddy would recover. The nurse, Irma Dos Santos, led them to the examining room and then returned to me.

"Sudden throat trouble, Miss Shane?" she asked. Irma's husband died in a factory accident years ago, and after a long struggle, with the help of Dr. Silver and the settlement house, she managed to complete a course as a trained nurse. She is one of the most cheerful people I know, and no doubt needs every ounce of that natural happiness in her work.

"No, thank goodness. I just want to have a word with Dr. Silver when I can. Nothing serious about me, just her medical expertise in the case of a former employee."

Irma looked puzzled, and no wonder, with my convoluted explanation. "I'll see if she has a minute after she sees the baby."

"Thanks."

Sure enough, after the mother left, looking much reassured with orders to give the little creature honey—and nothing else—for his cough, Irma guided me back to the doctor's private office.

Dr. Silver wears her dark, curly hair in a simple low knot, and inevitably a few strands escape to soften her face. Her eyes are hazel, and among the kindest I've ever seen. At that moment, she had a faint wrinkle between her brows, either concern or annoyance. "Ella. What on earth did you tell Irma?"

I took the report out of my bag. "I'm hoping you can take a look at this and tell me if you see anything."

"What is it?"

"The autopsy report on the soprano who died in New Haven."

Her eyes widened. "Poor girl. I read about that in the papers."

"There's a great deal more to it."

"Isn't there always?" She nodded and took the papers. "All right, let's see what we can see."

As she riffled through them, she smiled at me. "This is not a happy task, but I'm glad to see you're doing well."

"Thanks." I nodded. "It did take me far too long to get over my last throat infection before the tour."

She looked hard at me over her reading glasses, her eyes stern. "That, it did. You devote all of your energies to performing, and don't rest nearly enough."

I shrugged. "It's what I do."

"It does not have to be the *only* thing you do."

Dr. Silver is a widow with a teenage daughter, and she's a strong advocate for women managing both work and family. This was not the first time we'd had this conversation.

"Unless you can wave a magic wand and create a suitable husband, I'm afraid it does."

She smiled again, warming her serious features. "Well, you still do have some time if your fairy godmother sends one your way. But the older you get, the more dangerous that first childbed is."

"Childbed!"

"Well, yes. If you trouble to marry, I doubt you'll want to miss out on the pleasure of family life."

"I'm not *troubling* to do any such thing at the moment."

"I know." She shrugged. "I'm becoming a matchmaker in my old age. Let's have a look at this report."

Her brows drew together as she read. "Ella, does Romeo manhandle Juliet at all?"

"What? Of course not." I stared at her. "Hard to believe it as the great love of all time if he knocked her around."

"True." She smiled ruefully. "Now, if only I could get some of the women in this neighborhood to understand that."

"Some women everywhere, I'm afraid."

"Too true. At any rate, your poor Juliet had an ugly bruise on her upper arm, clearly a handprint, probably from someone grabbing her very hard."

"Very hard, indeed. I've had my share of rough-and-tumble in the street and on the stage, and no one's ever left a print on me."

"I imagine Toms would leave a print *on them* if they did." The doctor glared at the report. "It was quite recent. Probably within a few hours of death."

I shook my head. "None of the possibilities here are good. Either she was attacked on the way to the theater and didn't feel able to tell me for reasons of her own . . ."

"Or it was someone in the theater. In your company."

I bit my lip. While we were truly awful at choosing sopranos, I couldn't believe we would have hired anyone who would turn on his fellow performers. "I truly hope not."

She gave a faint nod and returned to the report. "Did she seem healthy to you, Ella?"

"Until that last scene, yes."

"Hmmm." Dr. Silver contemplated the papers. "Well, her stomach showed signs of irritation. And she was a bit underweight."

"Oh?" I had no idea what that might mean.

The doctor explained. "Now, considering everything, I'd be worried that she might have harmed herself because she was in a delicate condition—"

"Oh no!" And after I'd assured Saint Aubyn that she was virtuous.

"Don't worry. You didn't fail in your duty to protect her."

"No?"

"No. She was not with child, and was, in fact, *virgo intacta*. So that was not the problem."

"Then what?"

"I suspect something rather unusual." She contemplated for a measure. "I've had a few young lady patients who stop eating during times of stress, and one or two who actually vomit up what they eat."

" 'Vomit up what they eat'?" To a girl who grew up on the Lower East Side, where each meal was greeted with gratitude, it was inconceivable. I had heard of society women starving themselves because of some mental sickness, but never this.

Dr. Silver knew exactly what I was thinking. "Hard to imagine, I know, but it does happen."

"Why?"

"They tell me the vomiting purges whatever bad feelings they have. That it's relaxing, the way you and I might feel after a medicinal glass of sherry, say."

"Strange."

"To us. Not to them." She smiled a little. "Many people might find your fondness for fencing and the velocipede strange."

"Well, that's true. To each her own, I suppose. Surely, though, vomiting is a good deal more dangerous than a velocipede."

"It is." Dr. Silver's eyes narrowed a little. "Over time, it's really quite unhealthy. I don't think she was that far into it. From the report, the damage doesn't seem too serious. I suspect she'd only been purging for a short while."

"I never saw any sign of trouble."

"You probably wouldn't. Girls who do this are very good at hiding it."

"That's something." I shook my head. "I really feel that I failed her."

"You shouldn't. With all of our new science, we really have not learned much about the mind and its disorders. I can't say any more clearly than you can why she drank that nicotine."

"'Nicotine'? For some reason, I thought it was strychnine."

"No. Just as easy to get, of course, but less common." She shook her head. "But there's no doubt. She died of nicotine poisoning. There was nicotine residue in the vial, and as you know, she was the only one who touched it."

"'If all else fail, myself have power to die.'"

"Ah, poor Juliet. And poor Violette. She was only twenty-one, which seems almost as impossibly young as Juliet to me."

"And everything hurts so much more when you're very young."

"Some things hurt a great deal when you're an adult, actually." Dr. Silver's fingers strayed to her wedding ring. "But you're right. The very young don't understand that things will look different tomorrow—or have people depending on them to pull through."

"Too true." I knew she was thinking of her daughter. I was thinking of Tommy, and everyone else.

"However," Dr. Silver said thoughtfully.

"What?"

"I had a patient a while ago who overused emetics and purgatives. If she was using some patent medicine—which might have had nicotine in it—and put a dose in the vial by some mistake . . ."

I nodded. "It really could have been an accident."

"Yes. It's at least theoretically possible. Without seeing her things and knowing if she had any patent nostrums, we can't be sure."

I'd never seen her with any such thing, but then she would not have been swigging from the bottle at rehearsal, after all. I nodded. "But the possibility might certainly give comfort to the family."

"Perhaps." Dr. Silver smiled faintly. She put the papers

back together and handed them to me. "I hope I was of some help."

"You were. I just wish I had been able to help her." I sighed. Whether or not I had liked her, she was my employee—and to some degree, my responsibility.

"I doubt anyone could have." She shook her head. "Don't torture yourself. Doctor's orders."

"Thank you."

"And make sure you get some rest before your next tour."

"I will."

The faint smile became wider. "Oh . . . and if you wanted to devote a little more energy to finding that suitable man, I wouldn't argue with you."

"Doctor!"

"Just an observation."

Chapter 9

Candles for Remembrance

Technically, since my mother was Jewish, I am, too. I was also baptized Catholic and attend Mass. As I've said, I expect God will determine what I am when I meet Him. In the meantime, I do no harm observing both of my parents' faiths, where I can. So I light my Sabbath candles in the drawing room every Friday night, and usually go to Sunday Mass at Holy Innocents with Toms.

The Sabbath candleholders were small, and pewter rather than silver, but the only thing of value we'd had left at the end. Mama had sewn piecework, and, of course, she hadn't been able to work much. I'd taken up as much sewing as I could, but I was only eight. She'd sold the gold locket my father gave her, and pawned her wedding band, and the candleholders would have been next. Except that she just didn't wake up one winter morning.

By then, we were scraping by in a freezing corner room in a tenement. Mama was always thin and pale; a light silvery blonde, with brown eyes that shimmered with joy at the sight of me or the memory of my father. But in those last weeks, the consumption had worn her almost to trans-

parency—her hands skeletal, her face pared down to sharp cheekbones and huge, frightened eyes.

She never said a word to me about her fears. She just kept smiling, working as much as she could between the racking coughing fits, swallowing the blood and wiping her mouth quickly so I would not see, always pretending that everything was fine for my sake. For her, I pretended to believe it was, though I saw the blood and everything else. I didn't want to add to her pain by letting her know I was frightened, too.

But I was. So scared, so cold and so hungry.

Mama did the best she could, but there was barely money for bread, never mind heat. What warmth we had usually seeped from the walls of the rooms around us; once in a while, when we'd been able to do a lot of work, we had a small fire in the stove. We knew we might be paying for that heavenly warmth with hunger later, but sometimes people will do anything to escape the cold for a little while. All I could do to help was take up the piece-work, and I did as much as I could. I finally stopped going to the public school, telling Mama they were closed for some special American winter holiday. I know now she didn't believe me, but I also know she wanted every second with me that she could steal from the disease before it killed her.

The last night, we curled up together in the pile of old blankets on the floor that passed for a bed, drawing what warmth we could from each other in the freezing room. Mama told me the same comforting stories she did every night.

She always began with her first day in America, waiting at immigration, when young Malka Steinmetz shared a smile with a beautiful redheaded Irishman named Frank O'Shaughnessy. Months later, they met again, rushing to work on the Lower East Side, and started a brief, secret courtship. They were bashert, *she said, the Hebrew word for meant to be together, and they loved each other enough to defy their world.*

After the happy ending of the wedding, she always skipped right over losing my father and her own dreams to her hopes for me: the lives she imagined in the endless possibilities of this wonderful, new country. Maybe a teacher, a fashionable dressmaker—even one of those beautiful ballet dancers.

"You're an American girl, Ellen," she said in her soft, still-accented voice. "You can be anyone you want to be if you work hard enough."

The last thing I remember before we fell asleep was her kissing the top of my head and saying she loved me. I don't remember if I said it to her. I tell myself that I did.

It was colder than usual when I woke before dawn, and it took only a few seconds for me to realize that it was because my mother's arms were cold. I whispered "Mama," but I think I probably knew she wasn't going to wake. It didn't matter. I did the only thing that made sense to a scared little girl in the dark. I cuddled up to her, and hoped she'd awaken when it was light.

That's how my teacher found us.

Miss Wolff hadn't seen me in more than a week, and decided to check on me on her way to the school. I woke again to her gently pulling me away from my limp and cold mother. I knew for sure then that Mama was gone, and at first, I wasn't frightened, just relieved, because she looked so happy, not coughing or worrying any more.

The next several hours are a blur. There was a lot of wailing and crying from the neighbors, though Miss Wolff was very calm and quiet, and so was I. Someone wrapped me in a blanket; someone else made a bundle of the candleholders and the few scraps of clothing Mama and I weren't wearing. Miss Wolff took me to the school, and settled me in the teachers' room, where some very nice ladies fed me hot sweet tea and bread and butter while they tried to figure out what to do with me.

They told me my mother had gone to Heaven, and I didn't bother correcting them. She'd gone to join my father—and for her, that was heaven.

By the end of that first cup of tea, the first sweet I'd tasted since a stray piece of Christmas candy months before, I was starting to wonder what would happen to me. I knew Miss Wolff could not take me home, and that I had nowhere else to go. The poorhouse and the orphanage were terrifying things to children in the tenements. We knew they were likely the only places in the world worse than where we were. Worse because our families weren't there.

I didn't have a family now. I supposed I belonged with the orphans.

One of the nice ladies told me it was all right to cry if I wanted to, saying I did not have to be brave for her. I knew she could not have been more wrong. I would have to be brave for myself now.

I was afraid to cry because I did not know what would happen if I stopped being brave.

The other children had gone home, and the teachers were whispering over my head, as the late afternoon light started to fade, when I really started to worry. I was wondering what they did with children at the orphanage, and how I would survive there, when Aunt Ellen swept into the room, demanding to see the poor little creature. I'd never seen her before, never even known she existed—this tall, sturdy, auburn-haired woman in serviceable black, glowing with the fire and determination of some kind of magical Irish being, who had come to rescue me. She took one look at me with eyes almost exactly like my own, scooped me up, and announced to the ladies that she was taking charge of Frank's girl. Her namesake. And that was the end of that.

A Jewish charity made sure my mother had a proper funeral, with a rabbi, the next day, and Aunt Ellen and Tommy, already my protector, brought me. That was when I finally cried. And when I learned you can stop being brave for a while and then pick it up again.

Years later, Aunt Ellen gave me the letter my mother had sent her a few days before she died. Mama knew she didn't have much time, and she hoped my father's favorite sister would take me in for his sake, even though both families had cut all ties when they married.

"And, of course, little one," she said as my own fresh tears joined my mother's faint marks on the cheap paper, "I was happy to. Family is family, no matter how you talk to God."

One of the many reasons I love my aunt Ellen.

In addition to the Sabbath ceremony, I also light candles for my parents. For my mother, a *yahrzeit* candle on the anniversary of her death and when I need to feel closer to her. For my father, a votive at the feet of one of the saints at Holy Innocents. I could probably light one for her at church, too, or one at home for him, but it doesn't feel right.

On this particular Friday, I was grateful that Tommy and Father Michael were coaching a boxing tournament for some of the neighborhood boys. While candle lighting was usually warm and joyful, often with Tommy or any guests we might have, this week all of the upheaval associated with poor Frances Saint Aubyn and her cousin had left me in a sad, unsettled mood. It felt right to light my candles alone and think about things.

The main question for me was my responsibility. Had I done right by her? Had I done enough?

I had never heard of the problem Dr. Silver had mentioned, though I vaguely remembered hearing of that sickness of society women who outright starved themselves. It made no sense to me. This surely did not. I could not imagine why anyone might do such a thing, despite the doctor's explanation that it had some kind of calming effect. It must be some kind of sickness of the wealthy, which, of course, I would never have recognized.

But that didn't excuse me from knowing that Frances was in some kind of trouble. I should have seen something. At the very least, I should not have allowed my annoyance at her overacting and her disdain for my advice to blind me to the fact that she needed help.

I'm not a religious authority, but at least to my mother, her Jewish faith was about the way we live here, not winning mansions in some uncertain next world. She always told me that God cares much more about how we treat each other than about how and when we pray. On the holiest day, Yom Kippur, the Day of Atonement, she would say, it's not enough to apologize to God; you have to make it right with anyone you've harmed.

I could no longer make it right with Frances. Hopefully, though, I might give her family some consolation. At least the thought that it wasn't intentional.

Father Michael would approve of that, even if his fire-and-brimstone superiors might not, I thought, remembering his comment about being kind.

My eyes got a little damp as I sat alone in the drawing room, with my Sabbath candles and the *yahrzeit* votive for my mother. Most days, I felt she would have been very proud of me and how I turned out. I didn't know enough about my father to be sure . . . but based on how other Irishmen behave with their daughters, I would have expected him to be shouting from the rooftops about his girl the singer, and threatening to punch my stage-door Romeos in the nose.

That night, though, I wasn't so sure. Mama would have been very unhappy that I let my dislike for someone get in the way of helping her. And she would surely tell me to do better.

"Miss?"

Rosa stood at the door on her way out. She and Mrs. G always carefully stayed clear of me if I lit candles alone. It was neither fear nor distaste; it was just an understanding that it was a very emotional time for me.

"Have a good night." My voice came out a little thick as I brushed the corners of my eyes.

"Thank you, miss. Are you all right?"

"Just a bit tired, I suppose." I managed a small smile for her.

"Well, maybe you can get a little rest while Mr. Tommy is out." She smiled as she left, and I returned to my candles.

It was full dark, and the candles well burned down, when the boys appeared, a whirlwind of color and laughter. I walked out of the drawing room into the foyer, where they were refighting the tournament and planning the next one.

"Hello, gentlemen."

"Heller."

"Miss Ella."

Tommy looked past me to the dark drawing room, and his eyes lingered on mine. Of course, he knew. "All of this nonsense with the duke's cousin has upset you a little."

I shrugged.

"If I may, Miss Ella, I'd say one loss brings up another. Or many others," the priest said. "Not unusual at all."

"Perhaps."

"So tell him to go back to his castle and leave us out of

it." Tommy's frown told me this was a definite mark against the duke in his book.

"You know we can't do that." I sighed. "She worked for us. We're in it, whether we like it or not."

"I know." Tommy sighed, too. Because sighs are contagious among the Irish, Father Michael joined in as Tommy continued. "But try not to let it get you down, huh?"

"I won't." I did have something happy to offer. "Mrs. G was feeling ambitious this afternoon."

"Oh?" they asked in unison.

"I believe she tried a new recipe for penuche fudge. It smelled—"

I didn't get to finish the sentence, for they were already down the stairs. I followed them, a little more slowly. There are those who say fudge fixes everything. They probably are not entirely right . . . but it certainly does no harm.

Chapter 10

Madame Marie de l'Artois Plots Her Triumphant Return

Sunday midday, after Mass at Holy Innocents, I took a hansom cab over to Marie's brownstone in Brooklyn, where we'd do a light rehearsal of our duet, and, most important, catch up on events. I was especially looking forward to seeing Joseph, who'd been just a scrunched-up ball in a blanket the last time I saw him, and his older sibs, who were among the best-behaved small people I'd ever met. Of course, that was with the exception of Anna and Louis's son, the Morsel—real name, Morrie—who had the advantage of daily exposure to all manner of interesting people. The wee Winslows had a conventionally sheltered life, complete with nursery floor and nanny, thanks to their father's comfortable legal practice, and, not incidentally, the impressive fees their mother commanded when she chose to sing.

Marie, the former Maisie Mazerosky of Poughkeepsie—American sopranos tend to use French or Italian stage names to make themselves sound more credible and exotic—was sitting at the piano in her drawing room when the maid showed me in.

"Watch out!" she called. "Joey!"

I looked down to see a tiny, downy-headed creature with bright brown eyes barreling toward my ankles. Whatever else we might say about Joseph Winslow, he was mobile. With a vengeance. "All right if I pick him up?"

Marie laughed. "If you're fast enough, good luck."

I scooped up the baby, who let out a surprised squeak, clearly considered howling, but then looked me right in the eyes, smiled and gurgled. Joseph Winslow also apparently liked company. "Nice to see you, Master Winslow."

Master Winslow favored me with another gurgle and permitted me to carry him back to his mother. Sweet little kiddy.

Marie took him, gave him a quick cuddle and turned him loose again. "He's been crawling in circles for weeks, and only managed to go straight yesterday. So now he's exploring like mad. I'll have Marya take him back upstairs, but he was having so much fun."

"Not a problem. He's wonderful."

Marie gave me an appraising look. "Not too late to get one of your own, you know."

"Ah, but you've already married the only man progressive enough to allow his wife to maintain a singing career, so I'm sadly out of luck."

She smiled at the heavy truth behind that very light remark. "Well, when you finally find a man worth casting your eyes on, we'll send him to Paul for lessons."

"That could work." I sat down on one of the settees as she cornered Joseph and motioned to the maid. "I've missed you, Marie."

"I've missed you, too. And the stage. They don't call it 'confinement' for nothing."

"I gather not. The benefit will be a nice way to ease back to performing."

She patted her waistline as she walked back over to me. "Yes, now that I'm at least relatively presentable."

Marie is far more than presentable. Critics have described her as a jewel of a woman with a jewel of a voice, and they're not wrong. Tiny, with the palest blond hair and cornflower-blue eyes, she looks like an angel, and sounds like one, too. On this particular day, she was wearing a robin's egg blue dimity day dress with darker blue ribbon trim, perfectly chosen to emphasize her coloring.

We first met at an all-Mozart benefit show for a girls' school. She was singing the Queen of the Night, and I was singing Cherubino. We became good friends over backstage books, conversation, and snacks. The Queen of the Night, by the way, is the secret to Marie's magical ability to combine work and marriage. It's a fiendishly difficult role, and only a few sopranos in the world can sing it well. So she and her high F's can pretty much work whenever and wherever they like. She's used this to become New York's resident Queen of the Night, including several glorious runs at the Met. She also takes the occasional production in Boston, Washington or Philadelphia when her husband is trying cases or visiting family.

Marie doesn't perform often enough to be a star in the same sense that I am, but she has the respect of her peers and a good home life, besides. It says a lot about our world that a woman has to have such a rare talent to be able to have both a career and a family, doesn't it?

"You look wonderful," I assured her with perfect truth; her waist was slim again and her face had lost the puffiness it had in the weeks before Joseph's birth. "We really should do a limited run of the whole *Capuleti* sometime."

She picked up the score. "You're right. It would be a sensation, and do wonders for Polly's college fund."

"Not Jimmy's?"

She scowled. "His grandparents have already put aside the money and talked to people at Harvard. Polly, they say, will not need college to be a good wife and mother."

I sighed. "So much for the new century."

"New century, same people." Her husband Paul's parents, who actually fancied themselves modern and open-minded, were not especially delighted by her continued singing, either. However, they had become far more amenable to it after their Opera Guild friends were impressed by her Queen of the Night during a family stay in Boston.

"Well, you check your calendar, and I'll talk to Tommy about mine, and we'll see what we can do. Up to you if you want to put the Winslows in the good seats."

She chuckled. "I should've known you'd come up with something for me to do after the benefit."

"Well, if the Met isn't taking up all of your time . . ."

"They'd love to take up some of yours, you know. You don't have to be on the road all the time."

This was not a new conversation. Marie and the Met are much more the future of opera than traveling divas like me. And I've entertained more than one emissary from the Met. But Tommy and I have a very congenial life. I sighed. "Trust me, I don't enjoy being on the road with the unreliable Juliet du jour. It's going to be a long time before we take that on the circuit again."

"Yes, that poor girl in New Haven."

"Not so poor."

"Oh?"

"It's not public knowledge yet, but she seems to have been from a fancy English family. Ran off to pursue her singing career."

"Imagine having to run away to be allowed to work."

We laughed. If not for the gift of voices, I'd be cleaning or washing on the Lower East Side, and she'd be sewing in a shirtwaist factory in Poughkeepsie.

"Strange world we live in."

"Surely is." Marie studied me. "Weary of the road?"

"Not at all. We'll just take a different opera next time."

"You'll still have to find a soprano."

I sighed. "Yes, but maybe if she's playing something other than Juliet . . ."

Marie looked down at the score and nodded. "There is something awful about happily dying for love every night."

"What? I die, too!"

"But you have some power. You duel, you choose Juliet and you decide to come back for her. All she gets to do is pick up that poison and dagger. It's the only choice she has."

" 'If all else fail, myself have power to die.' "

Marie nodded. "If you're already a little desperate, for whatever reason, living in Juliet's skin for a while might just push you over the edge."

"Sad." I took a breath. "I don't know that I want to tell her cousin, the duke, that."

Marie's eyes gleamed. "A real Wicked Duke?"

"I've seen no evidence of wickedness so far."

"Is there a Wicked Duchess?"

"There is no such thing as a duke with honorable intentions toward an opera singer."

"Probably not." She shrugged. "But mistressing is a time-honored tradition, and—"

"Marie!"

"Come now. I saw the way you looked at Joseph. You are lonely. You are thirty-f—"

"Stop."

"Off stage, have you ever kissed a man?"

"I've never kissed a man *on* stage. I play boys, remember?"

"The question remains."

I was blushing, exactly the way every good Irishwoman does at the mention of such matters. "Enough. You can meet him before the benefit if you like. He's looking for insight into Juliet."

She grinned. "I'd love to give him some insight into the poor girl. And perhaps Romeo, too."

"Of course, you would." I waved the score at her. "Come along. We have singing to do."

"True. But let me tell you, as a married woman and a veteran of three childbeds, the body will not be denied, Ella."

"Women choose to live unmarried every day, and they don't explode or die, or whatever you may be suggesting."

"Most of the women I know who've *chosen* not to marry don't even acknowledge my children. You're different."

I sighed. "Can we practice now?"

"Of course. But it doesn't hurt you to think about things while you still can, Ells."

We ran our duet a few times; Marie felt the need for a little extra work because she'd been off the stage for a while. I couldn't hear anything in her voice; but then, I would not have. The singer knows first and best. I was well aware from my last visit before the tour, and much-appreciated letters on the road, that she'd been vocalizing at least lightly since Joseph was three days old. Even though she was still in bed, she was working to return to form. But it would still have taken some time to recover her normal level of power and support.

While no one would ever discuss such things in public, women singers will privately tell you that the early stages of a delicate condition can actually improve the voice; no one knows why, but it is true. Of course, the later stages aren't nearly so helpful, and the enforced rest of confinement can slow recovery. But Marie does her work, and to my discerning ear, she was right back at her usual level.

We ran through it a few times, each one better than the last. I didn't mind; with this work, I could skip vocalization for the day and just relax when I got home. This practice was really more for Marie, anyhow, to reassure her that she was indeed ready to return to the stage.

"Wonderful as always," I said after the third run.

She smiled. "It felt right that time."

I nodded. "Good."

"Better than good." She pulled the bell rope with a grin. "Would you like to spend a few minutes with the rest of the cast?"

"I thought you'd never ask."

Marya, the maid, carried Joseph back into the room, followed by his sibs: Jimmy, who was dark, and already working on his daddy's serious mien, but blessed with Marie's blue orbs and long lashes, and Polly, who was exactly the opposite hybrid of her parents: brown eyes, almost–white-blond hair, and her mother's impish smile. I was glad to see that both were in sensible, colorful play clothes instead of the befrilled white muslin things that many parents force their children to wear when they're showing them off to the world.

"Miss Ella!" the older two chorused.

I'd come prepared, as always. With Marie's permission, I'd bought interesting books for both on the tour. Jimmy got the story of Paul Revere's ride from Boston, and Polly, two years younger, a picture book about Betsy Ross from Philadelphia. I handed out the volumes, and hugs, and watched happily as the two slipped off to the corner to read. For Joseph, I'd brought one of those little cloth *ABC* books. He probably already had one; the Winslows believe every bit as strongly as I do in the power of reading, but considering what babies do to anything they touch, another was not unwelcome.

Joseph showed no interest whatsoever in his book, but was happy to sit in my lap and bat at the charms on my bracelet for a while as Marie watched with a knowing smile.

Soon enough, it was time for the small ones to return to the nursery, and the big ones to their busy day.

Marie walked me to the door. "I'm so glad you came over. It's so good to be back."

"I'm glad you're back. And the little ones are splendid, as always."

"You are always welcome to borrow them for a while. And you aren't required to bring books, you know."

"I enjoy playing fairy godmother."

"Maybe you should be working on the 'mother' part, Ells."

"This again?"

Marie gave me a long look as we embraced at the door. "The music is wonderful. It makes us who we are. But it isn't the only thing in the world."

Chapter 11

In Which Our Heroes Play Stradivarius

The *Beacon*'s music critic was delighted to join Tommy and me for coffee Monday, the day before the small benefit for the girls' school. I'd carefully locked the studio door so Montezuma would not make any unexpected appearances. Mrs. G, no mean judge of character, happened in with the coffee tray as Anthony Stratford made himself to home in our parlor; then she quickly reappeared with absolutely plain bread-and-butter sandwiches, instead of the cookies or other dainties she would normally produce. Tommy and I shared a smile at that. Stratford, utterly oblivious, or perhaps distracted by the excitement of refreshments at the Diva and the Champ's house, happily tucked in.

"So this is a treat," Stratford said around a mouthful. Even if we weren't aware of his repulsive behavior toward his female colleagues, he would have raised some flags. A small, skinny man, with a ratlike face and bony hands that continued the rodent theme, he had the same fanatic gleam in his eye as the worst of the stage-door admirers. But his reviews of my productions had always been merely complimentary if not enthusiastic, saving his best adjectives for the tenors and baritones, and leaving me mostly beside the point.

As I poured, I could tell from the way Tommy watched him that he was picking up something he didn't like, which I was sure he'd share once Mr. Stradivarius played on, so I simply picked up my coffee and offered an appropriate smile. "We are delighted to entertain you, Mr. Stratford."

"To what do I owe this pleasure?"

I looked to Tommy, but he was happy to let me raise the curtain. "We are hoping to gather a bit of information or insight from your wide experience."

Stratford preened a little. "Oh?"

Tommy nodded. "There are some questions about our late soprano Violette Saint Claire, and we wonder if you might have heard of her before she signed on with us."

"The poor little dolly who died?" Stratford took two more sandwiches and ate them simultaneously. "Yeah, she wasn't any Canadian."

"We are aware of that," I said coolly. "Her talent was at such a level that we weren't concerned with a little stretching of the truth on her curriculum vitae. Many singers do it."

Stratford laughed, giving us a lovely view of a half-chewed sandwich. "Isn't that the truth. You don't, though."

"I've been fortunate. I try not to judge others."

"Right, you don't. Nobody's that nice. What do you think she was up to?"

Tommy glared at him. "We don't know if she was up to anything. We're just trying to find any information that might comfort her family."

"Did they find her family?"

I kept my face and voice carefully neutral. "When they do, I would like to be able to tell her loved ones a bit about what she was doing."

"Nothing but singing, that I know." Stratford looked

hard at me. "A lot like you, huh? No rich swells sniffing about, no ill-gotten jewels."

"To the best of my understanding," Tommy began coldly, "she focused all of her energy on the music and becoming a better singer."

Stratford chuckled unpleasantly. "Would have taken a lot of energy. She was a light lyric soprano, and she wasn't going to be anything like Miss Shane here."

I sighed. "She was twenty-one. She had no idea where her voice was going to settle, and she was doing everything right."

"That wasn't what you thought when she was chewing up the scenery in Boston, was it?"

I glared at him over my cup.

"I happened to be in town last winter, thought I'd swing over and see how Arden Standish was developing."

"Yes, you like your tenors, don't you?" Tommy said, his voice neutral, his eyes absolutely not.

Stratford's face tightened for a moment; then he recovered. "It's no secret that I'm an authority on the male voice."

"Indeed you are . . ." Tommy agreed, amiably sipping his coffee.

"What do you think of Standish, Mr. Stratford?" I cut in.

"Well, Miss Shane." The critic smiled, clearly thinking that the poor foolish woman had missed all the subtext. Toms and I would have a nice chuckle over that later. "He was quite promising, actually. Though I thought he was trying for roles that might be beyond him. I see him as more suited for the lighter works, not as a heroic tenor."

"We agree. He was a fine Tebaldo, but I'm not at all certain he would have done well as, say, Radamès."

Stratford snorted. "No, I don't think so. And I think any impresario who gave him the chance would be sorry in the end."

I nodded and took another small sip of coffee, trying to remember what Arden had planned to do next. "He was looking to find a company that would offer him leading roles."

"Well, good luck to that company . . . and the ladies wherever it is."

Tommy and I both looked sharply at him.

"What do you mean?" I asked slowly.

Stratford gave me the unpleasant smile again. "Didn't check him out as thoroughly as you should have, maybe?"

"We took a good hard look at his history." Tommy's voice turned a bit cold.

"Well, it never came to a criminal charge, so perhaps it's only gossip in the singers' watering holes. Neither of you drinks with the tenors and baritones, do you?"

"What?" Tommy asked, his voice a little harder.

Even the persistently repulsive Anthony Stratford wasn't fool enough to ignore that note in the voice of the Champ. "The girl didn't bring charges, of course."

We waited. He was enjoying stringing it out.

"A camp follower, for lack of a better description." Stratford looked at me, clearly wondering if I knew what the expression meant. I gave no sign either that I knew, or that I was thoroughly disgusted by his use of it. "Claimed he'd gotten her, um, excuse me, Miss Shane, in a—"

Tommy just looked at Stratford.

"Sort of trouble," the critic said quickly. "And that he'd beaten her badly when she told him."

My stomach twisted, both at the realization of what kind of man I'd hired and worked with, and the terrible situation that poor girl had found herself in.

"What became of her?" I asked.

"She was just a bit of—" Stratford started.

"She was a human being created in the image of God,

Mr. Stratford." I scowled at him with all the dignity I could muster.

He turned to me with an ugly smile that quickly died when he looked in my eyes; he actually shrank back. I can be quite terrifying when I have to be.

"Um, well, I heard she threw herself in the East River. Couldn't prove it by me."

"I'll find out," Tommy said quietly. "Don't worry about that."

"I'm sure you will," Stratford replied. "I'm not sure what any of this has to do with Violette Saint Claire, though."

I shook my head. "It doesn't. But now that I know this, I can assure you I won't be seeking Mr. Standish's services anytime soon."

"I can give you a list of ten better tenors, none of whom have nasty habits."

I nodded. "That won't be necessary, Mr. Stratford. I will be having a word with my booking agent."

"I certainly would," he agreed. "What about poor little Violette?"

"Do you know anything else about her?"

"Sadly, no. Just that I thought she had a real problem with overacting. Which is probably no revelation to you."

"All young singers have a tendency toward overacting," I reminded him. "Most of us grow out of it with time and some schooling from our colleagues."

" 'Schooling,' " Stratford said, looking from me to Tommy. "That's a word for it. Most singers I know will tell you that they'd happily strangle a ham."

"A little excessive," I observed.

"Perhaps. But if anyone had reason to want her dead, it was you. After what I saw in Boston, no jury would have convicted you."

Considering that Frances had likely been her own judge,

jury and executioner, I did not find his comment amusing. "Apparently, she was a very troubled girl."

"Unfortunate," Stratford said.

"Very," Tommy agreed.

Stratford grabbed a couple more sandwiches and chewed thoughtfully and grotesquely. "So I've given you what I've got. How about you give me something?"

Tommy didn't actually growl, but it was a close thing.

"Information for information?" I asked. I'd been expecting this. "Well, why don't we tell you about our upcoming Western tour?"

"The Ella Shane Opera Company is going West again?"

"We plan to play San Francisco in the late summer." Tommy put on his manager's cool voice and smile.

"What's the repertoire? *Capuleti* again?" Stratford pulled a notebook out of his jacket pocket and started scribbling.

"No. I'm considering *Xerxes,*" I said, hoping it might be interesting enough to back him off. "We've never taken that on tour."

"I don't think anyone else even does it. It's been forgotten for most of a century."

I nodded. "All the more reason to take it on the road."

"Casting?"

"Not set yet. We'll start looking for singers soon."

"So you'll be needing tenors again."

"Not this time. The male lead is a baritone. I think it's important to give the heavier voices a chance, too, don't you?"

Stratford shrugged. "Not my cup of tea, but it's your opera company."

I smiled. "Why, yes, it is."

We forced a few more minutes of amiable small talk before Stratford looked at his watch and remembered his deadline.

Tommy and I walked him to the door, which is where I bowed to them, and Tommy shook his hand, very firmly, and didn't let go.

"I've heard that you're not very polite to your female colleagues."

Stratford went pale.

"You don't need to speak," Tommy continued, his voice as cool and pleasant as if he were discussing the spring weather. "But we'll have no more of that."

"Um, of course, right, then." The critic extracted himself from Tommy's grip and backed off.

Tommy smiled, not soothingly. "I will know."

Stratford swallowed and put on his hat.

"Good day, then." I gave him a polite smile as if I had no idea what had just happened.

"Right," he mumbled. "Good day."

Stratford practically ran out the door. I closed it, then patted Tommy's arm. "Well done, Toms!"

He gave me a sheepish grin, then started back into the parlor. "So, what do we do now?"

"Well, you'll tip a glass or two with the tenors, and in the morning, we'll have a serious chat with Henry Gosling."

"I'm sure he didn't know."

"I am, too. But he needs to know now."

Tommy nodded grimly. "I hate that we hired someone like that."

"I hate that someone like Stratford was the one to tell us."

"All the worse." He picked up his coffee cup. "He's a nasty piece of work."

"I understood that part, but there's more, isn't there?"

Tommy looked at me for a moment, clearly deciding how to phrase his explanation. "I know you're not an innocent little girl, Heller, but there are some things that are hard to explain."

"Well, tell me what you can."

"I'm not sure I understood it all myself." He paused and shrugged. "But I suspect that he's getting some kind of . . . consideration . . . from tenors."

"Oh." I knew he wouldn't tell me any more about what sort of consideration, and I really didn't want to know, anyhow.

"And I also suspect that he's chasing the girls at his office as a way to draw suspicion away from those other activities. He would not be the first man to do that."

"Oh."

"Really ugly things going on with that one." Tommy shook his head. "It's despicable enough abusing the women at the *Beacon,* but he's probably doing that to cover blackmail and worse with the tenors. And he didn't even know much about Violette."

"Except a few nasty comments."

"She *was* a rotten little show-off." He narrowed his eyes at me. "Don't turn her into a dead angel."

"She was also twenty-one. None of us is who we're going to be at twenty-one."

He chuckled a bit. "So true, my wise and ancient one."

"If I'm ancient, what are you?"

"Too damned old to care, Heller." Tommy put down his coffee. "I suppose I should get to work on finding the singers' drinking spot."

"I suppose I should just get to work. I should go over the lyrics for the *Xerxes* aria."

"Or maybe just take your book and go sit on the chaise." He stood over me like a good protector. "You work too hard, you know."

"Probably. You aren't going to be home by dinner, are you?"

"Not likely." He was almost pouting. "Believe me, I'd rather stay home and have something tasty from Mrs. G."

"I'm sure. Well, then maybe I'll just ask her to leave us some soup and send her home early. She might as well get an easy night."

"Glad someone will."

I picked up the library book. I'd gotten to the part where Anne had forced Henry to seek the divorce that would upend Christendom for the next three hundred years. "Now that you mention it, it may be a good night to just read."

Tommy smiled. "The exciting life of a diva."

"I have no complaints."

I didn't make much headway with the book, though. It was hard to care about historical upheaval when there were more current problems to consider.

Chapter 12

A Matter Not Good for the Gosling

Normally, when I am performing at night, I spend the day relaxing at home. I do a light vocalization session early, with help from Montezuma, some kind of easy exercise—a little dance or fencing, maybe just a walk around the block—and mostly simply rest my mind and body for the strenuous night ahead. But the situation on the day of that first benefit was serious enough to merit breaking my routine for a visit to Henry Gosling. Especially after Tommy appeared late for breakfast with a scowl that had as much to do with what he'd learned as the ale he'd tipped at a grubby spot on the edge of the Theater District.

"It was bad, but not as bad as Stratford said, and it took me two vile pints with a couple of equally awful chorus members to find out." Tommy glared at his eggs, over easy with bacon—a man needs his strength.

"Oh?" I asked, taking a small, careful bite of my coddled egg. Romeo, remember, not Brünnhilde.

"Yes. Standish jilted a girl in his hometown upstate, and her brother came to settle the matter . . . only to find he wasn't nearly as good a fighter as he thought he was."

I smiled a little. "There's a lot of that going around."

"Isn't there, though?" Tommy allowed himself a faint smile, too. "The upshot is, Standish isn't dangerous, he's just nasty." He took a bite of his bacon.

I let out a long breath in relief, and then saw Tommy's expression. I waited.

"And the girl?" he offered, a gleam in his eye.

"Yes?"

"Married a nice accountant, and by all reports will not be attending the opera anytime soon."

"I do not blame her, even if I'm sorry to lose a potential patron."

"Too true."

"We're still going to see Henry."

"Yes." Tommy took a sip of his coffee. "He missed this."

"He's not the only one." We might argue that our principal mistake was trusting Henry to do his proper diligence, but it didn't really matter in the end. I'd allowed a man who'd behaved dishonorably with a young woman to work with the ladies in my company. Quite unsettling.

Tommy and I were at Henry's office door when he arrived that Tuesday morning. That meant a walk through the Theater District shortly before eight a.m., when everyone is sleeping off the night before. Even the most desperate beggars were still tucked away wherever they'd managed to land, and the more fortunate were resting after long nights of performance on the stage, and quite possibly various celebrations off it. The only people moving were stage crews, setting up and breaking down, bringing in new sets or cleaning theaters. Even twelve hours before curtain, there was work to do for the show.

Henry's office was on a side street, two flights up from a store that sold musical instruments. His door, with his name stenciled on the frosted glass window, was closed when we arrived. We stood outside, waiting.

Neither Toms nor I had felt frivolous today, so we were in full dress as serious business owners. For him, a dark gray suit under his neat coat, with a tie in a slightly lighter gray, not even a pin dot for levity. For me, a navy-blue suit and plain shirtwaist, and a very simple midnight-blue hat. Anyone who knew us would be shocked by the seriousness and plainness of the attire, and probably more so by our very serious faces.

Henry certainly was, bustling up his stairs humming "Ta-ra-ra Boom-de-ay." An amiable and round little man, he was both intensely focused and intensely likeable, truly enjoyable to work with. He was also tremendously good at finding and bringing along new singers, so I really hoped we could resolve this well.

"Miss Shane! Mr. Hurley. A pleasure to see you, but why so early?" He got a good look at us. "And why so serious?"

"Arden Standish," Tommy said, the name clearly sour in his mouth.

"We have learned a few things," I said.

The color drained from Henry's face as he unlocked his door and motioned us in. "Please. Tell me about this."

"Apparently, Mr. Standish jilted a young lady in his hometown and her brother came to settle the matter. Unpleasantness ensued," Tommy explained carefully.

"Oh no."

"You were unaware?"

"Of course. I checked his references."

"So did we," I said quietly.

"And I talked to some of the singers who've worked with him, as I always do. Where did you hear this?"

"A friend of a friend put us onto the story." I would not go further, because we have to protect Hetty. Of course, Henry knows we have connections in the newspaper world, and might wonder, but he won't know who. "It wasn't nearly as serious as we first thought, but it still raises a concern."

"And I checked it out at the singers' bar last night," Tommy added. "It was apparently common knowledge. In some circles."

Henry shook his head. "I am so sorry. Especially to you, Miss Ella, I know how seriously you take matters of character, as, of course, you should."

"How did we miss this?" I asked.

"I don't know. But I will find out." Henry has three daughters he protects with the ferocity of a man who knows the world.

"Obviously, we will not be retaining Mr. Standish again."

"Of course not." Henry shook his head. "I doubt it will be an issue anytime soon. He's signed for a season in Philadelphia, and we'll see what happens after that." He nodded resolutely. "I will investigate this myself and we will talk again soon."

"Good." Tommy nodded.

"I was quite sure you were unaware," I said. "But I was very concerned. If we could miss this . . ."

Henry shuddered appropriately. "I know, Miss Ella. I'm going to have to take up drinking at the singers' bar."

"Don't you have a son-in-law these days?" Tommy asked.

The agent's serious scowl softened. "I will soon. And he's a smart, sharp fellow. Quite right. He can do his part in the family with a little information gathering."

"And congratulations on your daughter's engagement." As I offered the felicitation, I made a mental note to send flowers. "Your eldest, right?"

"Thankfully. Beatrice would never forgive my middle one, Corinne, if she'd gotten out first."

We all chuckled at that, balance restored for the moment.

"I'll take a good hard look at this matter, folks, and we'll see it doesn't happen again."

We both nodded at Henry.

"Thank you," I said with an honestly relieved smile. "I was just quite concerned."

"Understandably, Miss Ella. We have standards to maintain."

"That, we do." Tommy nodded.

We made our good-byes soon after, and we were both feeling far more optimistic as we headed back to the town house to resume our usual performance day routine. It could have been a great deal worse; and now Henry and his son-in-law-to-be were on the case, so it would not happen again. I felt almost relaxed as I settled onto my chaise with a cup of tea and my book for a few good hours' rest.

Chapter 13

Backstage Dramas

The girls' school benefit that Tuesday night took place at a fairly small, older theater very close to home, not a large Broadway venue like the one where Marie and I would sing a couple weeks hence. I was easily the marquee attraction, on a bill of mostly younger rising talents, and a couple of older singers who still enjoyed pitching in for a good cause with a piece comfortably within the range they had left. I had no doubt that I would someday be in that position, and I hoped to be able to handle it with similar grace, choosing repertoire suited to what I actually could do, not what I imagined possible.

As the top performer, I was last on the bill, and got a reasonably acceptable, if dingy, dressing room of my own. Anna and I arrived a couple of hours before curtain time, even though it was entirely unnecessary, because that's what professionals do. Of course, we also end up reading or playing cards backstage for hours, but we're there, warmed up and in full costume, ready to go on. I took a few moments to walk out on the stage and look around.

While I would wear my costume from *Xerxes*, all I would have behind me was one simple scenic drop Tommy had selected earlier, and I required no props. We try to make things easy for small benefits. But you still don't know a stage until you stand on it, tread the boards, if you will, and get the feeling of it. It doesn't hurt to sing a few bars at full volume, either, just so you know how the sound moves through the theater. That, of course, will be somewhat different when there are people in the seats.

As I stepped off the stage, I heard a strange creak, and reflexively moved away. Just in time to avoid the falling sandbag. It froze me where I stood for a second, even as I reminded myself that such things can happen in theaters, especially old, poorly-kept places like this one. I'd rather it didn't happen so close to my head, though.

As I caught my breath, I heard running footsteps.

"Miss Ella! Are you all right?"

I recognized the voice. Arden Standish. Clearly, not the person I wanted to see at this precise moment. Of course, I'd known he was also performing that night, and had a chance to steel myself after our conversations with Henry and Anthony Stratford. But, of course, that was before I almost got brained.

"Just fine. A little mishap is all," I called as he ran toward me.

"Are you quite sure?"

He put a hand on my arm, and I summoned all of my diva training to stay cool and friendly, and not slap it away. It did me no good to give any hint of the unpleasant things I had learned. Even if it wasn't the worst, it still put him well beyond the range of anyone I wanted to know, or wanted associating with my company.

But if I said so, it raised questions about my judgment. And Tommy's. Best to keep my own counsel.

I straightened myself, careful to detach from him without showing any sign of revulsion, and managed a polite greeting. "Good to see you again."

"You as well, though obviously not under these circumstances."

"Ah, well." Even as we spoke, I heard the stagehands scuffling and swearing behind us. "I'm sure it'll be taken care of. How are you?"

"Doing just fine. I've signed for a season in Philadelphia."

"Philadelphia?" It was only then that I remembered Violette was planning to go to Philadelphia too. I wondered if it meant something, and if so, what?

"They offered me several good roles, including Radamès."

Verdi's Radamès? I wondered. Surely, they didn't sign him for that. Arden might have been able to manage an audition aria for *Aida,* but as I'd told Stratford, I doubted he'd be able to handle the entire—exceedingly demanding—role, night after night. Not for me to say, though, and the chance to try would be enough to convince a man doing smaller roles in New York to head out. And getting him away from here would be just fine by me.

I managed a smile. "Well, that's wonderful. Congratulations."

He smiled back only faintly. "It's a great opportunity, and I need to lose myself in my work right now."

I looked sharply at him, puzzled.

"Violette, of course."

"Yes, a terrible loss, and an awful way to end our tour." More terrible than he knew. I kept my face as neutral as my response.

"Yes. An especially terrible loss for me." He started to say something else, but decided against it.

I watched him for a moment. To the best of my knowledge, they hadn't been close at all; I'd been taking consolation in the fact that I'd never seen her exchange more than a few words with him. Really, I'd have thought he was beneath her notice. Not that she had seemed the sort to hope for a fancy match. Rather, like many young ladies in the early stages of their careers, she seemed to be far more interested in the work than what any man might offer. I was—and still am—quite familiar with that idea. Nearly the only thing we had in common.

For my money, Arden was hardly the man to inspire a maiden to abandon her ambitions.

But the handprint bruise.

Still, breaking hearts, even in a thoroughly repulsive way, does not mean someone is capable of physical violence. "Did you know something bad happened to her just before?"

"What do you mean?" He looked stunned.

"She had a bruise, like a handprint, on her arm."

"How horrible! Was she accosted, or—"

"I don't know." And I did not know if his reaction was real or feigned. He was really only an adequate actor, but if he'd had something to do with it, he also had much better motivation than he did on the stage. "Did she say anything to you that last day?"

"Of course not. I'd have told you or Mr. Hurley immediately."

"I thought as much." I watched his face, which was tight and concerned, but his eyes were moving a lot. "I'm sorry to add to your pain."

He sighed, a bit too theatrically, but he would. "The thought of her suffering some insult, and then . . ."

"Very sad," I agreed. The thought occurred to me that whoever had left that mark on her arm could well bear responsibility one way or another. It might have sent her over the edge, or simply distracted her enough that she didn't realize what she was doing with the vial.

But I had no reason to believe Arden had anything to do with it, beyond my dislike and discomfort with him. And since I was already feeling more than a little guilty for leaving Frances to her own devices because I didn't like her, I could not allow my distaste for Arden to harden into accusation. It would not have been fair.

"If you hear anything else about her, Miss Ella . . ."

"Of course." *Not on your tintype,* I thought. "Well, I'm sure you need to do your own rehearsal. I'll enjoy hearing you tonight."

"And I you."

We bowed to each other, and I walked away, more unsettled than I'd been. I decided to ask Tommy to look into him a little more. With Henry's recommendation, and a fine audition, we'd hired him, and he'd proved a good, if not extraordinary, singer and a decent enough swordsman. On the road, if he wasn't as fun a touring companion as others I've known, he was certainly acceptable company. And while he wasn't my idea of handsome (you've no doubt deduced that I admire men who are tall, dark and all grown-up), his boyish blond good looks certainly didn't hurt with the ladies in the audience. Of course, none of that balanced out what we now knew.

As for that odd exchange about Violette, I hadn't had any sense of a broken love affair, but if he had hopes, and she squashed them in the sharp, imperious way she could well have, he might have done his best to make her life uncomfortable. Depending on what he did, I would likely never have known about it. And I did know that someone had put that bruise on her arm. I walked back to my dressing room, contemplating a number of unpleasant possibilities.

Despite that, once I returned, I pushed the odd conversation with Arden to a corner of my mind, where it could easily wait until after the performance. Even if I had wanted to chew over it, I couldn't have, because once the show began, it was all-consuming for me. When I'm on, I'm on. I assume that every person who is doing what they're meant to do, and doing it well, feels the same. It doesn't matter whether it's teaching children, singing or—hopefully—even digging ditches, because all honest work is honorable if it's *your* work. It is the greatest gift in my life, and the reason I will probably never marry. I can't imagine anything that would be a fair trade, no matter how poetically Marie talks about love, family or a man who would not expect me to make that trade.

Performers will tell you that some nights are better than others, whether the audience can tell or not, and some nights are extraordinarily good. It wasn't quite one of those special nights where it feels like magic, but it was certainly a very good one. My voice was in its best form, and the aria was just right for the range I had on that particular night; the audience was riding along with me. I took my bow, offered a very short encore, because it was already quite late, and walked back to my dressing room with a satisfied smile. This was one night that I'd earned the *"Brava, Diva,"* and I knew it.

As I stepped off the stage, I reflected that it was the kind of night that makes all the work worthwhile and reminds us why we love what we do. I hadn't known Frances well enough to talk about matters of feeling, of course, but I hoped that after everything she'd risked for her career, she'd at least enjoyed a few such nights.

She deserved that much.

Chapter 14

No Stage-Door Lotharios Wanted

The only real problem with small charity benefits is that all sorts of well-meaning contributors get to play stage-door admirer and we have to entertain them. I left my costume and makeup on because I knew there would be a procession of benefactors, and I was not disappointed. Most were overawed and boring, at worst, but there were a few bejeweled and overly-rouged society matrons who felt the need to glare significantly at my male dress, with an expression that would not have been out of place on Cotton Mather.

But the real stage-door Lotharios were the worst. I have a few excessively loyal and hopeful admirers, as does every performer of note, and one has to handle them with a certain degree of civility, no matter how annoying, and sometimes very nearly insulting, their behavior. Since this was my first performance in the city after the last tour, I was not surprised to see two of them.

First, with red roses clenched in his small, pudgy hands, came Grover Duquesne, "Captain of Industry," as Hetty had christened him. Duquesne was sixty, if he was a day, with an impressive belly straining at his brocade waistcoat, an egg-bald head under his perennial top hat, and truly intimidating white-and-brown whiskers. He culti-vated a carefully jovial and harmless air, but there was an oily appraisal in his narrow porcine eyes that made me want to go take a long bath.

The appraisal was, unfortunately, just part of the pack-age. Duquesne was from the earlier generation that col-lected chorus girls, and had dropped broad hints that he would like to be my "patron." So far, I had not given in to my desire to inform him that for that to happen, we would have to skate across the ice of Hell to wherever one kept a mistress, and that I would have to completely take leave of my senses, besides. But, considering the level of provoca-tion, I could not guarantee that my forbearance would hold forever.

Luckily, Toms arrived backstage at almost the exact same moment as the Captain of Industry, and engaged him in careful, amiable conversation with a distinctly intimidating undertone. This scene had played itself out many times in the past, with precisely the same outcome: Duquesne hand-ing off the roses to me, bowing over my hand while coming skin-crawlingly close to actually kissing it, and Tommy kindly, yet *very* firmly, escorting him to the stage door while I disposed of the roses and washed my hands. But my admirer apparently lived in constant hope that tonight might be the night that I would be swept away by his wealth and importance and abandon my principles. Hope, however misguided, springs eternal for the Captain of In-dustry.

Tommy was still taking care of vermin removal, Anna had helped me out of my cape and I'd loosened my hair from its tight stage knot to a more comfortable braid, when the second of my regular admirers arrived.

"The milksop and his mommy," Anna whispered as Teddy Bridgewater and his formidable parent swept in.

On his own (not that I'd ever seen him alone), Teddy was an amiable nonentity with a fortune that made Grover Duquesne seem like a pauper. But he came with his mama. Mama Bridgewater would have made an admirable Valkyrie, but instead of a horned helmet and metal breastplate, she wore a fashionable black mourning bonnet and a bombazine dress straining to do its yeoman's work. Teddy handed me a bouquet of lilies of the valley, his signature offering, with a smell that nauseates me, and bowed over my hand.

"Magnificent as ever, Miss Shane."

Mama B stood behind him and glared. She had never yet spoken to me, since as a person on the stage, I am beneath her oh-so-respectable notice. It always amused me to realize that, while she looked at least twenty years my senior, I was actually less than five years younger than she. Yes, I am aware that it would be (barely) biologically possible for me to be Teddy's mother. We will do well to walk right past that fact.

"Thank you, Mr. Bridgewater. Lovely to see you and your mother."

Teddy's beardless skin flushed and his colorless eyes lingered on my face. "Lovely to see you, too."

And so we made what must be smaller than small talk for a few moments while Teddy stared at me, and Mama B attempted to set my clothing on fire with her eyes. Anna made herself very, very busy with the costumes, so as not to giggle, and I conjugated Latin verbs in my head in hopes of distracting myself: *amo, amas, amat.*

"Yes, the weather has been rather chilly . . ."

After what seemed like an eternity, but was probably all of five minutes, Mama B reminded Teddy that he had to get home to bed, and I did my best not to snicker as they left. Teddy followed her docilely, but with a dusky flush creeping up under his collar. Even if I'd found him remotely appealing (not on your tintype!), there was no way

I would have allowed an adult man who permitted his mother to set his bedtime to court me.

I allowed myself a small sigh of relief as the door closed behind them, tossed the offending flowers to Anna, who threw them right out the window, and picked up my cold cream jar, in the hope that the worst of the night was at long last over. And, of course, there was still another knock.

"Come in," I called, only slightly wearily, shaking my head at Anna, who looked as disappointed as I felt at the thought of yet another visitor. Until I saw who it was.

Gilbert Saint Aubyn walked in. Of course, he was appropriate in black tie, and, thankfully, without flowers. He had an odd expression on his face, though, and I was afraid I knew what it meant. People I know socially always look at me differently after they see me sing. Sometimes it becomes very uncomfortable. Hetty had a hard time with Ella Shane, the Diva, until I showed up at her family's town house one afternoon on my velocipede and dragged her back into the park to remind her who we really are.

Don't be like those awful men, I begged the Fates as I looked at Saint Aubyn. *Please, please, don't be just another backstage Lothario.*

"Brava, Diva," Saint Aubyn said, giving me a wry smile that allayed my concerns. "General Shane wins the day."

I returned the smile, wondering why it had mattered so much to me that he not be another smitten fan. "Thank you, Your Grace. It was a good night."

"May I ask you a few questions about that?"

"Certainly." I motioned him into the room. "If you don't mind my taking my makeup off while we talk. I cannot stand another second with this paint."

He chuckled as he sat. "Fair enough."

I opened the cold cream jar, watching him in the mirror as he looked around the dingy and crowded space, and then returned his gaze to me. "This is not really about tonight's performance, is it?"

"Perceptive as always, Miss Shane." He nodded. "I am attempting to understand what might have drawn Frances to this life. And what might have made her desperate enough to end it."

"I don't know that she was desperate."

"What do you mean?"

"I've learned a few things about your cousin's death."

"Such as?" He sat down on the only other chair in the room, a spindly olive-green metal thing that looked as if it would barely hold him.

"A reporter friend of mine gave me a copy of the report from New Haven, and I asked my doctor to look at it."

Saint Aubyn's eyes narrowed. "You have a reporter friend?"

"We met on a settlement house committee. We have a great deal in common as working women."

"Aren't you uncomfortable with the idea that she might write about you?"

"People write about me often enough. And good reporters live by a code of ethics. My friendship with her is confidential, as any other friend would be."

"You've placed a great deal of trust in her."

I shook my head. "I have nothing to hide, Your Grace. If anyone looks into the deep secrets of my life, they will find nothing more than a fondness for shepherd's pie. And violet ice cream."

Saint Aubyn blinked. "Not together, surely."

"No."

"I do not fancy ices, having been forced to toy with far too many at various society balls, but I do enjoy a good shepherd's pie."

"Before you return to England, you should come to our

town house for luncheon or dinner with Tommy and me and sample Mrs. Grazich's version."

"I would like that."

"So would she. We'll never hear the end of it. 'I cooked for a duke!'"

He laughed. "Is everyone around you a character, or is it just the way you tell the story?"

"Both."

"I don't doubt it." He watched me in the mirror for a moment. "All right, so what did you learn from your friends?"

"I apologize for the indelicacy," I started.

His face tensed.

"Nothing like that," I said quickly. "She apparently had a sort of . . . nervous illness."

"What do you mean?"

"She was apparently vomiting up what she ate." I just forced the words out. Best get it over with.

"Again?"

That was probably the last thing I expected him to say. I simply stared.

"Perhaps five years ago," he started, "she got very thin, and her mother told me that she had a sort of eating problem. She started singing lessons soon after, and all I heard after that was about music, and how she wished she could make it a career."

So the music saved her, too.

"You are thinking that the music saved her, just as it saved you."

I blinked at him.

"I've checked your bona fides, as I'm sure you did mine, Miss Shane. I'm aware that you grew up a poor orphan girl on the Lower East Side. I don't doubt you believe you owe your life to the music, or that Frances did, too."

"True. I was thinking that."

"But you did not want to be unkind to me by saying so." He was looking much too deeply into my eyes.

"I try not to be unkind if I can avoid it."

He smiled. "That, you do."

"There's more."

"What else?"

"You will know this, since you saw the report, but it came as a surprise to me. She was poisoned with nicotine."

"Yes. I wondered why she chose such a nasty end."

"I'm no longer entirely certain she did."

He stood, knocking the little chair over, and took a step toward me. "*What?*"

The sound and sudden movement stunned me for a second. I found myself backing away, wondering where my sword was, and Tommy, too. I glanced at Anna, who was holding the clothing brush like a club.

"I'm sorry, ladies," Saint Aubyn said as he righted the chair and composed himself. "I didn't mean to startle you."

I wasn't going to give him that. "No offense taken."

Anna returned to brushing my cape.

"Perhaps I misunderstood."

"No. You didn't." I took a breath and a hard look at him as he sat back down. He was genuinely concerned and upset, as I surely would have been, and clearly hadn't intended any threat. Which, considering my skills, and the fact that Tommy would soon return to pick me up, was quite good for his continued well-being. "Dr. Silver says she may have been using some kind of patent emetic or purgative with nicotine in it, and there is just the possibility that she mistakenly filled the prop bottle with the medicine instead of water or whatever she normally used."

His eyes burned into mine. "Just the possibility."

"A possibility that might bring some comfort to a family in grief."

He let out a long breath. "Very true. Thank you, Miss Shane."

"I am glad to be of help," I replied, realizing how stiff it sounded as he watched me. "Losing a loved one is painful enough, without the added suffering of unanswered questions."

Saint Aubyn nodded, watched me. And then: "Do you know what she was taking?"

"I don't. From what my doctor said, I got the impression that nicotine is not an uncommon ingredient in patent medicines."

"Not as common as opiates, but I have heard of it. I'd never seen any sign of her using such things, though."

"Would you? Dr. Silver told me girls hide it quite well."

"A fair question, and one for which I don't have a good answer."

I looked away, and realized I still had a handful of cold cream and a face full of makeup. I left him to his thoughts as I got to work, well aware that he was watching as I wiped off the cold cream, revealing my normal face, with just a few smudges under the eyes from the heavy liner.

"You wouldn't really need to be beautiful, would you?"

I laughed. "As long as the people in the back row can see your eyes and mouth, it doesn't matter if you look like a pair of old shoes."

"And yet you are."

"A pair of old shoes?" I teased.

"No, a beauty." He looked a little flustered, but by now, I was used to his occasional awkward comments.

"Very kind," I said, turning away from my mirror. "We have also learned that your cousin was moving along in her career."

"Yes?"

"Her booking agent was ready to sign her for a four-role season contract in Philadelphia." He waited, so I continued. "It would have been exactly the perfect step in launching her."

"So whatever was wrong, it wasn't in the progress of her work."

"Likely not." I returned to my table, giving him a moment to contemplate. I thought about Arden, but remembered Father Michael's advice. "She was very gifted."

"But apparently not happy."

"Perhaps. Or perhaps careless. All of us mortals have our dark times."

"True." He was silent for a moment, thinking. "Artists more than others?"

I shrugged. "We do pour a lot of feeling into what we do."

"How does it feel when you sing?"

"Better than anything under Heaven," I told him honestly. "It's my gift. I hold the audience in my hand, and I can make them feel what I feel . . . or what I want them to."

He nodded gravely. "I trained as a barrister before I became heir to the title, and I've given the occasional speech in the Lords. There is something to be said for the limelight."

"It makes us more than we are." I returned the nod. "And it's very hard not to want to continue that feeling, once you've had it."

"Like love, perhaps."

"I wouldn't know." I picked up my charm bracelet and started putting it back on, but between the slippery cold cream and my tiredness, it was a struggle.

He watched me for a moment. "Here. Allow me."

I handed him the bracelet and held out my wrist. "I don't doubt your hands are steadier than mine at this hour."

He smiled and clasped it easily, running his fingers over the charms. "Are they all operas and roles?"

"Mostly." I shrugged. "Some personal mementoes from Tommy and my close friends."

"So the music is not the only thing you cherish."

"No." I suspected I knew what he was thinking. "But it is the center of my world."

"So you would have no trouble understanding why someone would run off and leave their family and world to do this."

"None at all."

"Especially if you thought the music saved you from a life you couldn't stand."

"Much as it did me. Without a voice, and a teacher, I'd be a washerwoman right now."

"I cannot begin to imagine that."

I shrugged. "I never forget that I am one of the lucky ones. There are so many other people whose gifts will never be known."

Saint Aubyn nodded. "Is that why you sang here tonight?"

"And why I will always sing for any school or settlement house that asks me."

"Impressive."

"I do very nicely with the paying customers. The least I can do is help others."

"Did you share this philosophy with Frances?"

I shook my head. "We never had a heart-to-heart conversation, I'm sorry to say."

"No?"

"We shared a coffee or tea a few times, and amiable chat during rehearsal, but it never went beyond the pleasantries. I'm older, I'm the company owner. I was not the one she would confide in." And I didn't like her, God forgive me.

"Probably true. And if you are trying to hide your identity, you would not be making close friends."

"Equally true. She did somewhat keep to herself."

"Did she have any friends?"

"As I said, she spent time with Anna and Louis, but I don't believe she was close to anyone else in the company."

He was silent for a moment as he thought about that; then he looked closely at me. "I'm sorry. I am probably keeping you from your rest."

"I am glad to help, but, yes, I'm quite tired."

"Understandably." Gilbert Saint Aubyn rose, smiling. "Thank you for your time, Miss Shane."

"My pleasure. Please don't hesitate to call on me if you have more questions."

"Thank you."

"You might, at least, gain some useful insight into Juliet soon."

"Oh?"

"Marie de l'Artois is joining me for the Balcony Scene at a benefit for the settlement house in about two weeks."

"I should see that."

"Would you also like me to ask Marie if she will talk to you about the role? Her time is limited because of her family responsibilities, but perhaps after our rehearsal session the day after tomorrow . . ."

Saint Aubyn looked either curious or shocked. " 'Family responsibilities'?"

"She has a husband and three children, and sings only occasionally. But brilliantly."

"Good for her."

"What?"

He shrugged. "I don't necessarily hold with all of that 'Angel in the House' swill. Why shouldn't your friend sing when she can, if she is meeting all of her family duties?"

I stared at him.

"My mother and aunts are absolutely angels, and they have always spent much of their time out of the house helping those in need." He smiled, apparently at the thought of those excellent ladies. "Perhaps we all must think of some new answers in this new century."

Will you marry me? I thought, and quickly shook that off. "It is good to hear a man with such modern ideas."

"Not that modern, Miss Shane. I'm not at all convinced about woman suffrage."

I laughed. "What? You don't mind the idea of a woman continuing to sing while raising a family, but you don't want her to vote?"

"Politics is a filthy game." Saint Aubyn shook his head. "I suspect women will not improve it, but be harmed by it."

I smiled. "I would very much enjoy having this debate with you when I am not so tired."

"I would enjoy it as well." He bowed. "Until next time, then."

"I shall look forward to it."

As he walked out, Anna shook her head. "That's some odd fish of a man. Not bad to look at, but one odd fish."

It was only as I took off my stockings that night, and saw the fading mark on my ankle from almost falling in front of the grocery wagon, that I remembered I hadn't mentioned the handprint bruise. I consoled myself with the thought that he'd read the report and must surely know.

Chapter 15

In Which the Agent Calls

People who do not know performers tend to think we lead lives of luxury and decadence, dancing all night and sleeping until noon. Even if I were inclined to late-night misbehavior, which I am not, I would not be able to engage in much of it and maintain a voice. I have no idea what's required to maintain a chorus girl's skills (whatever they may be), but an opera singer has to live quite a disciplined life. The instrument only works properly if the body in which it lives is in good health, and the voice is especially sensitive to lack of sleep. Which does mean, yes, that the morning after a performance, I might well sleep deep into the midday, simply to restore myself. Decadent, no. Disciplined, yes.

I do not, however, hold with breakfast in bed. Unless one is genuinely sick, decently-brought-up people get out of bed and eat at a table. Which, admittedly, may mean luncheon for breakfast. Not the worst thing, when Mrs. G is making it. And so it was that Wednesday, the morning after the girls' school benefit, I rose well after eleven. I buttoned my purple plush wrapper over my nightclothes, stepped into the matching purple slippers, with sweet pink flowers on the toes, and headed downstairs.

Needless to say, I was not expecting to find anyone but family about, or I would have put on an appropriate housedress.

"Heller? Is that you?" Tommy called from the parlor as I walked into the foyer.

I stuck my head around the pocket door, to see Henry Gosling and Tommy sitting with the coffee tray.

"Good morning," I said to Henry, trying for perfect diva aplomb—no easy task in my wrapper, with my hair straggling out of its night braid. The smell of good fresh coffee was too much for me, however, and I decided to brazen it out. I drew myself up to my full height and walked into the room with queenly demeanor, as if I were wearing coronation robes instead of a plush wrapper.

"Good morning, Miss Ella. I'm terribly sorry to trouble the two of you at this early—"

Tommy looked at me and chuckled; whether at my attempt at regality or Henry's discomfiture, I wasn't sure.

"It's only early if you've been singing all night." I offered a reassuring smile as I sat on the settee by Tommy. Thankfully, there was an extra cup on the tray. I filled it, doing my best not to huddle over the cup and sigh with joy as I sipped.

"That's right. You had a benefit last night," Henry said. "I'd forgotten."

"For the girls' school at St. Teresa's," Tommy said. "For some reason, it's harder to raise money for girls' education than boys."

Henry shook his head. Father of daughters, he didn't like it any more than we did. "Strange world we live in. You'd think we'd want the mothers of the next generation to be decently schooled."

"I certainly do." I smiled as the warmth of the coffee started to take hold.

"Indeed." Henry drank some of his coffee and picked up a snickerdoodle. "You do have an excellent cook. Mrs. Gosling would try to steal her away, if I told her."

"I do not think she'd be willing to move uptown." I shook my head. The Goslings live above Central Park.

"Probably just as well. I am told I already eat far too many cookies."

"We won't tell," Tommy assured him.

Henry nodded as he ate the last bite of cookie; then his face turned serious. "So, in light of our conversation yesterday, when I found this buried in my mail pile, I thought you might want to see it."

It was a letter from the coroner of New Haven County, Connecticut, thanking Henry for his help in identifying the unfortunate Frances Saint Aubyn. Tommy and I took only a few moments to read it, since it was but two or three simple paragraphs.

"At least we know she went back home," Henry said.

I took another look at the last lines: *We have sent her remains back to her family. Your help prevented her from resting in potter's field.* I remembered Saint Aubyn's comment about fighting the vicar. "Well, that's something for the family."

Henry nodded. "I'm glad I don't have to think of that poor child all alone somewhere."

"Thank you for telling us." I looked at the date on the letter—more than a month ago. It made sense now. Saint Aubyn buried his cousin; then he came over here to see if he could find out what happened to her. Poor man.

Tommy shook his head. "Terribly sad."

"Too true. I wish I'd known more about her," Henry said. "When she left that packet of papers with me because she didn't want to take them on the road, I never thought it was the last time I'd see her."

"We never do think it's the last time," I said quietly.

All of us sat there for a moment, thinking about any number of people who were not Frances Saint Aubyn.

"At any rate, Henry, it's a good thing you came by," Tommy said finally, holding out his cup to warm up.

I poured and pulled myself back to our cozy coffee. "He's right. We need to start looking for baritones."

Henry's brows went up. "Not tenors?"

"We're pretty well done with tenors." Tommy gave a wry shrug.

"No," I said. "We're done with one tenor."

"But we don't need one this time."

"It's probably going to be *Xerxes* in San Francisco," I explained, handing Henry another snickerdoodle and taking one myself. Surely, after all of this drama and emotion, we deserved a little treat. "The male lead is a baritone."

The agent took a bite of cookie, with a puzzled expression.

Tommy chuckled. "That was my reaction the first time I heard the name, too. It's Handel, and she gets to play a general. Hasn't been done much in the last century, so it's new and exciting to opera fanciers."

"Sounds like a winning idea."

"We think so," Tommy said, taking his own cookie.

"Well, then, all hail General Shane."

I laughed, since I felt anything but martial in my wrapper. "Something like that, gentlemen."

After Henry left, fortified with a basket of Mrs. G's snickerdoodles for the afternoon at his office, I neatened myself up in a blue-violet print housedress for a tasty luncheon of cold chicken and fruit macédoine. I then settled in for a quiet afternoon at home. The post came soon after we finished, with a special treat, a letter from Madame Lentini:

My Dear Child,

I hope this letter finds you and your cousin well. Amalfi is as lovely as ever, and Mr. Fritzel is in the pink of health, as am I. We do hope you children can manage a visit sometime soon. The sun and air will do you good.

You are probably working too hard, as always. Try to rest your instrument when you can.

And about the hard work, darling. Your voice will be reaching its peak within a few years, but you have plenty of time to sing. You may be running out of time if you wish to have a family. I remind you that we live in a much different world than when I started on the stage. Singers have every reason to expect to make an honorable marriage these days, and you should.

You will be rolling your eyes now, as you did when I reminded you to stand up straight. Roll away. I missed the chance to be a mother, and I promised myself as I guided you into your career that I would not allow you to do the same.

Just find a good man and marry him. You will know him when you meet him. And if you have already met him, don't fight him or make him wait. Too long, anyway. A man does like a woman who makes him work to win her.

In any case, keep taking proper care of yourself and your instrument, as you always do. Don't forget to vocalize every day.

Give my love to Tommy, and tell him and his writer friends to stay out of trouble.

With much love,
Madame

"How's Madame?" Tommy asked.

"Happy and healthy. She sends her love and reminds you and the sports reporters to stay out of trouble."

"Of course, she does." Madame had a soft spot for Tommy, like most of the rest of the world, and had been quite relieved when he retired. Even happier to know that he was devoting his energies to my career and to me.

"She also thinks I should find a good man and marry him."

"Does she, now?" Tommy smiled a little. "She may have a point. You could do with a little one or two."

"Not you, too."

"Heller, I'm not going to marry, because I'm not going to marry. That doesn't mean you shouldn't."

I just stared at him. We were rarely this blunt—though, of course, it was understood.

"I've seen you with the Morsel. I know. You know."

I shrugged. "I can't just go order a child from the stationer's."

"Well, no. But you could stop slamming the door on the fingers of any man who has the temerity to so much as smile at you."

"I don't—"

"Heller, we're two sides of the same coin. And both of us have a chip on our shoulders the size of the Lower East Side."

"Maybe."

"You assume no man can have honorable intentions because of who you are and where you're from. That's not fair to you, or to the many good men in this world."

"Oh?"

"I'm not suggesting you elope with one of your horrible hangers-on. I am suggesting you don't decide you know a man's intentions before you know him at all. You know I will be here to show your suitor the door if he turns out to be a bounder."

I laughed. "That, you will."

"Anyhow, nobody's sending you down the aisle tomorrow." He laughed, too. "Lentini's turning into a grandma in her retirement. Is she worried that you'll be too old to have a family?"

"I think so."

"Well, remind her that Grandma Bridey had Uncle David at fifty-two and tell her we'll see her in Amalfi next winter."

"Good idea," I said, skating right past Grandma Bridey. "We could just keep going after London, spend a few weeks in the sunshine before we come back here."

"Mother and our friends at the *Beacon* wouldn't like it."

"Neither would Father Michael."

We looked at each other and sighed. "Maybe next year."

Chapter 16

In Which Our Divas School
the Duke

Next day, Thursday, Marie appeared in the early afternoon; the small Winslows all take afternoon naps, and it's a propitious time to leave them to the nanny. I'd been taking a fencing lesson, and Louis arrived a bit early, so I hadn't had time to change out of my fencing breeches and oversized old shirt, leaving my hair in its loose ballerina's knot. Louis didn't even notice, but Marie chuckled and asked me if I'd deliberately stayed in boys' clothes to appear unattractive to the duke. Since I'd almost forgotten he was coming over to meet her, it clearly wasn't that.

In any case, she was lovely enough for both of us, in a cornflower-blue silk day dress, with white lace trim at the high neck, and a sweet matching hat. I know Hetty would not have wanted to write about it, but I resolved to make Marie tell me the milliner, and I would get one in lavender. She left the hat downstairs, with plans to put it on for tea with the duke; singing is much too serious business to worry about one's chapeau.

It didn't take long to run our duet; Marie and I had done it somewhere between dozens and hundreds of times,

122 Kathleen Marple Kalb

after all, and she was right back to top form. Montezuma, who has a bit of a crush on Marie, flew down to the piano, greeted her with a friendly "Love the birdie" and accepted a pat on the head. Then he sang along as we practiced, following Marie's melody line. Louis, who was used to having an extra performer, merely smiled and kept on playing.

After we finished, Montezuma returned to his perch, and Louis, as he always did, gave each of us a few notes and reminders. Then, as we were chatting around the piano, he pulled another score out from his music stand.

"I wonder if you ladies would try this for me and tell me what you think."

"You've been writing?" I asked. "About time."

"Past time." Marie's eyes took on a gleam many divas reserve for the offering of small velvet boxes. "What do we have here?"

Louis pushed his glasses up the bridge of his nose as he took a breath. "Well, Anna was reading a book about the Wars of the Roses, and I saw the painting of *The Princes in the Tower*, and thought it might just be perfect for you two."

I smiled. I knew which picture: the two blond boys in dark doublet and hose clinging together. It would indeed be a perfect visual for us: Marie as the delicate little brother, me as the older, regal king. And nobody knew our voices better than Louis.

"Since the princes aren't really interesting beyond the death scene, I thought I'd have you double roles. Madame Marie as Elizabeth Woodville, the princes' mother—"

"And me as Richard the Third?"

"No, Miss Ella." Louis blushed. "I'd never do that to you. Henry Tudor, the conquering hero."

I couldn't wait to hear what he had. Neither could Marie. She snatched the score out of his hands and started leafing through it. "Oh yes! Yes."

I peeked over her shoulder. "This looks marvelous."

Louis grinned, his face lighting up in relief and excitement. "Yes?"

"Yes, indeed," I said, looking at Marie.

"Can we sing it?"

"I hoped you'd want to. Would you like to try the death scene arias?"

"Please!" we called in unison.

He handed us the score, since he could play from memory. "It's just before King Richard's henchmen come to murder them. They fear—or know—what's about to happen . . . first Prince Richard, a scared little boy who wants his mother, and then King Edward, a teenager who realizes he will never know love."

It was all the direction we needed. Marie started in on "O, My Mother," a heart-wrenching soprano showcase even on the first read. Louis's music started gently and built along with the lyrics to a finish that left us all teary-eyed. Marie and I weren't really trying any acting just yet, but I ended up holding her like a comforting older brother as she finished the last few lines and crumpled onto my shoulder.

Then it was my turn. Following Marie is always a little daunting . . . and after that? As I started in on "Never Shall I Love," I questioned the wisdom of putting my aria last. I'd never be able to equal Marie, I thought, and it's always better to leave the audience with your best. But then the song drew me in. Perhaps too close to home: *I will never lie in the arms of one I love . . . I will never know the joy . . . or the pain—or any of it.* Again, set to Louis's glorious melody, it was placed perfectly in my range. It was an extraordinary piece.

Obviously, we hadn't blocked it out like a real scene, but when I finished my last notes, Marie and I were huddled together on the floor, holding each other for comfort and dear life. We sang the last few lines as a duet:

Marie, softly: " 'I am frightened.' "

" 'I am here.' "

" 'Help me be brave, brother.' "

" 'Remember who we are. Still, Plantagenets and sons of kings.' "

" 'So bravely . . .' "

" 'Bravely . . . we die.' "

Louis ended with a few ominous bars, playing in King Richard's henchmen to smother our poor princes, and Marie and I looked at each other, too impressed and moved to even speak for a moment.

"*Brava, Divas!*" called a voice from the back of the studio as someone clapped his hands.

It broke the spell and we looked up to see Gilbert Saint Aubyn walking toward us, unashamedly wiping away a tear. "Good heavens, ladies. What was that?"

I quickly stood and helped Marie up, taking a look toward Montezuma, who had been lulled to sleep by the music. Of course, he had.

Marie motioned to Louis. "His new work."

"Amazing." Saint Aubyn shook Louis's hand. "Absolutely astonishing."

"Thank you," Louis said, staring at all of us with the same dazed look I was sure Marie and I had.

"We should do this instead of *Capuleti* this fall for Polly's college fund." I took the score from Marie and handed it to Louis. "A world premiere? Two trouser roles and doubling, too?"

"An absolute sensation." She patted the accompanist's arm. "Louis, you're a genius."

He blushed and smiled. "I can't take all the credit. Anna writes the lyrics, you know."

"I thought I detected a woman's touch"—Marie smiled—"and a mother's."

Saint Aubyn was watching both of us with open curiosity. "Forgive me, ladies."

We turned to him.

"Are you both all right? You seemed quite—"

Marie and I both burst out laughing, a pretty standard reaction after plowing through all of that strong emotion.

The duke looked hurt. "I merely—"

Without thinking, I reached over and patted his arm. "It's all right. You'd have no way to know. We're fine. We just laughed as a kind of release after our performance."

I'm not sure how it happened, but he put his hand on my arm for a moment, and kept it there as he looked closely at me. "Understandable. I have never seen anything like that."

"I'm not sure we've ever done anything like that." Marie still seemed a bit dazed. "Louis is incredible."

"You ladies are rather impressive, too." The duke hadn't moved his hand from my arm.

"Thank you." I was enjoying the warmth of his touch, and the glow in his eyes as he watched me. It wasn't a besotted fan; it was honest admiration and respect.

"We like to think so." Marie's eyes sparkled as she carefully walked between us. "I don't believe we've met."

The duke and I broke apart, and I felt a horrible blush creeping up my face, which hopefully no one noticed as I made the introductions, not forgetting Louis.

Montezuma decided to join the conversation just as the gentlemen bowed. "English stick!"

Bloody blast it!

"Fine figure of a man!"

Yes, the only thing that would be worse.

Marie giggled.

Saint Aubyn laughed. "I beg to differ, Miss Shane. I may be a stick, but thank you, I am a *British* stick. My mother is Scots."

"Perhaps you would like to correct Montezuma," I replied, meeting his impish smile with my own.

"No, thank you. I have learned never to argue with a lady's parrot."

"Love the birdie!" Montezuma proclaimed as he preened.

Marie shook her head. "That bird will drive us all to distraction."

"Well, let's leave him to his contemplation," I said, motioning everyone out of the studio, and away from any further embarrassing comments. Of course, Montezuma started singing a raucous chorus of some drinking song the sports reporters had taught him, but at least I got everyone out of the room before he got to the really off-color part.

"Are you staying to tea, Louis?" I asked as we walked down the stairs, and I saw Mrs. Grazich setting up in the parlor on the first floor.

"Sorry, Miss Ella, I'd love to, but Anna is teaching an English class in an hour and a half, so I have to get back to watch Morrie."

"You probably also want to tell her how much we love *The Princes in the Tower*."

We three exchanged a grin.

"Yes, indeed." Louis picked up his hat and jacket.

"Then we'll all take this up later." I nodded to him and Marie.

"And we'll start working on learning the score as soon as we can," Marie added, as she finished pinning her hat at exactly the rakish angle that perfectly set off her blue eyes.

"I'll look forward to it," Louis agreed, beaming.

"Magnificent work, Mr. Abramovitz," said the duke, shaking his hand again.

"Thank you."

As the door closed behind Louis, I motioned to the parlor.

"I believe there's tea, although it's something of an anticli-max at this point."

Marie laughed. "A real cup of tea and grown-up con-versation are quite enough for me."

"Especially in this company," agreed the duke with a nod at me. "'Lead on, Macduff.'"

We went back in and set ourselves up in the parlor, Marie and I on the settee, the duke on a chair. All very for-mal and proper. Well, mostly.

Marie poured the tea, smiling as she glanced between Saint Aubyn and me. "It's probably more appropriate that I pour, even if we are at her home, since our Ella is a boy at the moment."

The duke nodded to me. "Never send a boy to do a woman's job."

I laughed and took my cup from Marie. "Something like that, Your Grace."

Mrs. Grazich, who is almost as fond of Marie as she is of Father Michael, had outdone herself with a series of plates of teatime dainties, all decorated with little veg-etable flowers and leaves, and even a couple of tiny carrot birds. Marie offered a plate to the duke, and he burst out laughing.

"Surely, you've seen tea sandwiches before," Marie said reprovingly.

"Sorry to disappoint you, Madame de l'Artois, but even in my rarefied circles, food generally looks like food, not objets d'art."

We laughed guiltily. I shook my head at him. "Please don't say that too loudly around Mrs. G. You'll hurt her feelings."

To his credit, Saint Aubyn nodded. "We can't have that." He gingerly picked up a sandwich.

"You don't have to actually eat any," I said quickly, "just don't insult them."

"They're actually quite tasty," he said after a bite. "As long as I don't choke from laughter at you. Did you quite seriously just tell me not to insult the sandwiches?"

"Not the sandwiches, their maker." I admit to being rather huffy about it. "There's more than enough unkindness in the world without you adding to it."

He studied me for a long moment. "You're right."

"Ella breaks quite enough hearts on the stage. She doesn't like to do it on her own time." Marie cut her eyes to me. "So, Your Grace, you want my thoughts on Juliet?"

"Yes, please."

"Well, it's a rather depressing role to play over a long period of time."

"All that dying for love?" he asked.

"Not really." Marie shook her head. "It's the powerlessness of it. Everyone treats her as a pretty ornament to be enjoyed and placed as they wish."

"Ah."

"Romeo here, as I pointed out to her a few days ago, has choices. He . . . she . . . chooses Juliet . . . chooses to duel . . . chooses how far he will go for love—and how he'll end it." Marie smiled ruefully. "Juliet quite literally has only one choice, the poison. It's the only power she has."

" 'If all else fail, myself have power to die.' " He clearly knew the line, but spoke it slowly, thoughtfully.

"Right." She sipped her tea. "Many women are powerless most of the time. For most of us, it's just life as we live it."

"Not you ladies."

I smiled at him. "Not as much."

"But legally, I'm still Paul's property, even though he hates the notion," Marie pointed out. "And all of us are at someone's mercy."

Saint Aubyn stared at us. "I had not thought of it that way."

"You wouldn't. You're a man."

He looked a little wounded.

"That's not quite fair, Marie," I cut in. "He's trying to understand."

Marie smiled, probably at my defense of him, and nodded. "No insult intended. Just an observation."

"No offense taken. Tell me more."

"Women don't control much. And playing a role that reminds you how little power you have?"

"Could help make someone desperate."

"Yes, I'm sorry."

He nodded and silently looked into his tea for a few moments, finally bringing his gaze back to Marie. "Tell me about something more pleasant."

"What?"

"How you manage to do all this."

"This what?"

"Singing and family life," Saint Aubyn said with a faint smile. "Miss Shane has told me you have three wee ones, which I cannot imagine."

Marie's serious expression gave way to a joyful smile. "Indeed I do. Being a mother is the most important thing I do, but not the only one."

"Clearly. You have a lovely voice."

"Thank you." She beamed at him. "I limit my engagements, choosing them carefully, and my husband is kind enough not to complain. I am lucky."

The duke nodded. "I suspect your spouse is the lucky one."

"Aren't you sweet," Marie said, picking up a very decorative cookie. "What about you, Your Grace? How do you feel about wives who sing?"

"That would depend upon the singing. And the wife."

As he said it, his eyes moved from Marie to me, and quickly back.

"No doubt, it would." She grinned and cut her eyes to

me. "I'm not the only singer who manages a career and children."

"No?"

"A fair number of women in the regional companies do the same. All that's required is a willingness to work hard . . . and a husband who won't stand in the way."

"Ah. That is probably the key."

"It is." Marie smiled. "Your cousin would almost certainly have known about such women. So she would have known that art does not have to be the only love in your life."

The duke nodded.

"It might—or might not—have been important to her at her age. I was far more interested in singing than in men until I was a bit older."

I nodded. "That was the impression I had of her. She was interested only in the music. But you're right, some singers do eventually widen their horizons."

Marie sipped her tea and watched me. "We all should eventually, unless we want to end up alone in a house filled with programs and old costumes."

I looked down into my tea. For a tiny second, I felt almost weepy.

"Perhaps a bit harsh, Madame?" Saint Aubyn cut in as I felt, rather than saw, his eyes on me.

She patted my hand. "No offense intended, Ells."

I shook my head. "None taken."

Marie once again glanced between Saint Aubyn and me, then just smiled at him. "At any rate, I hope I've been able to give you some insight."

"You've been a great help."

"Good." She looked down at the watch pinned to her bodice. "Heavens. I must be going home."

In the half second as she rose, she metamorphosed from diva to busy mother, and I smiled, having seen it many times before. Saint Aubyn couldn't help staring a little, but managed to keep his manners, stand and bow gracefully as she left.

After she was gone, we sat for a moment with our tea, enjoying the glow from Marie's presence, and perhaps trying to put off our other task.

"Thank you for introducing me."

"Marie is always happy to talk about her work. And she doesn't have many chances to do that. I suspect you did her as much good as she did you."

Saint Aubyn nodded. "She is a lovely lady."

"You'll get no argument from me."

"As are you." He took another look at the tea tray. "Don't insult the sandwiches?"

I shrugged. "There's nothing wrong with being kind when you can."

"It would be a far better world if everyone felt that way, Miss Shane."

Chapter 17

What She Left Behind

If tea and music had been all that were on the schedule for the day, it would have been a very happy afternoon. But before Marie arrived, a porter from the Waverly Place Hotel had dropped off Lady Frances's trunk, and there was another task waiting for us. Which is probably why we lingered over the tea longer than we should have. It certainly wasn't because he wanted to partake of more of Mrs. G's pretty sandwiches.

"I suppose we had best set to work." He put down his cup slowly, regretfully.

"I'll call Rosa."

It would not have been fair to ask Marie to help with this grim errand. I'd recruited Rosa, as the closest I had to a lady's maid, to provide insight on the make and style of the clothing, and not incidentally serve as chaperone. I didn't want to put Frances's dark fate so close to Marie and her sunny life, or bring her any further into this without asking the duke first.

I started dragging the trunk from the unobtrusive corner, where I'd had the porters place it this morning, and Saint Aubyn quickly moved to help me.

"Miss!" Rosa said reprovingly as she bustled in. She's a tiny, dark-haired girl, and while I know she has to be very strong to do the daily housework, I don't have to add to her burden.

I shrugged and knelt down beside the trunk. "I'm strong enough, why shouldn't I?"

Both of my companions glared at me, probably for different reasons.

"Fine." I looked to the duke. "Do you have a key?"

He handed it to me and got down beside me. "I don't think she left with a trunk."

"Probably just a small bag of essentials, and acquired the rest over time." I pointed to the stamp in the metal by the lock. "This is American-made, and good, but not expensive. I have a couple from the same maker."

"Practical?"

"Practical, and a common choice for traveling performers. Anyone wise in the ways of the road would tell her to get one. She probably bought it for the tour. That's when I got my first one."

He nodded.

I slipped the key in the lock and it turned easily. I felt Saint Aubyn tense beside me. I didn't blame him. These were his cousin's things, and he'd never see her again this side of Heaven. I hoped. My theology is unorthodox enough to admit the possibility that God takes in strays. I suspected the man who was ready to fight the vicar for Frances was probably a bit unorthodox, too.

Rosa tutted when the lid came up. "Badly packed, miss."

"True. The coat, like all heavy things, belongs on the bottom."

I handed the coat to Rosa, who started checking the linings and seams. It was a simple medium gray wool, which would have looked very good with Frances Saint Aubyn's pale skin and light eyes.

Under the coat was a light blue wool dress, also just thrown in on top, as the coat had been, and then we began with the lightest items. I didn't understand until I saw the dress.

"What?" Saint Aubyn knew I saw something.

"Well, she was packed to travel. She'd have worn the coat and dress after the show, so someone, I'd guess the police, just threw the clothes in on top. I doubt anyone searched the trunk at all."

His eyes narrowed. "Not exactly thorough, the New Haven constabulary."

"They had decided what it was, and weren't going to spend any more time." I shook my head. Tommy and I are probably the only Irish people I know who do not have a close relative who is a police officer . . . and that's only because Uncle Jim died a year after he retired from the force. Father Michael has brothers and cousins on the beat, and, like it or not, we're all versed in the ways of law enforcement. "Which does not make it right, Your Grace."

With his barrister's training, he probably had a bit of insight himself. "It certainly does not."

I looked to Rosa, hoping to change the subject, since we couldn't change what had happened. "Any thoughts on the coat and dress?"

"A dressmaker made it. It's good enough, but not really fancy. From the sleeves, I'd say a year or so ago. Probably made for the tour."

"That makes sense. I always purchase what I will need, and the singers get an advance so they can, too."

"'Advance'?" The duke looked at me.

"Most singers aren't especially well-off. You can't expect people to just run off without supplies, and they'll never tell you they can't afford things."

I thought of the first tour, when I had noticed a young

basso carrying his things wrapped in a bundle like a vagrant. He hadn't been able to afford a trunk and had no other options. Tommy and I bought him one and we provided a modest advance after that.

"Miss Shane, if I were a singer, I believe I'd want to work for you."

I smiled. "Lentini treated me well. The least I can do is be good to my company."

Saint Aubyn just nodded.

Rosa and I sorted through the rest of the clothes fairly quickly. Most were similar, pieces made by an American dressmaker, all about the same vintage. At the bottom, though, was a simple dark blue wool dress that was different. It was older and worn, but the fabric was noticeably higher quality, and the tailoring far better.

Saint Aubyn stared at it. "That looks somewhat familiar."

"I suspect it's the dress she wore when she left." I looked at the elbows and hem. "She wore it for a long time, and kept it after it was no longer in respectable shape to wear."

"Sentimental value, perhaps," he said.

"I'd guess. We women are like that. In a drawer somewhere, I have my dress from my first recital."

"Dress?"

I smiled. "Yes, Your Grace. I only wear breeches when I play men. For recitals, I dress like a lady."

"Silly of me. Of course, you do."

"You'd be surprised how many people who see me only on the stage are surprised to find out that I don't wear boys' clothes at home."

Saint Aubyn's eyes strayed to my shirt.

"Well, usually. I had fencing before I had rehearsal, and there's been no time to change."

"Ah."

I knew what was going on here. Any distraction from our task would do. "Not fair to ask the rest of you to sit here twiddling your thumbs while I scramble into something more appropriate."

"You're quite appropriate. As always, Miss Shane."

"Thank you." I handed the dress on to Rosa. "At any rate, she saved it as a reminder of where she came from, and who she was."

He nodded gravely. "So that's all we can gather from her wardrobe."

I opened the first of the three small drawers in the side of the trunk. Inside was sheet music: a *Capuleti* score, of course, plus one for *Aida* and several arias, including the Queen of the Night's rage aria from the *Magic Flute*. I looked through them, thinking of Stratford's dismissive assessment of her.

"What do you think?" Saint Aubyn asked.

"I think she was aiming high. Literally and figuratively. She might have had the range and skill to do the Queen of the Night someday. It's Marie's signature role, but it's fiendishly difficult. And *Aida*'s no walk in the park, either."

"Ambitious."

"Yes. Good for a young singer. But there's nothing in here that she could have comfortably done right now. I don't know who her teacher was, but she wasn't doing right by her."

"Did she have one?"

"I knew she was practicing with Louis on the tour. I don't know whom she studied with at home. I'll ask our booking agent if he knows, the next time I talk to him." Thankfully, no need to tell the duke that Henry was good and scared of us at the moment—or why.

"Could she just have been working on more difficult repertoire by herself?"

"Maybe. Or maybe her teacher told her not to work on these things yet, and she decided to do it on her own while she was away. It's a risk, though. Young voices have to be very careful."

"Why?"

"The voice isn't fully mature until a singer is around thirty. Sopranos can ruin their instruments if they push too hard, too fast."

"How?"

"Basically, you have to have all the technique in place to support those high notes. And even if your voice will go there, it may not be right for you." I pointed to the Queen of the Night aria. "I can hit most of those notes, most days—and often do in vocalization. But it's not just an athletic event. I have a big, dark voice, and I sound much better in my lower registers. Marie has that lovely bell-like quality, and sounds like an angel—or, in the case of the Queen of the Night, like a demon—when she goes up there."

Saint Aubyn thought about it. "Would she have been upset to learn there were roles she couldn't play?"

"I'm honestly not sure." I looked at the scores. "I was destined for trouser roles from very early on, and never really wanted anything else. Sometimes I think it might be fun to be the pretty princess, but it's not a deep wound that I can't."

His eyes lingered on the music. "And yet?"

"And yet, if I wasn't sure where my voice was going to settle, and what I might be capable of, and dreamed of things that could end up being beyond me . . . I don't know."

"What roles was she going to do in Philadelphia?"

"Pretty-princess things, challenging enough, but not heavy work. I know *Aida* is in the plan for Philadelphia— perhaps she was going to understudy."

"So maybe not all as rosy as we thought?"

"Well, this certainly suggests she wanted more than she

was doing. That's not unhealthy. That's evidence of ambition—and if I were her agent, I'd be glad to see it. As long as she wasn't pushing her voice too much." I would actually have been glad to know that my little show-off had lofty goals, and if she'd trusted me, helped her to grow safely. A missed opportunity for both of us.

"So we might do well to find her teacher."

"If she had one. I'll ask Henry, and Louis, for that matter."

He opened the next drawer. It held her makeup kit, and he looked down at it for several measures. "Her fingerprint is still in the rouge."

Without thinking, I put my hand on his back, a harmless reassuring gesture I would offer any friend in need of comfort. My friends, however, are not British aristocrats. After a moment, I realized what I'd done and quickly pulled back.

He looked at me and handed over the box. "No offense taken, Miss Shane."

I took it and almost immediately realized there was nothing but pots, powders and a small packet of hairpins inside. "I doubt we'll learn much from that. Other than that she used the same brand of stage makeup as I do—"

"Miss, there's something in the hem!" Rosa interrupted, holding up the skirt of the last dress.

"Get a seam ripper."

She went to the mending box and pulled it out. Saint Aubyn watched as I picked up the dark blue skirt Frances had brought from England and set to work.

"You're far too practiced at that."

"I did some piecework as a child." I spoke briskly, hoping to stop any further discussion. And the memories. I did not need to be reminded of sewing with Mama, during those last weeks in our cold tenement room. Often I'd put down my book and take the work out of her bony hands as she coughed, then just start in without a word. I'll never forget the look in her eyes as she watched me stitch, as fast and cleanly as I could.

I hope she can see me as I am now.

Saint Aubyn was studying me with an unnerving intensity. I just shook my head as I neatly ripped the hem, quickly revealing something shiny and hard. It came free easily enough; Frances had just slipped it into the sleeve of the hem without really securing it.

"A necklace. Or part of one." I handed it to him. It was an elaborate circlet of clear stones in white metal, but it looked to me like several pieces were missing. I'd have thought it was one of the paste gewgaws like Lentini wore while she was on stage, except that a couple of the stones caught the light. Paste doesn't flash like that.

"Well, now we know how she was funding her flier," he said dryly. "This was a wedding gift from Frances's father to her mother. Alberta didn't tell me it was missing."

"Would she even know? I know the ladies of the Four Hundred wear their jewels at all times, but I understood British women were more reserved."

"It is more suited to a presentation or coronation, and we haven't had any of that lately." He held the piece to the light. "I've never seen her wear it."

"So . . ."

"I believe her mother keeps her important jewels in a locked box in her dressing room. Probably simple enough for Frances to nick it."

I nodded as he studied the piece.

"It seems to me that four or five of the diamond drops are gone. I'm certain she didn't get anything near what they were worth," he observed.

"She wouldn't have to. And the individual pieces are unremarkable enough that she wouldn't excite much interest by selling them."

"I suppose pawnbrokers are as loathe to ask awkward questions on this side of the Atlantic as they are at home."

"You'd lose no money on that bet, Your Grace. But we also have no way to know when or where she sold them."

"I don't suppose you know anyone who knows a good pawnbroker."

"I did as a girl. Thankfully, I don't now."

Saint Aubyn smiled faintly and turned to the last drawer, which yielded programs, a box and a couple of envelopes.

The programs were from our tour, all the same except for the venue, with Violette's name on the front below mine and the title, and inside as Giulietta. Her biography was short, and I now knew, entirely false, listing a Canadian conservatory and roles in Ottawa, Toronto and Chicago.

Saint Aubyn took a moment to look at mine. It listed me as the final student and protégée of Madame Suzanne Lentini, and the highlights of credits from New York, London and other places I'd amassed before starting my own company. It made no mention of anything personal, and listed me only as a native of New York.

"You don't give much away, do you?"

"People aren't coming to hear about my life. They're coming to hear me sing."

"True enough."

The box and envelopes were still in my hands. The box, from a bottle of Mrs. Redfern's Beauty Tonic, whatever that might be, held *cartes de visite*. Our Violette had a fascination with the famous. Lillie Langtry, Sarah Bernhardt, and a selection of divas all stared soulfully from the small collector's cards. I handed them to Saint Aubyn.

"Some of these are British." I pointed to Langtry. "She may have brought them with her."

"I don't believe the box is . . . I've never heard of that particular tonic."

I remembered Dr. Silver. "We may wish to investigate Mrs. Redfern. It could have been an emetic with nicotine."

"A trip to the chemist may be in order." He nodded. "I have a good druggist. I'll take you to him."

"Once again, I'm in your debt." He nodded, then sifted through the cards, stopping at a picture of a woman in doublet and hose.

"Bernhardt's *Hamlet*?" I asked, trying to get a closer look. I knew the famous actress was tackling the great role, but I hadn't seen it.

Saint Aubyn grinned and held the card up to me. "Shane's *Romeo*."

I blushed, as only a pale Irishwoman can. "Yes, I did that one. Divas do."

"And a lovely one it is." He chuckled. "Just the one?"

"I hate standing around with a soulful look. I'll do it once in a great while to promote a tour, but . . ."

"Well, it's better than Langtry, for sure. She's been eating a bit too much at the Prince of Wales's table."

The squeak from Rosa, a fancier of the yellow press, reminded Saint Aubyn what he'd just obliquely referred to in the presence of females. To his credit, he managed a very nice blush of his own. "My apologies, ladies, I meant no offense."

"I didn't think you did." I took the apology gravely and Rosa nodded, as I realized I still had the envelopes in my hands. One seemed to hold pictures, the other was addressed in an unremarkable, but neat, copperplate hand to Lady Alberta Saint Aubyn.

I handed them over silently, realizing what they must be.

He took them and first opened the one with the pictures. It was exactly what I expected. Three family photographs: a group, a couple of boys, and a woman.

"Her family," he said slowly. "She must have taken them as mementoes."

"Yes."

He looked at the letter, then shook his head. "Not now, I'm sorry."

"It's none of my business. None of it is, really."

"I've made it your business by asking your help. And it's been invaluable."

I nodded quietly and helped Rosa finish folding the clothing and other things back into the trunk as he carefully put the necklace in his pocket; then he got up and walked to the window, still holding the letter and the pictures. It had started to rain, as it often does on a spring day in New York, and the room was turning dark.

I locked the trunk and walked over to him.

"I had this hope that we'd find some answer." As he spoke quietly, he kept his eyes on the wet cobblestones and deserted street.

"It may be in the letter. Or there may be no answer."

He nodded. "And I will have to live with that."

"Yes. I'm sorry." I handed him the key.

Our fingers touched, skin to skin for the first time; electricity suddenly arced between us, and we both froze for a moment as he turned back from the window to look at me. Neither he nor I moved; neither of us even breathed in that instant, and something changed in the balance between us. I didn't know enough about men to know what any of this meant, but for a fraction of a second, his eyes dropped to my lips, and I thought he might have been thinking about kissing me.

The amazing thing was, it didn't feel like an insult, but like what I'd been singing about all those years as Romeo. *The lightning bolt.*

I don't know what might have happened next, because he dropped the key, and Rosa called to me, and it all vanished as if it had never happened. Except that it had.

"Thank you for your kind help, Miss Shane." The duke

briskly pocketed the key and snapped back to his normal, cool demeanor. But I was relieved to see something different in his eyes, because it meant I wasn't the only one.

"Glad to help. I will let you know what I learn from my booking agent." I spoke equally coolly as I walked him to the door.

"I'll send a porter to pick up the trunk this evening."

"Thank you."

"Not singing tonight, Miss Shane?"

"Not for a few days. I will likely catch up on my reading, and my beauty sleep."

"Ah. Not out on the town with your many admirers?" He was teasing.

"I'm far happier with Anne Boleyn, and perhaps even Henry VIII."

"Well, now that he's safely dead, at least."

" 'I may be a big woman, but I have a very little neck.' "

"Marie de Guise." Saint Aubyn laughed. "Probably the single best refusal ever given."

"I think so." I was also more than a little impressed that he recognized the comment, which the lovely, and undeniably tall, Marie had made when Henry tried to come courting after "divorced, beheaded, died."

"In any case, I hope to see you soon."

"I'll look forward to it."

"As will I."

I closed the door after him, then leaned on it for a moment. "What in the name of Hades was that?"

Rosa looked sharply at me. "Miss?"

"Nothing. Sorry. Thank you so much for your help."

"Of course, miss. Wicked Duke, huh?"

"Maybe."

"Not my place, miss, but maybe you should find out."

And with that, and a cheeky little smile, she headed back downstairs.

Chapter 18

Milady in Her Bath

Tommy was spending that Thursday evening out with a bunch of old boxing chums, so I had a rare night at home alone, with no engagements or obligations. Other ladies may have their own ideas of what they like to do at such times, but my preference is very clear: I take a long bath and wash my hair.

In addition to Montezuma, the previous owner of our town house had left us with a modern water closet, to our eternal gratitude. But the bathing arrangements were pretty much as they were in any other comfortable, modern home. Which is to say, neither especially comfortable nor modern. We have hot water for a good basic wash each morning, but hair washing and a long soak in a hot tub are things that can only happen when the kitchen is quiet and no one else is around. It may be almost a new century, but no proper lady wants to be surprised in her bath by a bunch of reporters. I would have sent Toms out to play if I'd had to wait another day or two.

With the house deserted, I could drag the giant copper tub out into the center of the kitchen, fill it halfway with hot water from the boiler on the stove, then add cold water till it was comfortable. I added a little lavender oil to the water, an unthinkable luxury in a poorer home, where entire families would share the bath and be grateful for it, and happily sank in.

A hot, scented bath probably ranks as one of the greatest sensual pleasures available to humans, even in our modern day and age. No less authorities on decadence than the Romans considered a good soak a special, and healthful, treat. Whatever unpleasantness one may be dealing with in daily life, the luxury of being able to loll for a time in hot, scented water goes a long way toward easing it. And there's also the plain Irish practicality of it all. If you're going to all the trouble and expense of a hot bath, you'd damned well better enjoy it!

I made sure to do just that, soaking until the water started to cool, then washing my hair before it got too cold. Hair washing itself is a project, requiring a carefully calibrated solution of soap, thorough rinsing, and a light application of oil and combing through after, probably my least favorite part of the process, since my hair has more than a little natural curl, and it resists the comb. I put the oil on before I wrapped my hair in a towel, to let it sink in until I could get upstairs to my room. I could comb out at my leisure in front of the nice, hot fire I'd had Rosa set up for me before she left. Once the hair was all combed out into nice smooth waves, I'd sit in front of the fire and let it dry naturally for a few hours before braiding it up for sleep. All in all, a good night's work.

But, work or no, the evening was precisely what I needed after a trying few days. We've noted before that the instrument works best in a healthy and happy body.

Since I was, after all, staying in for the night, and no one would see me, I put a generous coating of almond oil on my face, to smooth and nourish the skin. Other ladies use all manner of exotic things to fight wrinkles or whiten their complexions—and it usually ends badly. I'll stick with the almond oil, plus rose water for cleansing, and cold cream to remove stage makeup. All of it comes from my druggist's daughter. Hermione Chalfont also makes a rose petal lip salve that is most definitely not rouge, but does give a natural glow where it does the most good.

A night like this is one of the great treats of being home. On the road, bathing arrangements are rather more primitive, and one manages what one can. Good hotels, of the sort we choose whenever we can, provide excellent facilities, of course, and anyone who tours learns to take full advantage. I've been known to soak in my hotel tub in the wee hours of the morning in San Francisco, simply because I could. That's my personal idea of the decadent pleasures of the road.

The most recent tour had been in large Eastern cities, so we'd been quite comfortable. I wondered, though, if Lady Frances had found it so. What I, a grateful child of the Lower East Side, consider a treat might well have been a comedown for her. But by the time she got to us, she'd likely have been used to life out of the aristocratic nest. And her things told me she'd been living quite simply, even by the standards of the road.

Poor girl. When I was her age, I was still working so hard I didn't have time to think. Or feel much beyond a burning desire to succeed. When I wasn't on stage, I was practicing my French and Italian, or taking dance and fencing lessons, or reading the literature and etiquette manuals Lentini selected. As I got a little older and more polished, I was allowed more freedom with my reading, but the lessons continued. Still do.

For me, of course, the prize was always in sight. If I did my part and worked hard, I would succeed. Lentini entertained no other possibility, so I didn't, either. Only now did I understand what a gift that was. Frances, of course, had no such certainty. I wondered if she'd had doubts, and if they'd helped destroy her.

The water was getting too cool. I carefully climbed out, dried off with a nice, slightly rough Turkish towel (good for the skin), put on clean cambric underthings and night-gown, and bundled up in my warm purple plush wrapper. Then I had to get rid of the water, first by scooping it up in a tin, then by dragging the tub to the kitchen door and dumping the last into the yard. Even the grass got to smell nice!

It was just starting to get dark by the time I was done. Mrs. G had left some good brown bread in the keeper and her excellent bean soup on the stove for dinner, and I made myself a tray. There were cookies in the jar, and I de-cided to have one. Why should the boys get all the treats?

As I went through the foyer to the stairs, in wrapper and towel turban, another thing I could only do when no one else was about, I noticed that Rosa had left a few cards and messages from the end of the day on the table under the mirror. Most were routine matters, invitations, calling cards, even a few advertisements, but one was a card from Gilbert Saint Aubyn, with a brief message on the back: *Thank you for your time and kindness this afternoon. I am in your debt.*

That was all it said, but the fact that he'd troubled to actually stop by the house and drop the card said a great deal more. I was smiling as I stopped in the drawing room to pick up the Anne Boleyn book, adding it to my tray and heading upstairs for my luxurious quiet night. And what— or who—I dreamed of is no one's business but mine.

Moreover, if it occurred to me later that Saint Aubyn was also a tall, dark man who might just bring me trouble, it was most definitely none of Aunt Ellen's business.

Chapter 19

A Fine Promenade in the Park

Saturday, the first one in May, dawned as yet another perfect morning for a velocipede ride, but since Hetty was at long last preparing for the Giants game, I would not have had my usual partner, anyway. I am, I admit, old-fashioned enough that I do not like to ride alone, and besides, it's much more fun to share the pleasure with a friend. So, I was at least a little disappointed about missing the chance, if glad for Hetty to finally cover her game.

My discontent had been somewhat eased by the duke's invitation for a walk in the park, which had arrived as I was again watching my candles burn and puzzling over matters Friday evening. This time, though, Tommy had joined me for the blessings before Father Michael arrived for checkers and an amiable argument.

All in all, a far less moody Sabbath than I'd passed the previous week.

Since I wasn't going to get the thrill of speed on my velocipede that day, I made sure to enjoy another treat: wearing a new spring morning dress in lavender silk, with only a little puff in the sleeves, per the current fashion, and some pretty ribboned trim in a slightly darker hue. I added a light wrap and pulled out my wide-brimmed straw hat and parasol for the first time of the season, since being a la mode was all well and good, but freckles and sunburn were not becoming on a diva.

His Grace, immaculately turned out in a light gray day suit with a silver-gray tie, and still the black armband, of course, was waiting for me at a bench near the fountain when I walked up, and this time, he stood when he saw me, smiling.

"I'm getting used to the sight of you in clothes."

I waited.

He laughed and shook his head. "I really did intend that to come out some other way."

"I'm quite certain that you did." I chuckled. "I'm getting used to your occasional odd comments."

"I thank you for your indulgence, Miss Shane." Saint Aubyn nodded. "Shall we?"

I took his offered arm and we started down one of the paths.

"The spring flowers are quite lovely here," he observed, making appropriate small talk.

"Yes. You are here just in time for the violets, and soon, roses and lilacs."

"Are you as fond of flowers as most ladies?"

"Yes. Except, of course, for red roses."

He looked at me, quite puzzled. "Surely, all ladies hope for red roses, the time-honored symbol of love."

"Also the time-honored signature of the stage-door Lothario."

"Ah." He smiled. "I shall never give you roses."

"Good." I took it as a pleasantry, since he would never have reason to give me flowers.

"Why, Miss Shane, how delightful." An oily voice from one of the benches made us both stop and turn.

Grover Duquesne, Captain of Industry, complete with

top hat and a newspaper in his pudgy hands, hoisted himself to his feet and looked up at me.

I felt the duke's arm tense as I made no move to let go of him. A lady has every right to stay with the squire of her choice.

"Good to see you, Mr. Duquesne." I bowed formally as those unctuous eyes swept over me.

"I don't believe I've met your companion," my admirer said, squinting at Saint Aubyn.

"Gilbert Saint Aubyn, Duke of Leith." He made no move to shake hands.

The Captain of Industry decided to play the jovial American. "Well, how about that. A real duke. You do have some interesting friends, Miss Shane."

"So I do." I smiled and left it at that.

The two sized each other up for a moment. Not a word was said, but Saint Aubyn was clearly backing Duquesne off. Very far off.

"Well, I must be going. I hope to see you and Madame de l'Artois at the settlement house benefit performance next week."

"Thank you." I bowed.

Saint Aubyn nodded coldly, and Duquesne walked away, clearly annoyed but hiding it as best he could.

"One of your stage-door admirers?" the duke asked as we walked on.

"Yes."

"It is not my place to say, but I would suggest your cousin be present whenever that man is nearby."

"He is."

"Do all of them look at you that way?"

"Thankfully, no." I couldn't repress a shudder. "The, ah, Captain of Industry is unusually persistent."

"Quite." Saint Aubyn looked at me for a moment, very

carefully making eye contact, his gaze somehow managing to erase Duquesne's filthy ogle.

As every woman knows, there are some men who make you feel dirty just by looking at you . . . and others who make you feel like something sacred, or a work of art, with the same mere glance. The duke was very definitely in the latter category.

His jaw tightened. "I considered teaching him a lesson in manners, but decided that since my last duel didn't go so well . . ."

I patted his arm and stifled my smile. "I'm sure I am a much better swordsman than our Captain of Industry."

"No doubt. But I also didn't want to waste my energy on the likes of him."

"Well, thank you for the thought, at any rate."

"No one insults a woman in my presence, Miss Shane. Especially not one so magnificent as you."

I had no idea what to say to that, so I merely nodded and allowed him to lead me down the path away from the fountain, surprised to share an almost-companionable silence.

"Miss Shane, fancy meeting you here."

Arden Standish almost walked into us as he strode up the path.

"Why, Mr. Standish." I gave him a cool smile. "How nice to see you again."

"Walking out with a gentleman friend?" he asked with an expression that was only a few notches above Duquesne's filthy gaze.

"Miss Shane is an old friend of one of my relatives," Saint Aubyn said obliquely, clearly picking up something from Arden. "We are catching up on the latest news."

"Ah. Well, I'll leave you to it." Arden bowed. "Many things to do to prepare for Philadelphia. See you at the benefit."

"I shall look forward to it." I bowed, and so did Saint Aubyn.

Arden was out of earshot before Saint Aubyn's next breath. He used it to ask the obvious question. "The tenor from the other night?"

"Yes. He was also in our company for the last tour."

Saint Aubyn's jaw tightened a little.

"And to the best of my knowledge utterly beneath Frances's notice," I assured him. "He may have had a crush, as we say over here, but she would undoubtedly have handed him his hat and sent him on his way."

A very faint smile played about his lips. "I expect she would."

"The music really was her main love. A pretty blond boy couldn't compete."

The smile widened. "You are not especially fond of pretty blond boys, either."

"Neither here nor there, Your Grace," I started rather reprovingly, "but men are far more interesting than boys."

That put a sparkle in his eyes for a moment, but then his face took on a much more serious cast. "Was he the only young man in the company?"

"We had a couple of others, young singers on their first tours, probably not even twenty years old. The rest of the company members are regulars, about a dozen chorus members, crew and helpers who travel whenever we do."

He nodded. "Would any of them have put that mark on her arm?"

Of course, he would ask. "I honestly don't think so."

"And that man, Standish?"

"Highly unlikely." I didn't want to tell him what I'd learned about Arden, because he would blame me for not knowing what a bounder I'd hired . . . and I was starting to care what he thought of me.

Why, of all things?

Of course, I never want anyone to think ill of me; certainly, it would do me no good professionally to have a duke with a grudge against me. But why did I care if he thought I had good judgment? I was never going to see him again after we determined what had happened to poor Frances.

Was I?

Well, I did find myself in London on occasion.

Neither here nor there. I took a breath and managed a cool, professional tone. "It's really very unlikely to have been a member of the company."

"But not impossible."

"Nothing is impossible. Anyone is capable of anything under the right circumstances."

He stopped walking and looked hard at me. "You say."

"I grew up in a hard part of the world, Your Grace. I know what people are capable of when they're desperate."

The cold blue eyes didn't waver.

"That said, I have no indication that Standish would ever physically harm a woman, and if I had, I'd have sent him away without a character at once."

"I believe you would."

"I don't lie," I said quietly. "I'm capable of a lot myself, but I don't lie."

"I don't lie, either." He met my gaze squarely. "But I've been known to leave out facts that might be hurtful or harmful."

"As have I."

We were silent for a few moments as we started walking again. This time, it was a tense and cautious silence, until he broke it.

"Well, at any rate, we should go to your chemist. Should I be concerned that you have one?"

"Nothing to worry about." I chuckled, balance restored for the moment. "I make my living with my voice. In addition to good technique, I also need a steady supply of pep-permint and horehound lozenges. Mr. Chalfont keeps me well stocked."

"Ah. Well, lead on."

Chalfont's Pharmacy was just a few blocks away, and Mr. Ernest Chalfont was busily compounding pills behind the counter when we walked into the quiet store.

"Miss Shane! Delightful to see you. Horehound or pep-permint this time? Or would you like a tin of my daugh-ter's new recipe rose petal lip salve . . ."

"The lip salve sounds perfect." I couldn't help smiling as he noticed the duke and broke off, probably to spare me any embarrassment about my beauty secrets.

"And the gentleman?"

"Some information, if I might," Saint Aubyn said.

"Certainly." Mr. Chalfont put his order of pills down and pushed his reading glasses up to the top of his balding head, giving him a good hard look. "I'm sorry, I didn't get your name."

"Quite sorry. Gilbert Saint Aubyn."

They shook hands. "Friend of Miss Shane's?"

"Yes."

"Good enough for me."

"Right, then. Miss Shane mentioned to me that she had heard that some patent medicines contain nicotine, and I wondered if you might know more about that."

My barrister friend did not need to treat my druggist as if he were a witness. I sighed. "A mutual friend is using one, and I am concerned."

Chalfont nodded. "You should be. Nicotine's dangerous stuff. In higher concentrations, it's an insecticide. It's also far too easy to overdose."

"Really?" Saint Aubyn asked.

"Really. If someone accidentally took even a slightly

larger dose, depending on their size, they could be done for. Tell your friend to stop taking it at once."

"Oh."

"Is the mutual friend a young lady?"

Saint Aubyn and I exchanged glances.

"Yes," I said. "One of the young singers I know."

"I stopped carrying the stuff months ago, when my daughter told me one of her friends got sick, but there's a tonic that some young women use. Supposed to make them paler and more beautiful or some such rot. It's actually an emetic and just plain nasty."

"That's probably it." It sounded like the sort of foolishness some girls would try.

"Well, get it away from her immediately and tell her to go for a good long walk." Chalfont smiled. "Or maybe lend her your velocipede. That seems to work for you."

I bought a tin of the newest rose petal salve while the duke looked around at the various other nostrums, and Chalfont grinned at me as he rang it up. "Quite a fine gentleman, Miss Shane."

"A relative of a friend, Mr. Chalfont."

"Too bad. He'd do much better with you than his little nicotine-drinking dolly."

I just shook my head at that, since it would take much too much effort to explain, and slipped my parcel into my purse. "I'll probably call for a new supply of lozenges for the next tour soon."

"I'll look forward to it."

Outside, Saint Aubyn offered his arm again, and I took it. "Shall I walk you home?"

"Thank you. I would like that."

We walked in silence for a few moments, enjoying the sun and the spring breeze a bit, despite the seriousness of the errand.

"Thank you, Miss Shane."

"I told you before, I'm glad to help."

"Well, I greatly appreciate it." He tensed a little. "Your reporter friend, is she expecting information in return for sharing that autopsy report?"

"No. But sooner or later, the story is going to come out. You may wish to control the circumstances of that."

"What do you mean?"

"If the New Haven authorities notified you, her legal name is known somewhere. And eventually a professional gossipmonger will recognize you wandering about town."

Saint Aubyn nodded. "There are only so many dukes."

"Exactly. If you talk to Hetty, and explain it to her as a family tragedy, she writes a respectful, sensitive account, and that's the end of it."

"If I wait for one of the yellow sheets . . ."

"Screaming headlines, sensationalism and Heaven only knows."

"Your friend is trustworthy?"

"Yes."

"She writes for a good paper?"

"The *Beacon*."

"I have read it." He nodded. "How is this done?"

"I invite both you and Hetty to tea at my house, away from prying eyes. You tell her the story. After that, it is out of your hands, but in her very good ones."

"I need to think about all of this."

We were almost to the town house. I checked the little watch charm on my bracelet. It was heading for noon now, and Tommy and I had to start our journey uptown to join Hetty and Yardley at the game.

"But not this instant perhaps." I saw no harm in adding to the party.

"Oh?"

"Would you care to do something very American this afternoon?"

He looked curiously at me.

"We're going to see the Giants at the Polo Grounds."

"Is that—"

"Baseball, of course. My reporter friend is writing a piece about lady fans, and we are going along."

"Perhaps another day."

"Not a fancier?"

"I don't know enough about baseball to know." He shook his head. "I have much to think about right now, and I would prefer to be alone."

"Of course." I nodded as I released his arm. "Well, thank you for a lovely walk."

"And thank you for all of your help."

We bowed. He moved slightly toward me, as if he wanted to shake hands, or something—who knows what British aristocrats do—and backed off.

"Until next time, Miss Shane."

"Until next time."

A tall, dark man who brings trouble, indeed.

Chapter 20

In Which We Pass a Pleasing Night at Home

The Giants had no trouble with the Spiders. One could not say the same for Hetty and the Baseball Writers. It turns out that one must be a member of the Baseball Writers to sit in the press box, and to be a Baseball Writer, one must be a man. This injustice did not sit well, even though she no doubt wrote a far better story because she circulated in the crowd and talked to female fans rather than lolling about the press box.

Either way, Tommy and I were just glad to see the game end without a rhubarb. Not on the field, but between Hetty and Yardley.

At a convenient corner, we paid off our driver and turned gratefully for home, leaving them to walk on to the news office, barely noticing our farewells as they sniped about whether Hetty's story belonged on the sports or the women's page. As for dinner, Father Michael wasn't in evidence; he'd apparently been invited to sup at some other parishioner's home. From the way Tommy told it, I suspected he'd be very grateful to return to us, indeed, and to Mrs. G's efforts.

But Louis and Anna were in the neighborhood, and likely to come over after sundown, formally ending the Jewish Sabbath with a family meal. It would probably be Tommy and me for dinner, and then the Abramovitzes—and maybe the adorable Morsel—for coffee a bit later.

That was as happy a plan as we could wish for, since Toms and I always enjoy our time together, with or without the supporting cast. Tommy and I were always close. He was my protector from the time Aunt Ellen took me in, a shy and scared little creature, nearly starved from the poverty of the last days of my mother's illness, and terrified of everyone. Aunt Ellen and Uncle Fred weren't well-off by any means, but no one went hungry in their home, and Tommy always hated seeing anyone upset, so he took it upon himself to make me smile that first night, pulling a silly face and sneaking an extra cookie for me. After that, I stuck to him like a limpet whenever he was within range, and God love him, he didn't shoo me away, as almost any other twelve-year-old boy would have done.

Soon enough, I was there when some of the neighborhood boys picked fights with him because he wasn't the kind of brute they were, and I started throwing in on his side. I figured his tolerance for me was part of the reason they thought he was soft, so it was the least I could do. There's more than one future Five Points gangster who lost a handful of hair when I jumped on his back and started doing my worst to help Toms.

Things were much quieter on this particular evening. As we waited for Mrs. G to do her magic, I was on my chaise with the library book on costume at Versailles, leafing through the plates and doubting that I'd have enjoyed wearing a *grand corps*, one of those heavily boned bodices that were a required part of court attire. Tommy was reading a study of the Wars of the Roses, research for *The*

Princes in the Tower. Montezuma was perched on a book-shelf, happily chewing on a carrot, and periodically making his own unique contribution to the conversation.

"Stays, Toms," I said, looking at a diagram of a particularly terrifying corset. "They're the principal reason men still rule the world."

Tommy looked up from his book. "I would have guessed skirts, but all right."

"It's all of a piece, isn't it?" I brushed my hand across my heliotrope-print afternoon dress, in a soft and comfortable, but definitely not fancy, delaine. Like most clothing meant to be worn only at home, it was cut loosely enough that I didn't need to wear stays, even though I don't really lace tightly at all, because I need to keep my lungs and diaphragm free for my voice. "We wear all of this pretty and impractical stuff, which makes us look very appealing to men—"

"Some men." Tommy chuckled.

"Too many. And most of us can't even walk quickly when we're dressed, never mind run for our own safety if necessary—or defend ourselves."

"Most ladies do not have to dress for a duel."

"Well, true. But it's the idea. We're all at the mercy of the world."

"Do you think taking off your stays and wearing breeches would help?"

"We'd be healthier without the stays, for sure. But we'd all have to agree to change clothes at the same time, or people would just laugh us off the streets like they did women who tried the Bloomer costume before we were even born."

"True." He laughed. "Probably better to win the vote in your current outfits and change later."

"Between you and me and the lamppost, I'm not even sure about the vote."

"Votes for women!" Montezuma called; there'd been

suffrage marches in Washington Square Park in recent years, and he'd picked up the chant. All he had to hear was the word "vote."

"Heresy," Tommy said, looking closely at me.

"I know the vote is what would make us real citizens, but some of us can't manage to get work to feed our-selves—or do it safely in these dresses. What good is being a citizen if you aren't even able to take care of yourself and your family?"

Tommy shook his head. "You are pretty pessimistic to-night."

"Discouraged, I guess, thinking about poor Frances. She tried so hard to become something else, only to end up dead, thanks to a beauty treatment."

"Not just a beauty treatment, if you've been telling it right. A sickness with food, and using a very dangerous emetic."

"Well."

"Don't overstate it, Heller. If she was using the medi-cine, she was already risking her life. She may not have thought the consequences through, but she wasn't a poor innocent."

"Maybe."

"It's an insult to her to deny her that much." Tommy shrugged. "Even if she thought she was better than us—"

"You felt the disdain, too?"

"At least once. It didn't make sense until we knew where she came from. Of course, she wasn't going to take anything, no matter how well meant, from a couple of jumped-up Lower East Siders."

"Even if they were paying her salary."

"Especially, then." He gave me a significant glance. "Nobody particularly likes criticism, and one way to dis-count it is to discount the people giving it."

"True enough."

"Looking down on us was probably the only power she had."

"Like Juliet."

He sighed. "I am incredibly sick of Juliet. There is no way we are touring with *Capuleti* next time."

"Never."

"Good." Tommy looked down at his book. "I could get used to the Wars of the Roses."

"Plenty of intrigue, blood and scandal."

"Not like our boring civilized time." He laughed at that. "Although, if I must choose between warring armies coming up my street and a little boredom, I'll take boredom."

"Very true." I held up a plate of Marie Antoinette's silver wedding gown, with panniers so wide she had to go through doors sideways. "See what I mean about the way clothes restrict the woman?"

"Well, you'd have a point if we still made you wear that."

"Miss, I think you should see this." Rosa walked into the drawing room. She was carrying the *Illustrated News,* one of her beloved yellow sheets. If she'd asked my opinion, I would have suggested the *Beacon* for reading to improve her English. Rosa's family came from Italy when she was just a babe in arms, and they still spoke Italian at home. But admittedly, the reputable paper wasn't nearly as much fun, and what really mattered was that she was reading.

"What is it?" I asked, putting my book down.

"I don't think you're going to like this." She handed me the paper, folded to the gossip column "The Lorgnette."

As a singer of some standing, I did occasionally find my various comings and goings chronicled there. But Rosa was right, this one was different:

> *Has someone touched our boyish diva's girlish heart? Miss Ella Shane has been seen walking out with*

a tall, dark gentleman with an unmistakable English accent. Surely, we cannot allow a foreigner to scoop up yet another of our treasures. "The Lorgnette" calls on all patriotic bachelors to do their part to keep our diva where she belongs!

"Argh." I tossed the paper to Tommy. "Thanks for showing me, Rosa. You know there's nothing to it."

She giggled. "Well, almost nothing."

Tommy chuckled. "I suppose we should brace for the invasion of the bachelors." He cracked his knuckles. "I do need to keep in form."

We all laughed, which was precisely what such foolishness deserved. Rosa took her paper back and scooted off, nearly mowing down Mrs. G as she stuck her head in the drawing room. The cook just laughed.

"Dinner is ready," she announced. "I'm leaving coffee and some nice gooseberry tarts if the Abramovitzes and their sweet little boy come by."

"Thanks, Mrs. G."

"A pleasure. You two are too quiet when you're alone. You need someone to liven you up."

We laughed.

"And really your wild friends aren't so bad. Even those hellion sports reporters are just good boys at heart."

"Thanks," Tommy said. "I'll tell Yardley that."

"Don't you dare! He'll come sniffing around for cookies more than he already does."

"Yes, ma'am."

"Now, that nice Mr. Dare is welcome anytime."

We looked curiously at her for a moment, but she didn't offer anything more than that as she swept out. She shared a small flat with a couple of nearly grown children within a reasonable walk. Rosa lived with her parents and five sibs, also not far away. Many people in the neighborhood still have servants living in the attics . . . but the top of our house is my studio, and it all feels too, well, subservient to me, anyway. They do very good work for us, we pay them well above the going rate in the neighborhood, and it's much fairer and more comfortable for everyone.

I know a lot of people who grew up as Tommy and I did would probably relish having their own servants to order around, but that's just not how either of us is made.

After saying good night to Rosa, I settled Montezuma upstairs; it was heading for his bedtime, anyhow, and while parrots are very pretty and interesting creatures, they do not mix well with small children. Tommy and I took our time wandering into the dining room and settling into the meal, both of us bringing our books as we often did when alone together. Dinner turned out to be a tasty chicken pie, simple and delicious. We'd had the traditional fish, of course, last night; no Catholic in the City would eat meat on Friday, even after Lent.

The meal was happily demolished, the dishes rinsed and stacked (not necessary, of course, but anyone who can feel comfortable leaving a mess for another person to start her day is not anyone I want to know). We'd returned to the drawing room and our books when the doorbell rang.

Louis and Anna would have been treat enough, but they had indeed brought the Morsel, who seemed to be in a surprisingly sunshiny mood for a three-year-old at nearly eight p.m.

"*Shabbat Shalom,*" I said. "Did you have a good Havdalah?"

Anna laughed. "We went to Louis's mother's to end the Sabbath. It's always crazy. More than this place when the Boston sports writers are in town."

Tommy grinned. "Nothing's as bad as that."

"Hey, Mr. Champ!" the Morsel said, walking up to Tommy and putting his arms up.

Tommy knows his place. He scooped up little Morris for a piggyback ride. Since Toms is far and away the tallest and largest person the Morsel has ever met, he's always pressed into service. I suspect it's also because if you're going to ride around on top of the world, you want to do it on the back of someone who makes you feel absolutely safe and comfortable—and that would certainly be Tommy.

I got Louis and Anna settled, then poured coffee, making sure to leave tarts for Tommy and his driver.

"So we are madly researching for *The Princes in the Tower,*" I said, nodding to Tommy's book. "Marie and I are both very excited."

Both beamed and Louis nodded. "We're looking toward a fall premiere, right?"

"Yes. I think you and I work on the score on the Western tour, and Marie and her teacher work back here. We'll be ready long before the fall, but it's good to start early."

He nodded gravely.

"And we can't wait, of course." I took a sip of coffee. "Anna, your lyrics are amazing. Of course, you'll be properly credited."

The two looked at each other. "Can we do that?" she asked.

"Should we?" he questioned her.

"Why not?" I shook my head. "She wrote it. Of course, she would be listed as lyricist."

I looked at the two of them for a moment, worried that this would somehow change the balance between them. I really hoped Louis was not one of those men who figured whatever his wife did was simply for his greater glory, and she didn't deserve acknowledgment of her own. Even in our more enlightened age, and even among basically good men, there are far too many who . . .

And he wasn't one. He took both of Anna's hands. "Abramovitz and Abramovitz."

She grinned right back. "Perfect."

"Baby pie!" the Morsel proclaimed, grabbing his tart with one of his chubby little starfish hands.

"That's one way to put it." Tommy straightened his hair and tie as he sat down with us. "Are we talking about *The Princes in the Tower*?"

"Yes. Lots of rehearsal and preparations."

Tommy drank his coffee thoughtfully. "And logistics. We'll be able to sell out a good-sized theater, so I'll get to work on that right now. Probably want to think about a little publicity. You and Marie should do a *carte de visite* like that painting of the princes."

I sighed. Posing for publicity photographs is one of my least favorite activities. I can't move and sing like I do in the role, so I have to stand there, looking somehow . . . interesting. *Horrid.*

"It's for the show. I know you hate being put on display, but you have to do it, Heller."

"I know. But I don't have to like it."

"I'll make you two the loveliest black velvet doublets and hose, and you won't mind at all," Anna assured me. "You know you'll be just beautiful together."

"Well, there's that," I admitted. It *would* be a lovely picture, if we could survive the posing for it.

We spent the next half hour or so happily planning the show, with the Morsel occasionally horning in, until Louis and Anna decided it was really far too long past his bedtime.

As they walked out, Anna scooping up her boy and rubbing his back as he dozed on her shoulder, I thought about poor Frances again. She had surely fit Marie's model of a woman who'd chosen not to marry and barely noticed children, including sweet little Morrie.

But as I shook off that sad thought, I realized that Louis might know better than Henry Gosling about her teacher.

"Do you know if Violette was working with anyone?"

"Yes. Desiree LaFontaine."

"I didn't know she was teaching." LaFontaine had been, if not exactly a rival of Lentini's, which implies someone on the same level, certainly a contemporary with no love lost.

"I don't think a lot of people do. But she takes on, as they like to say, a few promising students."

"Ah?"

"Ones who can pay, of course."

"Right."

"I wouldn't have recommended her," Louis said, his eyes serious behind his glasses. "I accompanied La-Fontaine a few times, and she's not a kind person. Not good for a young singer."

"Would she have pushed her into repertoire she wasn't ready for?"

"I honestly don't know. Why?"

"She had some pretty difficult music in her trunk."

Louis's brows drew together. "She was sounding a little raspy in her top register in those last few weeks, at least in vocalization."

"Really?"

"Yes. She didn't have a cold, so I didn't know what it was. Pushing her voice into something she wasn't ready for would do that."

"You're right." I nodded. "I guess I will have to talk to Desiree LaFontaine."

Louis's mouth twisted. "Hope you can find something better to do first."

Chapter 21

Shall We Dance?

Sunday morning found Tommy and me at Mass at Holy Innocents. One of the things I truly love about our neighborhood, and New York in general, is that while almost everyone knows who we are, nobody says anything at such times. I do my part by wearing a plain black silk dress and simple veil, to fit in with all the other respectable, but not rich, Irish ladies at the service. However, there's no doubt that my fellow parishioners are following an unspoken agreement. For my good neighbors, and many other New Yorkers, the famous are only famous when doing whatever it is they are famous for.

This Sunday was especially nice, since Aunt Ellen and the two youngest cousins joined us for Mass. They live in a very nice little brownstone a short walk away, and actually in a different parish, but Aunt Ellen still likes to come over and check on her oldest chicks on occasion. The last two cousins at home, both girls, are ten and twelve now, and she was taking them uptown to one of the museums for most of the day. We don't see each other every day anymore, of course, but Aunt Ellen is still very important to

Tommy and me. Going to Mass with her had that good old home-days feeling.

On the way out, she hugged us both, reminded me to watch out for the troublesome tall, dark man from her dream, then made us promise to come over for tea soon. It wasn't a request. After a few minutes of happy family chatter, I slipped away from her and Tommy to light a candle for my father.

I have only Aunt Ellen's and my mother's memories of him, and the vague idea that he probably looked a bit like a redheaded Tommy, but Mama always described him as a good man. He was loving and protective, to the last, when he ordered her to keep me, a weeks-old baby, as far from him as she could, lest I catch the typhoid that killed him. As I've been known to do, I reminded God that He brought them together, and He'd best let them stay that way in the next world.

Outside, Aunt Ellen had taken the girls off on their improving mission, and Father Michael and Tommy were standing on the steps, chatting with a few neighborhood children and their mothers. I joined in for a few happy sentences about the spring weather and when we might see lilacs. Then Tommy and I took the long way home through the park, soaking up a little sunshine, and, amazingly, not meeting anyone we knew, or who knew us. The fact that most of our friends would still have been asleep (for any number of reasons, not *all* questionable!) probably had something to do with it.

That afternoon, I had an unavoidable engagement. Appearing socially is part of a diva's job, but I've never been entirely comfortable with it, and certainly not with singing for my sandwiches at "little musicale tea dances." Society matrons are fond of holding these torture sessions in hopes of impressing each other with their good taste and—more to the point—social importance. But for the performers, it's awful; we're neither truly guests nor servants, and we must be on better-than-best behavior at every second. Horrid for anyone, but especially for a naturally shy girl who had to learn her fancy manners long after everyone else had. I was sewing piecework and scrubbing floors when Mrs. Corbyn and her ilk were starting dance and deportment lessons, after all.

So I prettied up with about as much enthusiasm as Anne Boleyn on that May morning when she was waiting for the warden to lead her to the scaffold. Probably less, since by that point Anne was ready to be a martyr. Not me, by a long shot.

"You don't have to go to Mrs. Corbyn's tea dance if you don't want to," Tommy assured me as I fussed with my hair at the foyer mirror.

I sighed. "You could come with me."

"Not on your tintype, Heller. I don't go to those dainty society things."

"More like open season for patronesses and stage-door Lotharios," I said irritably. "I'll have to sing something I hate, listen to the august ladies hold forth on their love of opera while looking down on me, and then dance with sweaty-palmed swells with nothing good on their minds."

Tommy scowled. "Maybe you should skip the dancing."

"Maybe you should come and glare at them."

"Sorry." He picked up his coat. "I promised Father Michael I'd go to dinner with one of the parish families this afternoon."

"Why did you agree?"

"He doesn't want to be the main dish at the Scaramuccis' Sunday meal. And who can blame him?"

It was true. The female Scaramuccis are the sweetest ladies you will ever meet, and terrific cooks, too. The male Scaramuccis are just as sweet, but at a significantly higher volume, and the entire family around a table can be intimidating. Father Michael, God love him, is a bit shy in crowds, as am I, and will bring Tommy along for moral support when he can.

"At least you'll be helping someone." I pulled the open neckline of my lavender taffeta frock a fraction higher. "I'll just be trying to stop Grover Duquesne from helping himself."

"I don't like that man."

"Neither do I. Hopefully, I can get away without a waltz. Rosa couldn't get the sweat stain off the waist of the last dress I wore for one of these things."

"Nasty."

"And then some. You boxers at least get to wear sports clothes for battle."

My hansom cab pulled up. Tommy handed me my wrap and looked down at me, quite sternly.

"Watch yourself, all right?"

"Always."

It was an amazingly short ride for such a jump in social prominence. The Corbyns have yet to escape to the toniest precincts on the edge of Central Park, staying in their older manse near the Ladies' Mile. That did not mean it was a simple cottage; taking up most of a block, it was a pile of expensive stone, three stories high, with two turrets, a columned portico and any number of embellishments whose names were not covered in my two years at the City primary school.

Mrs. Aline Corbyn, like most members of the Four Hundred, fancied herself a patron of the arts. She and her fellows each held these little musicale tea dances a few times a year, and competed to invite the best talent. I could have spent most of my afternoons singing in drawing rooms. Early in my career, I had, but as a star of my current stature, I was much choosier. Still, because it's very important to maintain goodwill with people who consider themselves great cultural leaders, I sang at each of the main hostesses' salons about once a year, even if it was rather a lot to give away.

Like all society events, these follow a rigorously set pattern. First the talent sang, in rough order of importance; then there was some sort of dainty repast; and lastly there was a bit of dancing, which was almost an afterthought, thankfully. We'd all be done in time for the socially important folk to make their fancy dinners, or whatever one does at that end of the class spectrum. I was going to be at home with my book and a medicinal sherry. Or two.

I usually ended up doing something from *Capuleti* and—bizarrely—"Ave Maria," which I hated, because it reminded me of my strange place between faiths. I either felt like a hypocrite singing angelically of a Holy Mother, whom I wasn't sure I believed in, or, far worse, found myself thinking of my own late mother. Not a happy event even before the Captain of Industry and his ilk started pawing me.

The Corbyn tea dance musicale unfolded according to pattern, at least at first. We presented ourselves at the door of her palace, to be guided into a drawing room the size of a small theater, only cluttered with antiques and objets d'art, any one of which might have cost more than we'd earn in our careers. I suspected Aunt Ellen and the small cousins were probably in the presence of fewer expensive relics at the museum that afternoon.

Once announced, we greeted the patronesses and their men, making careful conversation and accepting whatever condescension they heaped upon us with humor and grace. The young men pretended gallant flirtation with the ladies. We women did our best to ignore much less gallant glances and worse from the alleged gentlemen. Finally, and mercifully, it was time to sing.

A couple of new singers, a baritone and a very light lyric soprano, performed familiar arias, quite competently, but without any flash of star quality, and I doubted I'd be hearing from them again. A rising dramatic soprano I knew slightly, Alicia Ricci, gave a brilliant rendition of *"Suicidio!"* from *La Gioconda*. Not my wheelhouse, but I was very impressed. And then it was my turn. Sure enough, after my *Capuleti* death aria, came the request for "Ave Maria," this time from the elderly father of my hostess, so I couldn't even demur.

As often happens when I'm upset, I gave one of my best performances, but not without cost. It left me feeling unexpectedly weak and a little wobbly, wondering if I might plead a headache and slip away.

I was sitting on a quite literally priceless silver-gilt chair from Versailles, sipping a cup of tea and trying to settle my stomach a few moments later, when Grover Duquesne appeared to ask for the first dance. I assented, only because the first dance was a mazurka, faster and less intimate than a waltz, and to get it over with. It may have been less intimate, but the Captain of Industry still got to put his pudgy little hands on mine. He pulled me close enough that I nearly strangled in the cloud of cologne water that surrounded him. It did nothing to improve my mood—or my nausea.

As we spun around the floor, Mrs. Corbyn swept by in the arms of the baritone, clearly enjoying his attentions. Her necklace caught the light, and I couldn't help thinking that it was noticeably more elaborate than poor Lady Frances's piece. Nor was it especially unusual in that room, although most women had chosen large pearls, which when matched and sizeable are actually rarer and more expensive. A subtler way of flaunting one's wealth, I supposed.

I hoped they were using some of said wealth to help the less fortunate, but I had few illusions about that.

As the Captain of Industry and I continued our little terp-
sichorean tug-of-war, I consoled myself with the thought
that at least Teddy Bridgewater and his horrifying mother
weren't on hand. Most of the crowd was society types I
saw occasionally under these circumstances, maintaining a
polite acquaintanceship as required, but no one I would
have called a friend. At the end of the "Ave Maria," I'd
seen a very tall man walking in, and standing in the shadows at the back of the cavernous drawing room. I hadn't
gotten a good look at him, not that he would have been
anyone I knew or wanted to.

As the mazurka ended, I bowed to the Captain of Industry and pulled away, hoping to escape quickly. But then
the first bars of the waltz began. A gleam came into his
eye. "Miss Shane, would you favor me . . ."

Oh, good Lord. Must I . . . My stomach lurched, and I
decided this was quite enough. I am very legitimately nau-
seated and I am going home. I started my excuses: "I'm
sorry."

"My apologies, Mr. Duquesne, is it? Miss Shane promised
me the first waltz."

I have never been so happy to see anyone in my life.
There may have been a tall, dark man somewhere ready to
bring me trouble, but Gilbert Saint Aubyn was saving me
from it. His Grace, perfect in elegant black tie, bowed to
Duquesne and then to me. I didn't doubt that Mrs. Corbyn had sniffed out the presence of a duke in our fair city
and dragooned him into the party somehow. But it didn't
really matter how it had happened. I was just glad it had.

"Your Grace." I smiled, doing my best to hide my absolute relief as I took his outstretched hand. Thankfully,
this time there was none of that weird electrical reaction,
though it still certainly felt nice.

My previous partner did not take his demotion with
grace.

"Ah, well. Of course, you've got your duke now, don't you?" Grover said, his nasty little eyes narrowing as he made calculations that were both wrong and offensive.

Saint Aubyn wasn't having any. "I'm not certain what you're implying, Mr. Duquesne, but Miss Shane is a friend of my family, and any connection we may have is entirely honorable."

"Er, well," Duquesne mumbled.

"Not to mention none of your affair," my defender continued, his eyes freezing the Captain of Industry where he stood, his voice taking on the supremely cold, steely tone that only a righteously angry British man can produce. "And I would strongly caution you against impugning the reputation of a lady."

A nasty red flush appeared under Grover's collar as he backed away. "I had no intention . . ."

Saint Aubyn smiled . . . terrifyingly. "Of course, you didn't. We must have simply misunderstood each other."

"Of course, that's it. Have a nice dance now."

"A pleasure seeing you again, Mr. Duquesne."

We Americans simply do not have enough centuries of civilization to pack so much loathing and menace into polite phrases. It may be why we generally settle things with fists and guns.

Of course, my job as the duly defended lady was simply to allow my squire his waltz, so I happily complied as the duke swept me out onto the floor. He was not much better at dancing than fencing, but he would do. More than do.

"Thank you," I said as we settled into the dance. No surprise, my stomach had calmed right down once Grover and his vile cologne water were out of nasal range. "You have no idea."

"Isn't your cousin supposed to protect you from wretches like that?"

"Toms doesn't appear at society dances. I rather wish I

didn't." As he spun me around the floor, I noticed that while he, thankfully, didn't go in for cologne water, there was a very, very faint scent of something clean and herbal. And appealing.

"Understandably. And after you gave them such a lovely 'Ave Maria,' too."

"Well." I tensed a little.

"You do not enjoy singing that, do you?"

"No."

"Your mother, or your faith, or both?"

I just looked up at him; his cool blue eyes were close on my face, his expression surprisingly gentle.

"I observe, Miss Shane. Remember, I trained as a barrister. Very little escapes my notice."

I had no idea what to say to that, so I simply concentrated on the dance, which was well worth it. The waltz was, as it always is, a lovely dance with a partner who is at least reasonably competent. The duke wasn't the most graceful partner I'd ever had, but he held his own; more important, I didn't mind him holding me. Instead of praying for the end of the dance, and the moment when I would no longer have to hold his hand, or feel his hand on my waist, I found myself praying it *would not* end. *Oh, dear.*

"So I assume you are expecting a much happier time at the benefit this coming week."

"Yes." I smiled at the careful subject change. "You've met Marie. She's a joy to work with."

"She seems like a very happy lady, who shares her happiness with others."

"Exactly. It's the best way to use the gift, I think."

He smiled. "You ladies do see it that way."

"It would be hard for us to see it any other way. Remember, the music saved us from the laundry or the factory. We have a duty to use it well."

"Would Frances have appeared at one of these lovely soirees?"

"I'm not certain. She wasn't well-known, but she might have, as a rising new talent. Perhaps our good hostess will know."

"I suppose I must dance with her at some point." Saint Aubyn did not appear at all pleased by the prospect.

"I'm sure she'll happily tell you anything you'd like to know."

"No doubt. I shall beard that lion in her den later."

I stifled a chuckle at his beleaguered expression.

"I know you read a great deal," he said, firmly changing the subject as he watched me with what seemed like real curiosity. "I wonder if you have studied Japan at all?"

"'Japan'?" *That's an odd one,* I thought.

"Yes. I've never had the privilege of going there, but I understand that there are women who devote their lives to art."

"You aren't talking about the geisha?" I asked. I'd read a travel article once, and while the author seemed to think the women were courtesans, I'd come away wondering if they might actually be more like me.

Saint Aubyn nodded. "I should have known you'd read of them."

"Yes, but the travel author I read seemed to think they were, well, something else."

The pale blue eyes twinkled.

"But I wondered if perhaps he'd gotten them wrong, the way Mr. Duquesne persistently gets *me* wrong."

"That, he does."

"Well," I just kept going, "you're probably aware of this, but 'geisha' actually means 'art person,' and they spend their lives singing and playing instruments and so on, and usually do not marry unless they retire."

"It no doubt struck a chord, so to speak."

" 'Struck a chord.' " We shared a smile at the pun. "I suppose I am an 'art person.' "

"And are you planning to devote your entire life to your art, like the geisha?"

He studied me very seriously as the waltz reached its sweeping end. I was suddenly sharply aware of the warmth of his hand holding mine, and how close we were, even though he was very carefully observing the correct forms, not even attempting to draw me to him, as some men, notably Mr. Duquesne, have been known to do.

"At the moment, the art is the only thing on offer." I kept the reply light.

"Ah. And if life were to send something else your way?"

Tommy had said I should "stop slamming the door," after I read Madame's letter. "Then I would have to consider it, wouldn't I?"

Saint Aubyn smiled. "I should hope so."

And that was the end of the waltz. As we pulled apart, he held my hand for just an extra second, and there it was again, that damned electrical disturbance. We bowed to each other, very correctly, as if it hadn't happened. He went on to the next dance with our hostess, who seemed to be watching us with considerable interest. I allowed the young baritone who'd partnered her to scoop me up, knowing that he really was hoping to charm me into offering advice and connections—none of which I intended to share, having heard him sing.

After that, I found myself face-to-face with Mrs. Corbyn's father, a truly sweet old gent without an ounce of his daughter's pretension.

"A dance, Miss Shane?"

"Certainly, Mr.—"

"MacLaren, Emmett MacLaren. I do not usually enjoy my daughter's little soirees, but this one hasn't been too awful."

I laughed as he led me to the floor for another waltz. He had to be close to seventy, and he was still quite a good dancer—graceful, careful and respectful.

"Your 'Ave Maria' was absolutely angelic."

"Thank you."

"I'm sure you're asked to sing it a great deal, but it was very kind of you. Today would have been my mother's birthday, and even after all these years . . ."

Well, that changes everything, poor man. I nodded. "One always misses a mother. I'm glad to offer some comfort."

"You are the one who grew up an orphan on the Lower East Side, aren't you?"

"Yes," I replied very cautiously. This might go any number of directions, most unpleasant.

"Well, you've done very well for yourself. One good thing about this coming new century is that people are much less interested in where and how you're born . . . and much more in what you can do."

"Most days, I believe you're right." I nodded, hoping he would not ask what I believe on the other days.

"If I were thirty years younger, Miss Shane, I'd be competing with that duke to court you."

I gave the appropriate laugh at the pleasantry—which was, I'm quite sure, all he wanted. "I doubt the duke is courting me."

"It is a much different world than the one I grew up in, Miss Shane. In a new century, surely a diva can look at a duke."

"Perhaps." I shook my head.

"And the duke should count himself lucky if she does." MacLaren nodded firmly.

We finished the dance in amiable small talk, and Emmett MacLaren went away with a happy smile and, hopefully, a little balm for the sadness of his mother's birthday.

It did at least make the discomfort of singing the song worth it. I made my good-byes soon after that, pleading a busy day of rehearsal on the morrow. The duke was nowhere in evidence; I guessed he'd already made his escape, and well done by him. I was just relieved to make mine.

Chapter 22

Consolation and Confusion with Uncle Preston

After the trying tea dance, I did indeed manage to escape to the studio with a book and a medicinal sherry. A largish one, I will admit.

We have a sizeable, soft and exceedingly comfortable chair, upholstered in modestly hideous mulberry-colored plush, in one corner of the studio. It's often occupied by Tommy, when he sits in on rehearsal or practice sessions, and by me on nights like this, when I need to hide. I had very gratefully changed out of my fancy taffeta frock (and stays, ugh!) into a soft, warm and comfortable old violet cashmere housedress and had taken my hair down from the fancy Psyche knot into a more comfortable braid. I was wrapped up in an afghan against the chill of the big, empty room.

As it turned out, I did well to hole up in my corner, since I'd barely finished two sips of sherry and a chapter of the book— still poor Anne Boleyn—when Montezuma squawked and I heard the commotion downstairs. The sports writers. I should have expected it; Tommy hadn't had his fellows over in a while. A Sunday evening, when Mrs. Grazich was safely home, and there had been no baseball games, was just perfect.

"Extra! Extra!" Montezuma crowed. On some earlier visit, Yardley had taught him the newsboys' cry, and whenever he heard a lot of male voices and footsteps, he gave the warning.

"It's all right, sweetheart," I said, looking up from my book. "Love the birdie."

Montezuma made a slightly annoyed ruffling noise and settled back to his perch and carrot.

We really couldn't hear much from all the way downstairs; I suppose I might have turned on the phonograph, but why bother? Montezuma and I were quite happy as we were. I was through another chapter, and about halfway into the sherry, when the bird squawked again.

"Set the headline!"

That meant only one thing: Preston Dare, who knocked on the door frame as I waved him in.

Preston, the *Beacon*'s sports editor, is the dean of the writers. Or perhaps the ringleader. One of the other fellows, quite probably Yardley, had taught Montezuma to greet him that way, and Preston rather liked it. A tall, dapper gentleman heading for the golden years, he's taken Tommy and, to some extent, me under his wing. He watches over us with an almost fatherly interest, and after all that had happened while he was following the Brooklyn Superbas on their march to victory, I was especially glad to see him.

Tonight he was in a deep blue suit and red silk bow tie, with a red carnation in his lapel. His salt-and-pepper hair and mustache were perfectly trimmed, and his sharp gray eyes sparkly as usual. Also as usual, he looked a bit weary, but I was never entirely sure if it was lack of sleep or simply the world as he saw it.

"I'm not interrupting your reading, am I?"

"Not even a little. But I only brought the one glass of sherry upstairs." I smiled, knowing that Preston would require libation.

He held up his whisky glass. "Quite all right. Tommy has already made sure everyone is provided for."

"He would. Glad to see you back from the Superbas' road trip."

"It is good to go away," Preston reflected. "And much better to come home."

"Absolutely. How was it?"

"Suffice it to say, I am glad for my home, and a sip of whisky among friends."

"Nothing wrong with that."

He nodded gravely. "We do not get sloppy like those wretched writers for the yellow sheets, but gentleman scribes do enjoy a wee dram."

"Lady singers do not scruple at a medicinal sherry." I took a dainty sip of the same as he pulled the piano bench over and sat.

"I hear you need it. Another of those lovely soirees on Fifth Avenue?"

"We good little canaries must sing."

Preston laughed. "They usually don't bother you so much."

"It wasn't more horrid than any other one." I sighed. "Tea with a generous serving of snobbery on the side."

"They're the lucky ones, you know, kid."

"I tell myself this."

"It's one good thing about being a sports writer." He took a drink. "The swells stay away from us. They read our stuff, but we ink-stained wretches are well beneath their notice."

"Yes. No one puts you on display to show their friends how cultured they are."

"That would be a very unwise idea."

"'Unwise idea,'" Montezuma contributed.

Preston turned with a wide smile and held his hand out. "Love the birdie."

Montezuma swooped down to greet him and took a sniff of his drink. "Not for birdie!"

We humans laughed. Preston had said that, at considerable volume, the first time Montezuma sniffed at his drink, and it was now a tradition between them.

"No, 'not for birdie.'" He stroked the bird's head. "Good to see you, as always, Montezuma."

The bird whistled happily, then flew back to his perch.

"He is a sweet creature, for a parrot."

"That, he is."

"And you two are sweet kids."

Preston is probably the only person in the world who would describe Tommy and me as "sweet kids." We are, to some degree, substitute family. His wife and only child died in a cholera epidemic decades ago, and while he's apparently filled the emptiness with a succession of pretty and amiable barmaids, we are special to him.

"And you are sweet to us."

He grinned, and the laugh lines at the corners of his eyes crinkled. "It's nice to come home to you two for a change. No touring for a while?"

"San Francisco in the late summer. Just a few weeks. Then home to premiere a new opera."

"A new one?"

"Louis, my accompanist, has written a piece, *The Princes in the Tower*, to feature Marie de l'Artois and me as the princes."

Preston is not an opera expert, but he does know his English History. "Ah, two lovely blondes in doublets and hose singing away. A license to print money."

"That's what Tommy said. The music is good, too."

"It doesn't have to be," he said with a knowing smile, "but I'm glad for you that it is."

"It is. All of the elements of a great success are there, and Marie is willing, so it will be a very happy fall in the city."

"Excellent. Perhaps it will take away the sting of the Giants' inevitable decline."

I laughed. "Something will have to."

"At least we sports writers can drink."

"Just a drop, for medicinal reasons." We clinked glasses and sipped.

"Your friend Hetty turned in a bang-up article on lady fans, by the way."

"Oh, good. Do you think—"

"Morrison still has no idea what to do with her." Preston shook his head. "And baseball writing isn't the answer."

"After she was banned from the press box, I had my doubts," I admitted.

"She might do better to keep her eyes open for a good exposé story. It's worked for other women reporters."

"Good advice. Did you tell her?"

"You should pass it on, quietly, as a friend." He shrugged. "I don't have any doubt about her abilities, or about women's competence in general—"

"Good thing." I gave him a hard glance.

"But it's a harsh world, kid, and the world looks at women a particular way."

I nodded. "It sure does look at women in a particular way."

He heard something in my voice and gazed sharply at my face. "I don't have to have a word with anyone about that society party today, do I?"

"No, no. An acquaintance shooed one of my admirers away, and all was well."

I was perhaps too quick to offer reassurance, but I had terrible visions of Preston buttonholing the Captain of Industry. That was quite all any of us needed.

" 'An acquaintance'?"

"Ah," I started, trying to figure out how much I should explain, or could, without giving Preston the guilty knowledge of a story he should pursue, and would not, for our sake.

"Is this the duke that Tommy tells me has been visiting?"

"Yes. Exactly." I felt a trace of a blush as Preston smiled, and I quickly continued. "He's trying to find out what happened to a relative that I happened to know. Nothing interesting."

Preston's sharp gray eyes rested on me for a moment. "No?"

"*No.*" I looked away as I tried to skim swiftly over those odd electrical disturbances, not to mention the waltz.

"Ella, dear, you can sell that nonsense to Tommy and his priest friend, but I'm a man of the world. I know what it means when a woman doesn't want to talk about a man, the way you don't want to talk about your duke."

"And as a man of the world," I told him sternly, "you no doubt know that anything a duke would be willing to offer an opera singer is not something I'd be willing to take."

"Fifty years ago, I would have agreed with you. And probably punched him in the nose." He took a sip of his whisky. "Now, who knows?"

"What are you saying?"

"You would be furious if anyone judged you based on where you were born, and to whom, wouldn't you?"

"Of course."

"So . . ." Preston raised his glass to me with a smile.

I shook my head. "It's all probably just some kind of electrical disturbance in the atmosphere."

"Tell Uncle Preston."

My blush bloomed into full, embarrassing effect. "It's nothing. Just some sort of strange . . ."

He smiled as I trailed off. "Some kind of electricity when your hands touched?"

"Yes, all right?"

"And you strongly suspect he's feeling the same."

"At least once."

Preston grinned. "This has never happened to you before."

"Ever."

"Well, life comes for us all, Ella. Now you and your duke will have to decide what you do about it."

"He's not *my duke.*"

"Yet." He took another sip, then looked at me for a long second and shrugged. "On to far more important matters. I hear the lovely Mrs. Grazich was kind enough to leave some kind of cake for us starving scribes."

"Yes." As I took a relieved sip of my own, I remembered that odd comment from Mrs. G a few days back and watched him. "I believe it involves gingerbread and lemon curd."

He beamed. "Now *that* is a worthy topic of discussion."

"Preston!" Tommy called. "We're starting the card game!"

The writer stood and gave me a slightly teasing bow. "My public calls."

"Indeed. Good luck."

"I'll need it with that crew."

"Set the headline!" Montezuma called after him.

I was smiling, too, as I returned to poor Anne Boleyn in the tower.

Chapter 23

At Her Mentor's Knee

Next morning, I set out to beard the lion in her den, rising early and dressing in my very best off-the-stage diva style. I knew I would need it when I met Lady Frances's vocal teacher. As Lentini's protégée, and a considerable success in my own right, I was automatically on the wrong side of the discussion. Even in our enlightened age, men still tend to intimidate in very blunt ways: size, status, weaponry. Women are more subtle, but woe be unto she who goes into battle without the proper armor. For me, that cool and sunny Monday, it meant a lilac-striped silk morning dress, covered by a short, soft wool cape in a deep purple, with black nutria fur trim, and my best new spring hat. My chapeau was a lilac confection piled with ostrich feathers, barely purple at the tips, to deep heliotrope at the ends. No jewels—we know I don't go in for that, but the latest fashions in the finest materials made the point well enough.

Tommy drifted past as I checked myself in the hall mirror. "Who's earned this? Is the duke's mother in town?"

"Indeed not," I snorted. "Madame LaFontaine."

Tommy grimaced. Being a manager, he heard things I didn't. "Not a nice lady."

"So I've heard."

"Why are you poking that particular hornet's nest?"

"She was Lady Frances's teacher."

He shook his head. "I think I'd drink nicotine before I'd take a voice lesson with *that one*. The book on her is very short, and not sweet."

I turned to him.

"Poison mean, Heller." He looked me over. "At least to anyone who can't fight back. You should be all right, as long as you don't let her get to you."

I nodded.

Tommy leaned against the banister and studied me for a moment. "You're going to a lot of trouble for this duke character. He'd best appreciate it."

"You're not going to have a word," I told him.

"No." He smiled. "But I will permit him to have a word or two with you if he asks nicely."

"I'm not sure I want him to."

"You're not sure you don't, either."

I sighed.

"Ah. Well, he is a tall, dark man, and Mother said . . ."

"There is no second sight."

" 'There are more things in heaven and earth, Horatio . . .' "

I glared at him. "And Horatio is probably a tall, dark and troublesome man, too."

"We can only hope."

"Have a lovely morning." I got on tiptoe and kissed him on the cheek, then swept out, chuckling, as Toms had no doubt intended.

Madame Desiree LaFontaine (also probably not born with that name, not that I had any idea what it might once have been) had spent an eminently respectable career in the opera houses of Europe and across the United States. A coloratura soprano, with excellent range and crisp technique, she'd done quite nicely for herself. However, she was just that one tiny notch below Lentini's level. Close enough to see the Promised Land, but not to sing there, if you will. If Lentini hadn't discovered my gift for the trouser repertoire, I might well have found myself in a similar position. As I'd told Saint Aubyn, I was vocally capable of singing many important soprano roles, just not with the amazing quality that separates the star from the merely good. Unlike me, though, LaFontaine never found a place to show off her special gifts. It's entirely possible she never had them.

With that insight, I was not unsympathetic when I walked into Madame LaFontaine's apartment, on the middle level of a town house much like mine, though about twenty blocks farther up the island of Manhattan. It was still a respectable area of town; my favorite bookstore was a few doors down from her home, and a music store that I occasionally frequented was a block or so away.

LaFontaine, who was likely just a bit older than Lentini, had apparently retired without anyone's noticing a few years before, which, in itself, would have been painful. When Lentini retired, there was a gala final performance in New York and a farewell tour. It was undoubtedly satisfying to bask in the praise, but it was also very helpful in setting her up for a prosperous retirement in Amalfi. As a lesser light, LaFontaine had apparently taken her final bow with no such parting gifts, and was now, as Louis had put it, teaching "a few promising students." Financially promising, at least.

A very, very young and beleaguered-looking maid, probably Irish, answered the bell; she guided me into a dingy foyer. I gave her my card and asked if I might call on Madame La-

Fontaine, and she whispered a "Yes, miss," which confirmed my guess about her country of origin, and scuttled away.

A few moments later, an impossibly small, but ramrod-straight, woman walked into the room. LaFontaine was wearing a wine-colored crepe tea gown, with her steel-streaked iron hair in a low knot. She had extraordinary eyes, brown and bottomless, and she was unmistakably wearing kohl around them. A dab of lip rouge, too, unless I missed my guess.

"Ella Shane," she pronounced, looking up at me with poisonous intensity. "Or should I say, little Ellen O'Shaughnessy?"

It wasn't a happy-home-days moment. It was a deliberate effort to slap me back to where I'd come from. I kept my gaze steady. Better than she had tried. "Madame LaFontaine."

"Do you ever hear from Lentini?"

"We correspond frequently." I smiled politely. "She is like a second mother to me."

"She's in Amalfi now, with that awful little Fritzel?"

"I would rather say, retired to a sunny place with the love of her life."

"'Love.'" LaFontaine's still-generous mouth twisted. "Never mind that. Get the jewelry. And if he can't give you any, don't love him."

I felt my eyes widening, but I replied coolly, "I've never been fond of jewels."

"Then you're a fool." She shook her head. "The only reason to do this is to do well for yourself. And singing alone won't do it."

"That may have been, so many years ago. It is not now." I returned, denying her any reaction. "In any case, I am not here for advice on ordering my life."

LaFontaine snorted. "Then what are you here for?"

"A little insight on your late student, Miss Saint Claire."

"The pretty one who ended up dead."

She did not seem especially bothered by the fact as she shrugged and waved me into her studio, a dim room dominated by an old piano, with a lovely view of the wall of the town house next door, seen between dusty velvet curtains that had probably once been a reddish color. La-Fontaine stopped at a peeling ebony veneer occasional table, turned over a chipped glass and picked up a clearly well-used decanter of amber liquid. "Would you like a brandy?"

"Thank you, no. I have fencing practice later today, and brandy and swords don't mix." *Especially at ten in the morning,* I thought.

"Suit yourself." She motioned me to a somewhat-worn red plush chair, then poured the tumbler halfway filled before settling onto the matching settee opposite me. La Fontaine took a sip, gave a faint smile and squinted up into my eyes. Her smile was replaced by an appraising scowl. "What are you looking at? Judge when you're in your seventh decade with no family, and nothing but the memory of a career."

That was rather awfully close to home, but even so, I could not imagine what brandy at breakfast time would do to improve my lot. Other than perhaps dull the pain, which might well have been the point. I wanted to dislike her, but instead I pitied her.

And she saw it, which only made her dislike me more. "All right, get to it and get out. I don't wish to look at Lentini's last protégée any longer than I have to."

"I merely wanted to know how long Miss Saint Claire studied with you, what you were studying and what you thought of her talent."

"I thought she should go marry a man who sounded as posh as she did and stop taking singing jobs away from women who need them."

I just stared at her, feeling almost assaulted by the poison in her voice.

"I taught her because I needed the money. She wasn't any better or any worse than a hundred other singers."

"I found some music in her things, sheets for *Aida* and the Queen of the Night."

LaFontaine was midway through another slug of her brandy, and she laughed, choked and coughed. "That one?"

"Yes, I think she was trying to learn them."

"Good for her," sneered the teacher. "Strain the top register and have nothing left."

I nodded. "That's what I'd have been afraid of."

She looked at me, the poison momentarily ebbing away to a canny assessment. "You're quite sharp. Don't put anything past those Lower East Side kids."

"Something like that. So you wouldn't have worked on those with her?"

"Hell no." The profanity came all too easily to her lips. "And I'd have told her to stop at once. Understand, I didn't like her. I don't like anyone. But I also wouldn't help someone destroy herself."

The choice of words was a stopper, since, accidentally or not, that was exactly what Frances had done. I took a breath.

LaFontaine took another drink. This one ended up where it belonged. "I told her, take it slow, wait for your voice to mature, see what you can really do."

"Good advice."

"Only if you take it." She shook her head. "If she was working on those roles that young, she was taking a terrible risk."

I nodded. "What should she have been doing?"

"Exactly what she was doing with you. Nice light role, get used to the strain of performing. Then slowly start working your way up to harder things."

"Was she planning to come back to you after the tour?"

"Probably not. She wrote me asking if I could recommend someone in Philadelphia. And, of course, there is no one. There's barely civilization in Philadelphia."

I couldn't entirely suppress a chuckle. We'd played the City of Brotherly Love on the last tour, and it was actually a very acceptable place, with sophisticated and appreciative audiences. But, of course, it's not New York. Nothing is.

"So that's all?" LaFontaine asked, looking into her almost-empty glass.

"I think so."

"Good. I've got a contralto coming at ten-thirty. So go."

I rose and managed a social smile. "Thank you for your time, Madame."

She gave me a nod and growl, and I didn't look back as I walked toward the door. But her voice rang out again as I put my hand on the tarnished brass knob.

"You think the music saved you, don't you?"

I froze.

"Don't count on it, Ellen O'Shaughnessy. It just might eat you alive."

I straightened my spine and just kept moving as her bitter cackle followed me out the door.

Her laugh was still echoing in my head as I walked down the stairs and turned the corner—to nearly walk into three little girls standing in front of the bookseller's window.

"I'm so sorry," I said quickly as they looked up at me. They weren't from one of the most unfortunate families; they were clean and their clothes, while worn, were neatly kept. They didn't look hungry, either, at least not for food. The oldest one, who might have been ten, was looking in the window of Harrier's Bookstore like it was the Promised Land.

"Sorry, miss," she said, pulling the smaller ones closer.

"No, no. It was my fault." I smiled reassuringly. "Are you going to buy a book?"

Her clear hazel eyes dropped. "No, miss. Just looking."

"Ah. What's your name?"

"Alice. And this is Josie and May." She indicated the other girls, dark-haired and light-eyed like her, probably six and four.

"Nice to meet you all." I bowed very seriously. "Do you go to school?"

"Not anymore. Me ma does piecework and me da's working on the railroad, so somebody's got to watch the little ones."

I nodded. "Would your ma mind if I bought you a book, maybe once in a while?"

Her eyes widened. "Um, I suppose . . . I don't know, miss."

"All right, then, let's go inside and talk to Mrs. Harrier and see what we can do."

Sometimes I love my life and the good it enables me to do. Twenty minutes later, Miss Alice Shay had a copy of *Little Women* and an agreement to get herself a new book whenever she finished one, with Mrs. Harrier sending the bills to me. On one condition: she had to read to the little girls and make sure they read, too, once they were old enough. And I had a smile to replace the chill from my visit to Desiree LaFontaine.

It didn't last, though. Coming out of the music store a few blocks after the bookseller's was Arden Standish.

"Miss Ella." He greeted me with a bow and a smile, but once again, there was that weird tension, some of which was no doubt only in my mind—from my knowledge of his indiscretions.

"Good to see you again, Mr. Standish. Buying scores for Philadelphia?"

"And beyond. I need to expand my repertoire. I'm sure you understand."

I managed a social smile. "I surely do. I am always looking to add new roles."

"We must all grow as artists." His brownish eyes scanned my face closely as he clearly forced himself to stay and converse.

"So we must."

"You have learned no more about poor Violette?"

"No." *Not that I'm going to tell you,* I mused silently.

"Does the man you were walking out with have something to do with her?"

Something in the tone of the question unnerved me more than a little, but I managed a cool and neutral laugh. I shook my head. "We were catching up on old acquaintances."

"Ah. It is a very small world."

"That, it is." He didn't believe me. But I didn't believe he was asking casually, so we were even. "Good luck with your preparations for Philadelphia."

"Thank you. I'll see you at the settlement house benefit this Saturday."

"Yes. That's right," I agreed.

"My last New York engagement for a while."

"Philadelphia's gain is our loss," I offered.

He smiled. I smiled. We bid each other good day, and, thankfully, it was over. I tried not to think of him, but of Alice Shay's beaming face, and the way she hugged her new book, stroking the cover like it was the treasure of the world, which for her—and for me when I was that age—it absolutely was.

Chapter 24

No Dollar Princesses
Wanted, Either

After that Monday began in such eventful fashion, I was more than happy for a good hard fencing lesson to clear my head. That was precisely what Monsieur du Bois provided; he is probably the only opponent I have ever had who is unquestionably my superior. Although I did give him a worthy challenge that day. And then a pleasant surprise. Early in the afternoon, as I was seeing Monsieur out, the duke appeared at my door.

The introductions did not go well. Monsieur, a small, mustachioed, dark-haired man who generally very proudly bills himself as *"Le Comte du Bois,"* took one look at His Grace and quickly scuttled off. He was no doubt worried that a real British aristocrat would have no trouble recognizing a fake French one. I smiled to myself as I guided my latest visitor into the parlor.

"You do know that man is a count the way I am president of the United States." Saint Aubyn seemed personally offended by the *comte*'s existence.

"Are you quite sure?" I laughed. "I'm well aware that he's actually Mr. Mark Woods from the Bronx. He's also a marvelous fencing master, so he can call himself 'Queen Victoria' if it pleases him."

Saint Aubyn's scowl softened into a smile. "No fool, you."

"You're not the only astute observer around here, barrister. I grew up on the Lower East Side. If you couldn't see a con coming, you didn't last long."

"Fair enough."

"May I offer you coffee?"

"Thank you, but no. I hadn't intended to stay. I merely wanted to leave a note that I would be happy to meet your reporter friend at her convenience."

"Ah."

The weight of it hung between us for a moment. I knew this was a very serious matter for him, and I just hoped I was steering him in the right direction. I had no doubts about Hetty, but once the train leaves the station . . .

"Thank you. I will send word to her."

He nodded. "I appreciate it."

"I have spoken with your cousin's voice teacher."

"Oh?"

I decided to spare him the worst of it. "It's as we thought. She should not have been working on those pieces. Louis told me he was not practicing them with her, so she was working on them alone at some point. Very dangerous for the voice."

"And no one would have known?"

I shrugged. "It's of a piece with her, ah, eating problem, I'd imagine. Doing things she knew to be dangerous in secret."

Saint Aubyn absorbed that. "She really was quite troubled."

"I wish I'd known. I truly do."

"I don't blame you, Miss Shane. If we, her family, didn't detect the problem the first time, how could you?"

"Well," I said, taking a breath, "I should've twigged to the singing somehow. And that was career-threatening."

"That serious?"

"We have to be so careful." I shook my head. "Every day, I do my vocal exercises."

"Other exercises, too." He smiled a little as he nodded at my outfit—today an old, well-washed white broadcloth puffy-sleeved shirt from a previous season's Romeo and black serge breeches, my hair in a neat dancer's knot.

"Yes, that too."

Saint Aubyn looked at me with a gleam in his eyes. "Are you quite done with fencing for the day?"

"Perhaps a rematch?"

"I shouldn't," he admitted. "I am expected soon at Mrs. Corbyn's. A tea I must not miss, she said, with people she wants me to meet."

I was quite sure he knew what that meant. "No doubt, there will be a few lovely dollar princesses and their equally charming mamas."

"When you put it like that . . ." Saint Aubyn shook his head. "You don't really think—"

"I don't think anything. I only know that you are a duke and unmarried, and Aline Corbyn is a society hostess. Everything else is math, and I was never as good at ciphering as I was at reading."

He absorbed that, his face tightening. "I am not unaware of the whole American industry of title shopping."

"I have no way to know what Mrs. Corbyn is planning. And it would be unfair for me to suggest—"

"Well, I have no intention of allowing anyone to throw insipid young ladies at my head in hopes of winning a coronet."

"You have to be polite to people like Mrs. Corbyn, though."

Saint Aubyn looked down at me with a wry smile. "You may have to be polite to Mrs. Corbyn, Miss Shane. *I* do not."

The smile widened into a cheeky grin, and he looked like a misbehaving little boy. "You know, Miss Shane, I could use some fencing practice, if you would do me the honor."

"It would be my pleasure."

"I assume your cousin or other suitable chaperone is about somewhere? I doubt the parrot would cover the forms."

I chuckled. "Montezuma would take issue with that, but Tommy's in his study. We'll pass by on the way up to the studio, so you can make appropriate greetings."

"Winner and still champ-een!" Montezuma called out as Tommy led the way into the studio.

Toms had decided that propriety required him to bring his biography of Richard III, research for *The Princes in the Tower,* and park himself in the chair in the corner. Or he just wanted to see the show. I wasn't sure which, and didn't especially care. Neither did Saint Aubyn, who took off his coat and jacket and draped them over the piano bench, then looked to me. I'd forgotten just how appealing he was in shirt and waistcoat, truly a fine figure of a man. Which would not prevent me from defeating him. I tossed him a foil.

This time, he caught it as Montezuma crowed: "English stick!"

Saint Aubyn shot the bird a glance and put the foil down. "I'm very sorry, Miss Shane, but this is quite enough." He turned to Montezuma, holding his hand out. "Love the birdie."

Montezuma, the little wretch, flew right over to him.

"Excellent." He stroked the bird's head. "Now, my fine green friend, repeat after me, '*Alba gu bràth.*'"

"*'Alba gu bràth.'*"

Tommy and I exchanged glances, trying not to laugh as Saint Aubyn and the bird repeated the phrase a few more times, clearly starting a mutual-admiration society as well. Then he sent Montezuma back to his perch, turning to me with a truly wicked smile.

"What have you just taught my bird to say?"

"'Scotland forever.' In Gaelic. Of course."

"Of course." I couldn't help laughing as I handed him the foil. "Ready?"

"Never more so."

"*En garde,*" I said, tapping my foil on his. "Think you can defeat me this time?"

"We'll have to see, won't we?"

He was a little more in the game for this match, and perhaps I was a bit more distracted by his attractiveness. But it wasn't enough to change the outcome. Much.

We were both silent and quite concentrated at the beginning, Saint Aubyn once again having trouble adjusting to the idea of dueling a woman, particularly one so much more skilled than he. But he quickly started holding his own.

"So you'd rather duel with me than find yourself a dainty dollar princess?" I asked as I backed him across the studio.

"I'm not looking for a wife." He managed to back me up a little. "At least not one who brings nothing but her bank account."

"It seems to work for many aristocrats."

"I'm *not* many aristocrats."

"Duly noted."

"What about you?" Thrust. Attack.

Block. Parry. "Me?"

His eyes gleamed above the swords. "You'd surely have a more comfortable life with a rich husband."

"Either you're teasing or you weren't listening when

you talked to Marie. Husbands are usually more trouble than they're worth."

"Depends on the husband, I should imagine."

"I doubt there's the man living," I started as I pressed my advantage, almost cornering him.

"Who what?" he asked, backing out of the corner and now pressing his own attack.

"Who could live with both me and the music."

"Some men might find it a pleasing challenge."

"Not for long. Men like their wives at their service."

"Do we, now?" Parry.

"Don't you?" Attack.

"Not all of us. Some men actually enjoy taking care of their women instead of being tended by them."

"Oh." I saw the look on his face and almost missed the parry.

"Just an observation, Miss Shane."

We were at crossed swords in the middle of the studio then, eyes locked, waiting for the next move, nothing to do with the match at all.

"Well, then. That looks like a draw to me, again," Tommy called, breaking the moment.

This time, he'd earned the draw.

Saint Aubyn bowed to me. "Thank you, Miss Shane."

"*Alba gu bràth!*" Montezuma put in. "Fine figure of a man!"

"My pleasure." I glared at Montezuma over Saint Aubyn's shoulder as he handed me the foil, but the bird just blinked back at me. "I hope you will not be too late for your tea."

"I find I am somewhat indisposed," he said as he picked up his jacket from the piano bench. "And at any rate, I have to prepare for my talk with your friend."

I nodded, trying not to watch him too closely as he re-assembled himself. Meanwhile, I brought my breathing back under control and silently prayed that my face wasn't flushed utterly magenta from the fencing, and more.

Tommy walked down the first flight of stairs with us, then nodded to me. "I'm sure you can manage to walk your guest out. Good to see you again, Your Grace."

They shook hands, and I had the sense of some genuine warmth and respect there. Only a fool would not like Tommy, but I was glad Tommy had decided to at least tolerate the duke.

I did feel a bit guilty as I saw him to the door. "I do hope I didn't ruin anything for you," I said as we walked through the foyer. "There's no shame in—"

He stopped cold and very deliberately looked me in the eye. "Miss Shane, the only reason to marry is love."

"I quite agree." I quickly continued to the next thought, lest I trap myself here. "But I have no way to know if Mrs. Corbyn really was throwing pretty misses at you, and if I caused you—"

"No, you called it exactly right. A tea you must not miss, with some people I'd like you to meet, means only one thing from a society matron to an unmarried duke. I should have seen it coming. I'm in your debt, yet again."

"Not at all."

We walked out onto the step. I was glad for any chance to get some air, even if the sky was a bit threatening.

He bowed. "Have a lovely afternoon, Miss Shane."

"And you." I bowed as well. "Thank you for an excellent match."

"The pleasure was mine."

We stood on the step for a moment, looking at one another, some sort of current crackling around us. Perhaps it was just a storm on the way.

"And what have we here?" a familiar voice called from the sidewalk.

"Preston!" I turned. "Are you coming for tea?"

"If Mrs. G will permit me."

"I think she'll be able to find another cup."

Preston and the duke studied each other, and I was briefly reminded of how fighters size each other up at the start of a match. They, however, seemed to like what they saw. Or at least not want to punch each other immediately. I jumped in.

"Gilbert Saint Aubyn, Duke of Leith, may I present Mr. Preston Dare, the sports editor of the *Beacon,* the dean of the writers' corps and a dear friend and mentor to Tommy and me."

Saint Aubyn gave him a cordial nod. "Delighted to meet you."

"Likewise." Behind the duke's head, I mouthed, "Your Grace."

"Your Grace," Preston added smoothly.

They shook.

"After such a glowing introduction . . ." Saint Aubyn smiled.

"Ella is a little too kind to those she loves." Preston beamed right back at him. "If you're lucky, you'll learn that in time."

"I shall hope for it."

They were silent for probably a full stanza, still quietly assessing each other under the cordiality. Preston finally spoke.

"Not staying to tea?"

"Sorry, no. I would enjoy discussing what you Americans consider sport at some later date."

"Baseball, my British friend, is highly overrated," Preston observed.

"So, too, cricket."

They laughed, and it was genuine and amiable.

"All right, then. Next time I shall stay." Saint Aubyn

nodded to us both. "If only to see how much Miss Shane knows about her American pastime."

"Just don't say a word against her beloved Giants and you'll be fine," Preston assured him.

He looked puzzled for a moment.

"Baseball, Your Grace."

"Ah. Of course. Miss Shane and I have tended to confine our conversations about matters of sport to fencing." He cut his eyes to me, with a trace of a smile.

"I'd guess she's better than you."

"She is, indeed. And I am honored when she's willing to tolerate me as a sparring partner."

Preston grinned. "I bet you are."

I just stood there blushing, hoping that the conversation would soon be over.

Saint Aubyn decided to be merciful. "I really must be going."

"A pleasure to meet you."

"For me as well. A good day to you." The duke bowed to us both and walked off.

Preston carefully waited till the duke was out of earshot; then he turned to me with a gleam in his eye. "Is that the one you don't want to talk about?"

"Yes, all right?" I shrugged, wishing the blush would dissipate.

"Well, for a British toff, he seems decent enough."

"Don't want to punch him in the nose?" I asked, mostly jokingly.

"Not yet, anyway." He smiled. "He looks at you like you can do no wrong. Give him a chance, kid."

"Preston."

"I'm not telling you to have Father Michael post the banns. I'm telling you not to slam the door in his face."

"Do you and Tommy compare notes on what to say to me?"

He laughed, the big explosive guffaw that I love. "No. It's just that we're always right."

"Come in for tea. I'm sure Mrs. G will have something lovely for you."

"Mrs. G is lovely enough on her own."

I caught a whiff of something again, and looked sharply at Preston. "Has she won your heart with her hermits?"

"Mrs. Grazich is a very pretty and kind lady, not to mention an amazing cook. It's a shame she's not baking those cookies for a houseful of adorable grandchildren instead of a bunch of hungry sports writers."

"Why, you fraud," I teased. "Telling me to—"

Preston suddenly looked quite serious, and it crossed my mind that he might have spent the last few decades chasing barmaids because he was actually afraid of catching a good woman. I was not the only one who felt safer at arm's length.

"I will make you a deal," I said as lightly as I could.

"What?"

"I will leave the door open if you will."

He gave me a rueful smile. "Well, kid, when you put it like that . . ."

Chapter 25

Worth the Candle

Tuesday afternoon, Hetty agreed to meet the duke for tea at my house. "Agreed" was a pale word for it. She'd have walked through the fires of Hell, and who could blame her? A chance to break a good and interesting story, make a connection with British aristocracy and impress her editor? Any reporter who was compos mentis would have jumped at it.

She arrived a half hour before the duke was due, so I could bring her up to date on what I knew, and also give her a sense of how to treat him. There'd be no point to any of this if it all fell apart, after all.

"No Montezuma?" she asked, looking around the parlor.

I shook my head. "The last thing we need is him piping up in the middle of the interview."

"Isn't that the truth."

"So have a seat and we'll talk."

"What do I need to know about dukes?" Hetty asked as she made herself comfortable on the settee, smoothing her neat gray skirt. She was in her usual simple serge suit, but she'd put on a shirtwaist with a lacy collar in honor of the duke. She didn't have to tell me that she'd carefully thought it out, deciding in favor of a businesslike suit, instead of a perhaps more elegant dress, to set the right professional tone. Her wire-rimmed glasses gleamed, and were actually staying in place for once. And, of course, there were no visible ink stains, though she admitted she'd already gotten one on the cuff of her shirtwaist and had to tuck it up into the jacket sleeve.

"Well, dukes in general tend to be stuffy old men. Let's stick to this duke," I said, taking a sip of my tea. I'd chosen a very simple lavender-and-lilac sprig-print day dress, and even though I certainly could have used the excuse to wear one of my spring hats, I was taking the hostess's privilege and going without. Etiquette notwithstanding, I feel silly wearing a hat indoors.

"Does he have a name?"

"Not that you'll ever use. Or me, either." I shrugged. "He's not as much of a stick as most British aristocrats, but if you want him to be comfortable and talky, you'll observe the forms."

"Of course."

"You'll quote him as Gilbert Saint Aubyn, Duke of Leith. Probably 'the duke' on second reference. He's from the north of England, so you may notice a faintly different accent."

Hetty nodded, watching me carefully.

"You don't have to curtsy."

"Like I would!" she snorted.

"Americans," I continued rather stiffly, "are not expected to curtsy to British—or any other—aristocrats or royals, for that matter, even though many do."

"I'd hope not. We fought a war for that."

"Well, exactly. Try not to remind him of it, though."

"All right. What else do I need to know?"

"Most of us ordinary mortals are expected to address dukes as 'Your Grace.'"

She snickered. "'Your Grace,' really?"

"Really, Hets, that one's an absolute requirement, so make yourself sound comfortable with it."

"Yes, *Your Grace.*"

I glared at her.

"Just trying it out. If you married him, would I have to call you that?"

"You'd call me 'crazy,' because that's what I'd be."

"Ah." Hetty's face turned serious. "Tell me about the poor dead sister."

"Cousin. Lady Frances Saint Aubyn. Don't ask me how she was a 'Lady.' It's a courtesy title, and something to do with the family tree."

"Please don't make me figure that out."

"Don't worry. Lady Frances is accurate, and that's all you need."

"Saint *A-u-b-y-n?*"

"Yes."

"She sang as Violette Saint Claire, right?"

"Right."

Hetty looked thoughtful. "A lot of people who use false names choose something with an echo of their true name. She fits the pattern."

"Interesting."

"Pretty brave when you think about it. Running off from a safe and comfortable life in England to America, all alone, to sing."

I nodded.

"Was she good?"

"Good enough to work for me," I said carefully, "and good enough to get an offer for a season in Philadelphia. She was on her way."

Hetty's no fool. "What are you holding back?"

"Nothing, really. She was very young. We didn't know what she would turn out to be."

"Who does at twenty?"

"Twenty-one, I think."

"I'll check the records. Either way."

I nodded. "You couldn't pay me enough to be twenty-one again."

"But the men love the pretty young dollies. At the peak of their loveliness, they say." Hetty's mouth had a bitter twist that negated the joking tone.

"*Fools.*" I shook my head and poured some more tea. "He'll answer your questions about what kind of girl she was. I don't know much more."

"No heart-to-heart talks or velocipede afternoons?"

"Not even close. She pretty much kept to herself."

"All right." Hetty took a few notes and contemplated. "So it was poison?"

"Ruled accidental, as you know. And we recently discovered that she was apparently using a patent medication with nicotine in it. So it might really have been an accident."

"There's enough nicotine in patent medicines to kill?"

"Mr. Chalfont says nicotine's a close thing, anyhow, and a small woman who mistakenly took a larger dose might get enough to do it."

Her amber eyes widened. "But that's a scandal."

"You know there can be anything in those bottles. Think of the soothing syrups they sell to help babies sleep."

"And the ones who don't wake up from the opium." She nodded. "But still, Ella, the patent medication is the hook here."

"What do you mean?" I remembered Preston's comment about an investigative piece and the germ of an idea sprouted.

"Well, it's interesting that the dead girl turned out to be the runaway cousin of a duke. Good story, for sure. Our readers will lap it up—and forget about it. But if she died from an accidental overdose of something that's on their own dressing table?"

"We aren't sure which one it was. She had a box from something, but it was old, and who knows?"

"But you know there is some beauty tonic with nicotine in it?" Hetty asked.

"Yes. And that's enough of a start for a good exposé, isn't it?"

"Surely is." She nodded and I could see her wheels turning. "I'll do some research. That'll be our second-day story. And a good one. 'Duke's Cousin Killed by Dangerous Beauty Treatment.' Maybe girls will stop playing with those things."

"I could not agree more." A quiet, unmistakable voice from the doorway.

"Miss! He's here!" Rosa proclaimed needlessly, appearing behind Saint Aubyn.

"I figured that out." I rose and walked over to him. "Your Grace."

We bowed, no handshake, as usual, and I hoped Hetty picked up. I'd forgotten to warn her about handshakes.

"And may I present Miss Henrietta MacNaughten from the *Beacon*."

Hetty stood and bowed gracefully. She didn't curtsy, but I could tell she was thinking about it. I could also tell she was enjoying a good look at Saint Aubyn. As she absolutely should.

"Nice to meet you, Your Grace."

"A pleasure, Miss MacNaughten."

We sat, and I poured, swallowing my smile at the memory of Marie's taking over during his first visit because I was still in breeches.

Once all were appropriately refreshed, the silence descended, thick and uncomfortable, as everyone waited for everyone else to speak. In theory, Hetty should simply start in with her questions. In practice, Saint Aubyn probably expected to take charge of the event.

"What do you want to know about my cousin?" he finally asked.

"Anything you'd like to tell me. Let's start with how she left to come here."

"All I know is that one morning, her mother came to me in a panic. Frances had gone, leaving a note that she was following her talent, and a few small valuables were gone, too."

And one not so small *valuable, of course,* I silently parried. I assumed he wasn't mentioning the necklace for reasons of his own, so I didn't say anything.

"Naturally, we looked for her, and asked after her in opera circles in London and Edinburgh, without success. We eventually figured out that she'd left the country, but weren't sure where she'd have gone. Since she spoke French and Italian, she could have gone to the Continent equally well."

Hetty nodded and took notes, keeping her eyes on his as she let him spool out the story.

"It was about two years after she left that we got the letter from the coroner of New Haven. She'd died in a mishap on stage, and they managed to trace her true identity by finding a few papers she'd left with her booking agent."

I remembered the letter of thanks the New Haven coroner had sent Henry, and once again, I wished I'd done more. I wondered if I'd ever stop feeling that I'd failed her.

Violette Saint Claire started out the same as every other Juliet, except Canadian—we thought. Very pretty and young, of course; shy, at first, like everyone is in their first lead. We were playing opposite each other, which meant we had to develop some kind of rapport, at least on the stage, so I did what I always do with new young singers: I told funny stories about my own awkward moments. Usually, my tale of losing my balance as I climbed over the balcony, tripping over my sword and sliding on my cape to land in a graceless heap at Lentini's feet is enough to thoroughly break the ice.

Not with this girl. She laughed politely, said she was glad not to have to manage a sword and left it at that. I assumed the reserve was just shyness and hoped it would wash out with time.

Soon after, I decided to try a different tack. Since I'd never played Canada, I asked her about it during another rehearsal break. After just staring at me for a second, as if she never expected to be asked about her homeland, she gave me a few sentences about the cold and the provincial fashions, then quickly changed the subject.

Now, of course, I know why. Back then, I'd taken it as a very clear snub, which I put down to pretour nerves. I gave her a wide berth for the first few weeks. In the early performances, she was very good, if clearly unused to large, appreciative audiences. At one point, I saw her pale and shaky backstage, taking deep breaths just before going on.

I went over to her, put a hand on her arm and offered a little reassurance with a wry grin. "They can't kill you. And it's not you, anyway. It's Juliet."

She returned a wobbly smile, then turned in a perfectly fine aria. Looking back, I wonder what might have happened to cause the upset.

At first, I thought the over-acting might be a way of fighting stage fright. So one night before the show, I asked her to my dressing room for tea and a chat. Once again, though, it was very hard to get past the first few sentences and develop any kind of rapport. As gently as I could, I urged her to back off the overacting a bit, and to relax into the role.

Mostly, she just nodded and looked at me. I remember thinking that even though she seemed respectful, there was a definite undertone of disdain there. As if she knew more than I did, as if she were better than the likes of me. Of course, considering her true pedigree, she might well have thought she was.

Despite all of that, we were still on the road together, and we still shared the experiences of the company. Probably the best night of the tour was the snowstorm during the Boston stand. After the show, the cast stepped out of the theater to find that there were no hansom cabs in sight, so we had to walk to the hotel.

The streets were nearly deserted, and the fluffy snow glittered in the gaslights as the lot of us slipped and slid on what sidewalks there were. It was not a short walk, and soon the young singers of the chorus were looking scared and cranky. Anna and Louis were just exhausted, desperate to get back to the hotel, where the nursemaid was watching the Morsel. Violette gazed up at the sky and muttered the same curse I was thinking.

It was very cold, the one thing I cannot stand because it brings back memories of my last winter with my mother.

That's when Tommy threw a snowball at me.

Our eyes met, and we started laughing. I grabbed up my own handful of snow and threw it right back at his head— and before you could say "Molto Presto," our entire elegant opera company was in the midst of a truly hilarious snowball battle.

Soon Violette yelled, "Girls versus boys!" and the distaff side unleashed a merciless onslaught. Naturally, we won.

Covered in snow, laughing like fools, we finally made it to our hotel. The staff took pity on us and sent a huge tray of cocoa and cookies to my suite, and we stayed up into the wee hours, drinking and eating and telling funny stories. Violette happened to end up sitting beside me, not *saying much, but joining in the laughter and camaraderie. Her eyes were sparkling, and her black hair curled damply around her flushed face.*

As we relaxed and joked in the lamplight, I really thought she and I might become friendly, if not exactly friends. That girl, the girl we saw that night, was someone I would want to know, and work with again.

Until the next performance, when she once again showed up in the full flower of overacting, and brushed off my very careful comment with a curt "Yes, Miss Ella."

After that, I left managing her to Tommy. He didn't have much success, either, and we decided to just ride out the tour. We both knew we were missing something, but with everything else that happens on the road, we didn't have much time to think about what it might be.

In retrospect, I wonder if the overacting was a kind of cry for help . . . and if she was afraid to get close to anyone, for fear of giving away her secret.

My mistake, I think, is very simple. I never asked the next question, never said the next sentence. She pushed me away and I let her, because I was busy, because she made me uncomfortable, because I did not want to give her the chance to insult me. Instead, I left her out there alone.

From now on, I ask the next question.

Saint Aubyn was still explaining to Hetty what happened. "So, after the funeral, I came here to find out what might have led to this."

Hetty chewed on the end of her pencil. "With Miss Shane's help."

"Yes." His eyes lingered on me for a moment.

"What was she like, your cousin?"

"Determined. Talented. What's the word you Americans use for spirited women? Fiery?"

"Feisty?"

"Yes, that." He smiled ruefully. "And absolutely in love with her music. I'm sorry I didn't see how important it was to her. I wish we could have found some way for her to continue without running away."

Hetty's eyes were sharp on him. "Could you?"

Saint Aubyn sighed. "Her mother would have said absolutely not. And I imagine I would have agreed. Knowing what I know now, I believe I would have helped her find a way."

"Knowing . . . that she died?" Hetty asked carefully.

"No. Actually knowing singers, knowing what kind of people they are, and knowing how they live." He looked around the parlor. "This is hardly a den of iniquity."

She laughed. "You haven't been here when Tommy, Yardley and Father Michael are having a three-way checkers tournament."

"Duly noted."

They smiled at each other for a moment, and I knew this was actually going exceedingly well.

Hetty pulled it back. "Do you know what patent medicine she was using?"

"No. Only that she was using something with nicotine."

"And that . . ."

He nodded. "An unfortunate accident."

"Would you say people need to be much more careful about patent medicines?"

I knew what she was doing, and I suspected he did, too.

"Indeed. I would suggest parents of young ladies take a very good look at what's on the vanity table. And I'd suggest young ladies ask their chemist before they take anything."

" 'Chemist'?"

"A 'druggist,' " I translated. "British."

"Ah. Are such things available over there?"

"Yes. Probably just as dangerous." He shook his head. "I will be looking into the laws covering them when I return."

"Can you do anything about it?"

Saint Aubyn smiled faintly, then responded far more gently than the question deserved. "Yes, Miss MacNaughten, I am a member of the House of Lords."

Hetty flushed, and I quickly jumped in. "My fault, Hets, I didn't mention that part, did I?"

"You left that out." To me, with narrowed eyes. To Saint Aubyn: "I apologize for my ignorance. I'm quite sure you aren't prime minister, at least."

"No." He gave her a real smile at the parry. "Nor even in the government. But I do have a certain access to the levers of power, which I will be happy to use to prevent another family from knowing this pain."

Even though I am a diva and not a reporter, I know a quote when I hear one. Hetty, of course, took a moment to make sure she got it precisely right, then nodded to the duke.

"I believe I have what I need," she said. "Anything you would like to add?"

Saint Aubyn thought for a moment. "Many young ladies would like to be more beautiful. It shouldn't cost them their lives."

Speaking of quotes, I thought.

Hetty wrote that down, too, then closed her notebook. Saint Aubyn and I both stood.

"Thank you, Your Grace." She held out her hand, in a lacy half-glove, to shake.

He did. It meant he was treating her as a professional, just as he would with a man. I don't know if she understood how important a gesture of respect that was, but I certainly did. I'd tell her later.

"Thank you, Miss MacNaughten. I'll look forward to reading your article."

"I'll have a copyboy bring you a bulldog edition late tonight." She smiled. "It's the least I can do. Where?"

"I would like that." Saint Aubyn nodded. "Waverly Place Hotel, then."

"Why, we're all practically neighbors." Hetty grinned. "Perhaps you'd like to join us for a velocipede ride one of these days."

His eyes widened. "I leave that to the ladies."

"Probably wise." I could not imagine him on a velocipede. "Later this week, Hetty?"

"Yes. I suspect we both need a good ride."

Saint Aubyn refrained from comment, but one eyebrow flicked almost imperceptibly.

"Ah, well," I said quickly. "We can talk about that later."

Hetty nodded, tucking her notebook and pencil in the pocket of her jacket, moving on from the awkward moment to the work at hand. "Yes. I've got to get back to the office."

As she headed out, Hetty turned to the mirror to make sure her hat was properly in place. And then came the whirlwind. Tommy and Father Michael blew into the foyer, laughing about something. Tommy popped up behind Hetty in the mirror, making her laugh, too, as he said, "Lovely as ever."

Father Michael saw Saint Aubyn and me, and tried for a little ecclesiastical dignity.

"Hello, Miss Ella and . . . ?"

I laughed, too. "Glad you and Toms are having a good day."

"It will be a better day after I beat him at checkers." Tommy smiled evilly as he held the door for Hetty, who cut her eyes to me as she made a hasty escape. "We've got enough time for at least one game before dinner." He only then noticed Saint Aubyn. "Hello, Your Grace. How's your checkers game?"

"I usually play chess, actually."

"Why am I not surprised?" Tommy chuckled. "Well, you're still welcome to join in."

"I don't think we've met. Are you the duke that Tom has told me about?"

He nodded. "Gilbert Saint Aubyn."

"Father Michael Riley."

They bowed, but didn't shake hands, and carefully assessed each other for a moment, with some unmistakable tension simmering below the surface. From Father Michael's teasing comments about the matter a few days ago, I'd never have expected this.

"It's the Irish Question, isn't it, Father?" Saint Aubyn finally spoke quietly.

"All due respect, Your Grace, it's not a question for us. It's your grandfather letting my grandmother die in the road."

Tommy looked at me. The Hunger is always a wound for the Irish, but we rarely speak of it. Perhaps the presence of a British aristocrat had sparked something in our usually genial priest.

"Father, that's not quite fair," I spoke up. "You don't hold the alleged misdeeds of my ancestors against me."

"And I don't hold whatever his family did or didn't do against him, Miss Ella. Prejudice does none of us any good. I'm just not sure how I can have a friendly—"

"All due respect, Father, you know nothing about my family. Or, for that matter, my views on Ireland." Saint Aubyn was radiating tension right back at the priest.

"I don't, for a fact."

The tension eased a tiny bit, but I knew I'd best pour some oil on these troubled waters.

"I do, however, know both of your views on shepherd's pie, and that happens to be what Mrs. Grazich is making for dinner tonight," I offered, looking from one to the other. "What do you say?"

"Miss Shane is always right," Saint Aubyn said, offering a hand to Father Michael.

"That, she is." The priest took it and gave him a significant glance. "Well, you've clearly learned the most important thing about dealing with Miss Ella."

"And what is that?"

"Her word is law, of course."

They exchanged a smile, and while the tension wasn't entirely gone, they'd at least made a move in the right direction.

"Heller thinks she's running things, but we all know who's really in charge." Tommy looked every bit as relieved as I felt.

"Not you," I replied cheerfully, as he knew I would.

"Never challenge an Irishwoman's authority in her home." Father Michael laughed.

"I would argue, never challenge any woman's authority in her domain," Saint Aubyn said. "My mother is Scots, and rules only slightly less imperially than our queen."

All three sighed, looking like little boys who'd been ordered to come home from the playground. Nothing unites men like feeling henpecked by their women.

Father Michael smiled. "Half Scots?"

"Yes."

"It's not as good as being Irish, but at least you've got a little of the Celt in you."

Saint Aubyn knew a large olive branch when he saw it. "Highland Scots, at that. She even taught me a little Gaelic."

"The Auld Tongue?" The priest's smile widened, and I knew he was reevaluating his opinion.

"My French and Latin are far better, Father," the duke demurred.

"No matter. I won't make you speak it at dinner." Father Michael took a moment and studied Saint Aubyn. "Look, I was probably a bit hard on you."

"It's the disgrace of the world what the British government allowed to happen in Ireland in the forties." He shook his head, and something in his face suggested he knew a lot more about it than the average aristocrat. "I understand it's an open wound."

"But not one you inflicted. So I apologize for prejudging you."

"Thank you, Father." Saint Aubyn nodded gravely. "I will tax you with only one thing."

"What?"

"You surely haven't been troubling Miss Shane with your coreligionists' views on Jews?"

Father Michael looked like he'd been slapped. "Never. I don't know how—"

"My fault, Father," I jumped in quickly. "Remember, I said you don't hold my ancestors' alleged misdeeds against me."

"'Alleged,' indeed," said the priest. "You know I skip that part in the Good Friday liturgy, bishop be damned. Er . . . sorry."

Saint Aubyn just watched us all, unsurprisingly speechless. I doubt he'd ever had preprandial conversation like this. I shook my head. "We are all at a pretty mess of cross-purposes, gentlemen."

"We surely are," Tommy said. "And you still owe me that checkers game."

"Well, not now, you don't." I looked at the clock. "Mrs. Grazich will be setting the table any second."

"I guess we shall have to call a truce for the moment, Tom," Father Michael said.

"Enjoy your dinner, because you're going to taste defeat later."

They fell into their usual amiable bickering as they headed for the dining room, and Saint Aubyn turned to me.

"Is this the typical evening at your home?"

"Pretty much. They play cards, too." I laughed. "It's often rather like having two very, very large seven-year-olds running about. And sometimes the sports writers come over."

"Like your dear Mr. Dare?"

"No. He's special, a sort of surrogate uncle, who watches over Tommy and me."

Saint Aubyn nodded. "No doubt, good to have an older and wiser protector about."

"Yes." I decided he'd best know the rest. "Preston lost his wife and child in a cholera epidemic many years ago. We are good for him, too."

"Poor man." He was silent a moment. "My late wife. Influenza."

"I am sorry."

"I still have my sons. I cannot imagine losing a child, too."

I had nothing to say to that, the unthinkable that so many families must face.

"Well," Saint Aubyn said finally, studying me with that barrister's appraising glance. "I understand why he watches over you."

"Tommy too. And, as you can tell, he's very good company."

"He does seem quite interesting."

"He is, on his own. It's only when the whole sports department comes over that things get a bit loud."

The duke smiled. "No wonder you go on tour."

"I'm used to it. I often hole up in the studio with Montezuma and a book, and I'm free and quiet, unless they need someone to referee."

Saint Aubyn shook his head, and offered his arm, formal protocol for dinner, even on a typically crazy night at the town house. I took it, not missing the twinkle in his eyes.

"My stars and garters!"

That would be Mrs. G, at her first view of me walking in with our guest. The exclamation was followed by a thud and the tinkle of bouncing silver. She'd just dropped the shepherd's pie onto the trivet at the center of the table when she saw him. Not my fault, since I'd warned her he might stay; but I guessed the sight of both a duke and a priest at her table was simply more than she could stand. Either that, or she was as fond as I am of tall, dark-haired men, and less shy about showing it.

"Thanks, Mrs. G, it looks wonderful." I nodded to her as she straightened the dish.

"Not the only thing that looks wonderful, miss." She grinned. "Enjoy the night."

Thankfully, my squire had decided to be amused, favoring her with a smile as she made for the door.

"This is not service *à la russe*," I observed as Saint Aubyn held my chair.

"Fortunately, I had no such expectations."

The boys took their seats as well, and I dished up plates of the main dish, as is usual practice for the lady of the house, and made sure the salad was passed.

Father Michael offered a brief and not especially Catholic grace, probably in deference to our Protestant guest, and we tucked in.

"You were not exaggerating about the shepherd's pie, Miss Shane."

"Mrs. G is an amazing cook." Tommy took a breath as he happily demolished his own. "Even when the father isn't here."

Saint Aubyn's eyebrow arched.

"A lot of women take pride in cooking for the priest. It's a pleasure when it's Mrs. G, not always with others." Father Michael's beleaguered expression said far more than the few diplomatic words. "You don't want to know about the alleged delicacies I've been forced to enjoy over the years."

They laughed.

"This actually rather reminds me of home, Miss Shane." Saint Aubyn had a wistful look.

"Really?" Tommy asked. "Surely, arrangements are far more elegant at the castle."

"I grew up in a town house in York, with my Scots mother serving meals very much like this. And when we have to be at the family seat, she usually holds our meals in a small room. There are even books."

I blushed a little as he looked at the stacks of library books on the sideboard, where Tommy and I usually left them so they would not get mixed in with our own volumes.

"No criticism intended. I do not trust people who don't read."

"Neither do we," Tommy said. "What are you reading now?"

"General Grant's memoirs. Seemed appropriate for a trip to America."

I nodded. "A good and improving book, and such a brave man to write it all out as he was dying."

"Indeed." Saint Aubyn looked thoughtful. "The last thing he could do for his country, perhaps."

"Perhaps." Tommy smiled. "I'm actually much more of

a Lincoln man. I will happily read absolutely anything about him."

"Lincoln probably is the finest man your country's produced so far."

"And you'll get no argument at this table," Father Michael put in. "He was truly God's gift to our nation when we needed it the most."

"But if your Prince Albert hadn't been wise enough to ameliorate the *Trent* crisis, we wouldn't be here now," I pointed out, a nod to our British guest and Queen Victoria's husband, who'd kept Great Britain out of the Civil War.

"Prince Albert was a bit of a stick," Saint Aubyn said with a faint smile, "but a gifted diplomat."

That sparked a discussion that consumed the rest of the shepherd's pie, and lasted us into coffee and Mrs. Grazich's tasty lemon cake. I do not know how it happened, but I found myself reciting the end of Mr. Whitman's lovely elegy on Lincoln, "When Lilacs Last in the Dooryard Bloom'd."

Saint Aubyn knew it, too, and we gave the last few lines together, like a duet:

> *Lilac and star and bird twined with the chant of my soul,*
> *There in the fragrant pines and the cedars dusk and dim.*

We sat there for a few measures, just looking at each other, encircled in the beauty of Whitman's words.

Tommy broke the spell with a laugh. "And that, I strongly suspect, is why Heller is so fond of lilacs."

I shook my head. "You recite well, Your Grace."

"As do you."

"No achievement there, I'm afraid. Just part of the package."

He nodded, looking a bit dazed, as I felt, too.

"Miss Ella, I believe you're going to have to do that for the history class this year," Father Michael said. "The students might not understand opera, but they surely understand Lincoln."

"We can only hope," I said, making sure to take a bite of my cake before Tommy got any ideas.

Saint Aubyn returned to his cake, too, and the rest of dinner passed in amiable and inconsequential conversation. Soon enough, we were finished and moving toward the drawing room.

"My apologies, Miss Shane, I'm quite tired, and I think I should return to my hotel."

"Of course."

Saint Aubyn paused at the drawing-room window as I walked him to the door. "It's another rainy evening."

"It's spring in New York." I couldn't help laughing at his scowl. "Surely, it rains just as much in London."

"But one expects it there. One hopes for better from New York."

"Of course, one does." No doubt our City should order its weather for his pleasure.

"What's this?" he asked, pointing to the votive I'd forgotten to move after I lit it Friday night.

"It's called a *yahrzeit* candle. I lit it for my mother on Friday."

He nodded gravely.

"Traditionally, they're only lit on the anniversary of a death, but I do it sometimes when I need to feel closer to her."

"Does it help?"

"It does." The thought made me smile faintly. "I light a votive for my father at Holy Innocents on occasion, too. It's the ceremony of stopping to remember them that gives comfort, I think."

"That makes sense."

"I'm not a theologian, and your vicar would probably label it 'popery' or 'idolatry,' but I don't know anything wrong with taking a moment to light a candle, remember and ask God to take care of our lost ones."

Saint Aubyn's eyes were a little too bright. "I am not especially interested in my vicar's opinion at the moment."

I remembered he had narrowly averted a fight over poor Frances's burial. If he was anything like Tommy, he probably felt he'd failed her. With far less cause than I had to feel the same. I turned to the whatnot and pulled another candle out of the drawer. "Here, if you want to try it yourself."

"Thank you. I just might. Is there a special prayer?"

"Not one I can teach you. My Hebrew is awful."

"Really?" He smiled at that. "You, who have Italian, French, even Latin?"

"Hebrew's different, special, and fiendishly difficult. Someday, I suppose."

We were silent for a moment, watching the rain.

Then he spoke again, turning the candle between his long fingers. "So, what do I do?"

"Light the candle and say whatever prayer is right for you. I usually just pray that my mother is safe and happy and with my father."

"Perhaps safe, happy and singing for Frances."

"Whatever feels right. You'll know."

"I suppose I will." He started walking for the door again. "Thank you again, Miss Shane."

"Glad to help."

"You really are, aren't you?"

"I've told you before, there's not enough kindness in the world. Where I can, I try to add to it."

Tommy and Father Michael appeared in the foyer as Saint Aubyn put on his coat and slipped the candle in his pocket, then picked up his umbrella. I knew what the boys were doing, however unnecessary it might be, and it made me smile.

"Good night, Your Grace," Tommy said. He had a bright and friendly expression that didn't diminish the vague and, I was quite sure, intentional menace of his large presence. He hadn't felt the need to do this a day ago, but perhaps now that it was after dark, he was concerned that the duke might be swept away by the moment. Or perhaps Preston had said something? Who knew?

Father Michael added his own good night with a grin; he'd clearly twigged onto the idea that nothing untoward was going to happen here, and was simply enjoying the show.

"Good night, Mr. Hurley, Father Riley." Saint Aubyn bowed to both, then turned back to me with an impish grin of his own.

"Good night, Your Grace." I shared the grin, glad that he found the situation as amusing as I did.

"Good night, Miss Shane. Thank you for a lovely evening."

"And you."

I heard Saint Aubyn's laugh bubbling up as I closed the door, and I couldn't control my own amusement anymore, either.

"Really, boys," I said through a giggle. "Did you honestly think there was some danger to my virtue?"

Tommy had the good grace to laugh, too. "I wasn't taking any chances. He's a nice fellow and all, but he's got that look. There's no guarantee he might not try to steal a kiss."

"And Miss Ella would flatten him!" Father Michael said. "Tom, you missed that one pretty wide."

"Probably. But there's nothing wrong with letting people know Heller's properly defended."

I patted Tommy's cheek. "Indeed there isn't."

We three stood there for a moment. Then Father Michael smiled. "Would Mrs. Grazich have left a bit more cake?"

"Probably," I said. "I'll investigate."

Tommy piped up, turning to Father Michael with a competitive gleam in his eye. "And I believe you owe me a rubber match on checkers."

Father Michael stayed behind as Tommy went to set up the board. "I am sorry I was a little—"

I shook my head. "He understood, and, more important, I do."

"He's a good man, for a duke."

"I agree."

The priest's perceptive brown eyes focused on my face. "He pinned me right back on your faith. He didn't have to stand up for you like that. Didn't even have to notice it."

"He's not your usual duke."

"I'm not familiar with the run of dukes, but I'd have to agree."

"Rematch, *now*!" Tommy called.

I sighed. Just another typical night at the town house. I hoped Saint Aubyn would get some comfort from the candle, but I suspected the good laugh at Tommy and the father's expense might help just as much.

Chapter 26

Perfidy and Prejudice
Among the Lilacs

I walked out to Chalfont's Pharmacy next morning to place an order for a new supply of throat lozenges, and, not incidentally, just to enjoy a stroll in the spring air. Even though it was a little chilly, and there were a few clouds at the edge of the sky, it was still a May morning. Since it would be a busy afternoon of fencing with the *comte*, vocal practice with Louis and fittings with Anna, the errand might be my only chance to get out and smell the flowers.

Mr. Chalfont was behind the counter again when I stepped in. He finished with his customer, then glanced over at the few other people browsing amongst the nostrums and turned to me.

"Miss Shane. Delightful to see you."

"Thanks. Yourself as well."

"Perhaps not so delightful alone?"

I narrowed my eyes.

"I saw the paper this morning. So your friend is a duke. And the dolly was his cousin, wasn't she?"

"All true."

"Well, I did a little checking around after I talked to you

two. There are several patent medicines with nicotine in them, but the only one popular among young ladies is Mrs. Redfern's Beauty Tonic. Nicotine and an emetic, among other things. Nasty stuff."

"I'll say." *Later I will ask Saint Aubyn to check the box in Frances's trunk,* I thought. I remembered it was a Mrs. Something's Something, but that was all. I looked at the druggist. "Have you ever heard of young women vomiting up what they eat?"

He thought for a measure or two. "I've heard of it a few times. Obviously, for most people, not getting enough food is a bigger problem than not keeping it in . . . but once in a great while, I've seen a mother or father who's trying to stop a daughter from doing it."

"Is there a cure?"

Mr. Chalfont sighed, much as Dr. Silver had. "Not that I know of. I think it's a problem of the heart and mind. We don't know nearly enough about that."

"Isn't that the truth."

We shook our heads in silence for a moment, and I finally moved on. "Anyway, I find I am running low on throat lozenges, so I might as well put in the order for the tour, as well as the usual beauty supplies."

He smiled. "We'll get right to it. Still prefer my daughter's cold cream to that stuff they sell at the theatrical supply house?"

"Of course. My skin is happy. I don't argue."

"Indeed. You could probably make a few dollars endorsing cosmetics the way some actresses do."

"They're actresses, Mr. Chalfont," I reminded him.

"Of course, they are. And you are not." He gave me a wry smile, having heard my thoughts on the topic more than once. "I'll send your delivery around in a few days."

"Thank you."

"And give your duke my condolences."

"He's not *my* duke."

"Don't tell him that."

I took the long way home, through Washington Square Park, enjoying the flowers in bloom, and the scene, with little boys chasing each other on the paths, a few ladies on velocipedes, and the elegantly-dressed women risking the weather to show off their spring hats. I'd only worn my second-best, because I did not like the look of those clouds.

I walked on, turning down the side path that would lead me toward home. The lilacs had just come out, and I stopped to smell a cluster, bending to bury my nose in the soft, pale purple flowers, and breathing deeply of the heavenly scent that can't be distilled or simulated. Lilacs are the only flower I really love.

"Miss Shane, is that you?" called a carefully-cultured voice behind me.

I turned to see Aline Corbyn, garbed in *eau de nil* silk and matching hat, with ostrich plumes; her youngest, and only unmarried, daughter trailed behind her in a suitable white dress with straw hat. I believed the last Corbyn was coming out this year. Her older sisters had married appropriately, but not brilliantly by mama's standards.

And suddenly even a product of a Lower East Side primary school could do this math. I stole a glance at the daughter as I rose to greet her mother, and I came away with an impression of limp sandy hair, bored grayish eyes, and a sullen pout. Yes, no doubt, Gilbert Saint Aubyn would be entirely swept away.

"Mrs. Corbyn, how nice to see you. And your lovely daughter." I smiled and bowed appropriately.

"Yes. Pamela came for a walk with me. It's so important for young ladies to get their fresh air."

"All ladies, really," I said with a light laugh. "I know I need mine."

Pamela just gave me a leaden glare.

"Why don't you go draw the roses, dear?" Mrs. Corbyn said to her daughter as she moved toward me. "I'd like to walk a bit with Miss Shane."

"Certainly." I fell into line beside her, wishing I'd worn my best hat despite the risk of rain. Pamela took her sketch kit and scuttled away to a nearby bench. I hoped she was better at that than conversation. "A lovely musicale the other day."

"Yes. My father was quite transported by your 'Ave Maria.' "

"Thank you. It was a privilege to give him some comfort. I understand it was his mother's birthday."

Mrs. Corbyn nodded. I waited. I knew something was going on here, probably a request for a performance at a special soiree or some such thing, and I hoped she'd just get it over with.

"He also told me what he said to you, and I'm terribly sorry if he gave you the wrong impression."

No? Really? I managed a light social laugh. "I'm well aware of the pleasantries, Mrs. Corbyn. I don't expect your papa to show up at my door with roses, and, in fact, I quite hope he doesn't."

"No, dear. I meant his comment about a diva can look at a duke."

Oh. Well, meet the society mama, I thought. I looked at her face, which I'd always thought seemed kinder and friendlier than some of the other matrons, who made no bones about looking down on the likes of me. But that, of course, was before there was a coronet at stake.

"Of course, he was being kind, but I wouldn't want you to get the wrong idea, dear. Just for your own good."

My own good, or that of your surly daughter . . . and your social standing? I nodded carefully, keeping my eyes on her face. I was going to make her say it. Make her look me in the eye and tell me I was not worthy.

"You know a man like the duke can't marry outside his own circle. If he's spending time with you, dear, it's not because he wants to court you."

Tommy and his boxer friends would have had many suitable words for her at that moment, none of which would have been appropriate for me to use. I contented myself with the thought that even if Mrs. Corbyn did think she was clearing the field, her sweet Pamela would not catch Gilbert Saint Aubyn's eye unless she accidentally stuck one of her colored pencils in it.

"Thank you for your kind concern," I said with a polite smile—and the cool voice that only years of training can produce. "I've merely been helping the duke find out about an unfortunate relative's life in America. I have no interest in courtship or anything else, as you no doubt know."

"No?"

"No, Mrs. Corbyn. I am married to my art."

She didn't even try to conceal her relief; I had the distinct impression she wanted to do a cartwheel right there on the cobblestones, but she hung on to some filament of demeanor.

"I do hope you're not offended. I know you did not grow up in the highest circles, and I did not want you to be led down the primrose path."

"Thank you for the warning." And for slipping in yet another reminder that I was not *quality.* I looked at the watch on my charm bracelet. "I'm so sorry. I have a full afternoon of rehearsals and practices."

"I wouldn't want to keep you. Are you singing at the settlement house benefit?"

"Yes. The Balcony Scene, with Marie de l'Artois."

"She's returned from her indisposition? Splendid." Aline Corbyn's face lit up with genuine interest. "I will look forward to it."

We bowed, and I walked on toward the town house as the sun faded from the sky, and the temperature seemed to drop ten degrees. I'd held my own in the heat of battle, but, good Lord, it was crushing.

Not that I had any real desire for Saint Aubyn to court me, or any idea what might come of it if he did. What hurt was the attitude that I was unworthy. No matter what I do, no matter how well I do it, no matter how much the world changes, I'm still just an orphan girl from the Lower East Side, and there will always be someone to remind me of that fact. As I turned for my street, with the first drops of rain starting to fall from the heavy gray clouds, I could cheerfully have burst into tears myself.

I wasn't really wet at all when I walked in, but I was pretty miserable. I took off my pretty hat, now a little damp, and just sat down on the chair in the foyer for a moment.

"Heller? Is that you?"

Tommy bounded down the stairs, smiling, newspaper in hand. "Hetty did well by your man, the duke."

"Not *my* man," I said slowly, Mrs. Corbyn's sleek well-fed face still too fresh in my memory.

"What?"

"Nothing. Just another little reminder of who I am and where I'm from served up by someone I thought was better than that."

Tommy stood over me for a second, then took my hands and pulled me to my feet, dragging me over to the hall mirror. "Come here. Look at us."

"All right."

Weepish as I was, we did make a handsome, prosperous pair—a far cry from the tenements of our birth.

"What do you see?"

"The Champ and the Diva." I smiled in spite of myself. "A couple of Lower East Side kids made good."

"Damn good."

"Yes. Damn good."

"And what do we Irish say to anyone who tries to make us feel inferior?"

"The hell with you."

"Exactly." He pulled me into a hug and I put my head on his shoulder. "I don't know who it was, or what they said, but the absolute hell with them, sweetheart."

Chapter 27

In Which We Make Our Duke Useful

The cold rain continued falling that afternoon, but thanks to Toms, I quickly recovered my balance after that nasty run-in with Mrs. Corbyn. I put my wet hat in a window to dry and hung up my damp clothes. I changed into my breeches for my fencing lesson with the *comte* (Mr. Woods!), and the whirl of the busy day quickly spun away the low spirits.

Most of them, anyhow. With a sad little look on her face, between my fencing lesson and vocalization, Rosa brought me the latest edition of the *Illustrated News*. "I hope it ain't true, miss."

"'Ain't' *ain't* a word, Rosa, and very little in the yellow papers is true, anyway."

She just nodded at "The Lorgnette":

> "The Lorgnette" breathes a sigh of relief with word that there is no danger of losing Miss Ella Shane to the Empire. We hear that her gentleman friend is merely an old acquaintance from London, a genuine duke who is actually in town to pay court at the Corbyn manse. A happy announcement may be coming soon. We hear

Miss Shane is likely to sing at the blissful occasion, since she is known for her transcendent "Ave Maria."

My compliments, Mrs. Corbyn, for that extra little twist of the knife, I thought. I just shook my head at Rosa, then tossed the paper down on the side table by the chaise, on top of Hetty's article, reminding myself of Toms's excellent phrase: "the absolute hell with them."

Henry Gosling appeared after my fencing lesson with a list of baritones for the tour. He quickly assessed the whirlwind of the house and decided not to stay for coffee, though he did accept a small plate of Mrs. G's raisin bars. He also assured me he'd thoroughly checked their professional references, and his new investigator, the future son-in-law, was taking an equally careful look at their personal habits. We'd probably start auditions within the week.

Preparations for the big settlement house benefit were in full swing when Gilbert Saint Aubyn appeared at the town house a bit later. Louis was pushing me into top form with a good vocalization session, with Montezuma, of course, following along, when Rosa dashed upstairs. I'd been hoping it would be her younger sister, Sophia, whom I'd asked her to send for—so she could watch the Morsel for Anna and Louis while we worked. But . . . no.

I ran down the stairs, laughing when I realized I was still in my breeches from fencing practice the hour before, with my shirt and hair more than a little disheveled. Poor Saint Aubyn will never get a chance to get used to me in clothes, as he puts it.

He didn't seem to mind when he saw me, smiling as I walked him into the parlor.

"I came over to thank you for introducing me to your reporter friend. Her article this morning was kind and sensitive, and certainly seemed to shut the door on the matter."

"She's rather wonderful. I wish they'd give her something more to do than features on parties and hats." I sighed, glad to think about a different newspaper item.

"But, surely, she doesn't dream of covering politics and murders."

I smiled at that. "Of course, she does. She's a reporter."

"And a woman."

"The two are not mutually exclusive."

"I suppose not." He shook his head. "Is this yet another area where we will need to adjust our attitudes for the new century?"

"Probably."

"New women, new world, what next?"

I had nothing to say to that, so I just laughed. As I did, I felt a tug on the untucked back of my shirt. Little Morrie had gotten away from Anna, not surprisingly, since she was busy with some very fine needlework. I scooped up the little cherub.

"Miss Ewwa," he said, cuddling into me and turning his face up to mine.

After rubbing noses, I tried to figure out what to do next. I'd have happily enjoyed a few moments with the Morsel, but there was far too much to do on this day. As I cast about for a solution to this particular babysitting conundrum, my eyes landed on the duke. Well, time for His Grace to make himself useful, as well as ornamental.

"What's this?" he asked, not unkindly, looking at the little fellow.

"A child."

"I am aware of that. What are you—"

"Here." I handed him the Morsel before he could protest.

To his credit, he didn't drop him. "What am I supposed to do with . . . him?"

The Morsel batted his big blue eyes at Gilbert Saint Aubyn. "He-wo, Mr. Man."

Like all other humans when confronted with the Morsel in full effect, the Wicked Duke melted. "Ah . . ."

"Watch him. Anna's taking in Marie's costume, I need to do my vocalization with Louis, and Tommy's meeting with the theater owners about the tour, so you'll have to do."

The Morsel snuggled into Saint Aubyn's arms and smiled up into his face, which actually spoke very well of the duke. Young Master Abramovitz is an excellent judge of character.

"How long—"

"Until Rosa's sister Sophia gets here. May be a while."

His eyes widened in absolute terror. "I don't know anything about children."

"You managed to produce an 'heir and spare.' I have no doubt—"

"I didn't *care* for them!"

I should have been moved to pity, or something, by the note of panic in his voice, but I found myself devilishly amused. "Well, you men like to tell us that taking care of children is the most important and sacred job there is." I allowed myself a wicked smile. "I'm sure you're up to it."

"But—"

"The Morsel's a good sort. Just don't let him near your watch or anything else mechanical you may have. He'll take it apart."

"The Morsel?"

"As in little morsel of humanity. Full name, Morris Abramovitz."

"Cookie?" asked the young gentleman in question.

"Absolutely." I grabbed the plate of cookies off the table and handed it to His Grace. Mrs. G had prepared a nice nursery tea for the little fellow. "There's milk in the carafe. He can drink from a cup just fine."

The Morsel took his cookie and smiled radiantly at the duke. "Thanks, Mr. Man."

"You're very welcome." The icy blue eyes narrowed at me over the curly blond head.

I just grinned at him. "Thanks. Enjoy."

Little sister Sophia never did get there. She's a bit flighty. It was nearly dark by the time I got back downstairs, halfway expecting to find a battleground.

Instead, Gilbert Saint Aubyn was asleep on the chaise, with the Morsel happily curled up on his shoulder. Both had gone to dreamland, and were utterly adorable. The sight brought up all sorts of unfamiliar and uncomfortable feelings. I took a deep breath, trying to tamp them back down into the lockbox where I keep the things I can't afford.

Gingerly I put a hand on Saint Aubyn's free arm and leaned down to try and wake him. His eyes opened halfway and he smiled sleepily up at me. "Shane."

Oh, my. This must be what it's like waking up with a man. I pushed the thought away and cleared my throat as I pulled back, putting some safe distance between us. "Looks like you and the Morsel managed to make a truce."

"Um, right, *Miss* Shane." He blinked a couple of times as he fully awoke. "He isn't a bad sort, as you said."

I smiled. "Neither are you. Thank you for watching him. Anna will be down to collect him in a moment."

"I actually rather enjoyed it. I haven't spent much time around wee ones. They're quite nice in small doses."

"The Morsel isn't representative. Most of them are nasty, snotty little beasts." Unless Marie's bunch is counted as well.

He laughed lightly, not enough to wake the Morsel. "Voice of experience?"

"My aunt took me in when I was eight. I helped care for the babies, a new one every year."

"Ah. That's why you've never married."

242 Kathleen Marple Kalb

I shrugged. "Marriage is a rotten deal for a woman."

"Depends on who's setting the terms, Miss Shane."

Our eyes held for several measures. In another world, another life, this might have been important, the moment where acquaintances move to something else. But for the Duke of Whatever and an Irish-Jewish "theater person," it was nothing at all.

"I'm sorry, miss." Anna burst in. "*He's* been watching Morrie?"

"And quite competently, too." I cut my eyes to Saint Aubyn with a conspirator's smile.

"Well, thank you, sir," Anna said, settling on an ambiguous honorific, since she didn't know for dukes, and—as we've already established—considered him one odd fish.

"It's been my pleasure." He had an almost wistful expression as he carefully handed over the still-sleeping boy, then looked again at me over his head. "Truly."

"He's a sunshiny little fellow, for sure," Anna said with a smile as her boy snuggled into her shoulder, recognizing his mama even in sleep, then relaxing in her arms.

Louis came down the stairs. "Looks like he's gotten his nap, at least."

"Indeed," Saint Aubyn said as he stood and straightened his tie.

"Thank you again. See you tomorrow, Miss Ella." Anna very deliberately looked from the duke to me and gave me a bright smile. *Odd fish, but good catch?* I wondered. I shook my head and handed the Morsel's bag to Louis.

"Thank you. And thanks for an excellent vocalization session, Louis."

"You were very good." He grinned. "Montezuma was not in his best form."

We all laughed softly, so as not to wake the Morsel, and I watched them go, fighting down a wave of unfamiliar emptiness.

"These days, I believe, it is possible to stop at one." Saint Aubyn was standing behind me, his voice gentler than I was used to.

A respectable maiden lady should have slugged him for even hinting at such matters. Especially a respectable maiden lady who was quietly supporting Dr. Silver's efforts. But I'd opened the door with my earlier comment about my youth, and he clearly didn't mean it as any sort of insult.

He turned to pick up his jacket, then saw the newspapers. "Your friend really did write an admirable account."

"She also wrote the intriguing item two columns over." It had caught my eye because it hadn't been in the bulldog edition and probably came in later.

"Ah, yes. 'Theater District Pawnbroker Arrested With Stolen Goods.'"

"Should I suspect that someone tipped her off?" I watched his face.

"One wouldn't give a friendly lady reporter flowers, would one?"

"One would give her information."

"One would." He shrugged. "Frances sold two of the drops there. If we assume she sold another to pay her passage, there are two unaccounted for."

"It raises a question."

"One that I'm trying to answer now." He looked down at the other paper in his hand. "I didn't know you read the yellow sheets."

"I don't. Rosa does."

Saint Aubyn's face tightened as he read the item. "You were absolutely right about Mrs. Corbyn."

"There's a dollar princess for the taking, if you want her."

"I'd rather let the castle crumble over my head, thank you. I can always earn my living as a barrister, if it came to that, and the rest of the clan can shift for themselves."

The comment was so shocking that I laughed.

"I'm quite serious, Miss Shane. I don't need some grasping mama feeding gossip to the papers in hopes of a coronet."

"Of course, you don't," I said. "I wasn't laughing at you."

"I know." He scanned the paper again, then looked at me very closely. "Does she know that you don't enjoy singing 'Ave Maria'? Or why?"

"I don't know."

"Well, in the absence of proof to the contrary, we will add it to her account."

"Oh."

He looked down at me, suddenly reminding me of Toms or Preston when they're offering to "have a word" on my behalf.

"It's one thing to try to play the press. It's another entirely to be deliberately cruel. Especially to someone who does her best to be kind."

At that, I felt almost weepy, and if he'd been Tommy, I probably would have put my head on his shoulder. As it was, Saint Aubyn made a vague move in my direction, and I didn't back away.

Fortunately, Tommy himself blew in just then.

"Heller, how do you feel about the opera house in San Francisco?"

I stepped back, took a breath and forced myself into some kind of demeanor. "Somewhat overrated, but they paid well last time."

The duke stepped back, too, looking almost guilty.

"Perhaps you would like to stay for dinner," I offered, "since we never did get a chance to discuss—"

"I have an evening engagement." His voice was cool and polite, despite his strange unguarded expression. "I'm sorry."

The duke bowed to me and shook Tommy's hand. He was clearly still quite displeased about "The Lorgnette" item, and who could blame him? As I saw him to the door, I realized I was shivering and picked up the afghan from the chaise where he and the Morsel had been napping; I wrapped it around myself. It was still warm and smelled faintly of milk, cookies and also something very definitely adult male.

"Cold?"

"A little."

"Stay warm, Miss Shane," Saint Aubyn said as we walked into the foyer. Something flickered in the icy blue eyes, and I knew he was thinking some of the same things I was, none of which were appropriate.

"You too."

He pulled the afghan a little tighter around my shoulders, then rested his hands over mine where I was holding the fabric, and just left them there for a moment. This time, it wasn't electricity, but the simple warmth of his skin soaking into mine, the two of us comfortable and safe and together. It was nothing, and it was everything.

Finally he took a breath and backed away.

"Good night, then." He bowed gracefully again and walked out.

I watched him go, trying to figure out what on earth had just happened to me.

"Heller, do you want him?"

Trust Tommy to get to the heart of the matter. But "want" was such a small and basic word for whatever this was. It didn't feel like some dirty little bit of business that should rightly be ignored by a respectable artist. It felt more like whole pieces of the earth shifting beneath my feet, rearranging themselves in some entirely new pattern, all somehow related to what was probably desire for Saint Aubyn, along with warmth and admiration for his gentleness with the Morsel. A shocking combination of feelings, accompanied by an incredibly shocking thought: *I'm nobody's whore, but I wouldn't mind being the mother of that man's child*. Even though I knew there was almost certainly no honorable way for that to happen.

Worse, I found myself thinking about how it might actually happen, honorably or not. I may be active in helping married women *not* have children, but like any nicely-brought-up unmarried woman, I have only the vaguest idea of how exactly the *having* takes place. "Your man will tell you what you need to know on your wedding night" was all the information Aunt Ellen had offered me years before. I had never cared to pursue the matter further. I wondered what exactly Saint Aubyn might tell me if he were my man. *If he were* my *man*.

Deep and dangerous ideas, these.

I turned, quite honestly stunned by my thoughts, and tried to snap back into my normal self. "I don't need that kind of trouble."

"But what *fun* trouble it would be." Tommy grinned. "Mother said a tall, dark man would bring you trouble."

"Trouble, indeed."

"Admit it. You're at least a little smitten."

"Neither here nor there." And it was leading nowhere good.

"You'd make a lovely duchess, after all."

"I doubt that's on offer, and I'm a much better diva, anyway. Besides, I like our life."

"So do I. But we may want to expand the cast a bit." He looked hard at me for a second. "He may not be the one you choose, but sooner or later, you're going to come down off the barricades, Heller."

"Not tonight, though." I stiffened my spine and smiled at him. "I believe Mrs. Grazich made her famous roasted chicken for dinner."

"Excellent."

"And you can tell me what we're doing in San Francisco . . ."

Chapter 28

All a Lady Has Is
Her Reputation

Next morning, the rain, the cold and the weird and un-comfortable ideas they'd brought with them were gone. With the return of the sun came the return of my senses. No doubt, I enjoyed the duke's company, and, no doubt, I was indeed giving some contemplation to the idea that I might want to take Lentini's advice and make sure I did not miss out on motherhood. But these were two entirely separate things, and it was wise to keep that in mind. And it's a well-known scientific fact that all manner of electrical disturbances take place during rainstorms.

In any case, I had more pressing matters to consider. I was at my dressing table, getting ready for a velocipede ride with Hetty, when I picked up the tin of lip salve. I then remembered the box of *cartes de visite* in Frances's trunk. Upon reflection, I was quite certain it had been Mrs. Redfern's, the tonic Mr. Chalfont had mentioned. I wondered if that would help Hetty in her exposé efforts.

I found out soon enough, when she insisted on parking her velocipede at the town house and walking over to Dr. Silver's clinic, still in our sports costumes and straw hats.

"And let's stop at a druggist along the way to get a bottle of this poison."

"Mr. Chalfont won't sell it, as you know. I don't know where the next nearest is."

We ended up walking a bit out of our neighborhood, to a slightly less respectable block, and finally found one. It was nowhere near as clean and elegant as Mr. Chalfont's establishment, but we were able to purchase a bottle of Mrs. Redfern's evil potion from the shopgirl, who was a little wide-eyed at the sight of two nice ladies in velocipede costumes looking for beauty tonics.

"That's a good one," she assured me as she rang it up. "You definitely know it's working."

Hetty shook her head. "It's not working. It's making *you* sick. A girl who took too much of this died not long ago."

The shopgirl, who was younger than Lady Frances had been, stared at Hetty. "They can't sell anything that's dangerous, can they?"

"Actually, they can. That's the problem."

"Well, that's just wrong. And this one . . . they make it right here in the City." She pointed to an address on the back of the box, just a few more blocks away.

Hetty and I exchanged glances. We might have to pay a visit after our talk with Dr. Silver.

"Look," Hetty said to the girl, "just be careful of yourself and don't use things like this."

"You're beautiful enough, as it is," I added with perfect truth. Her skin was golden rather than fashionably ashen pale, and her hair curly and black, so she may not have felt like a beauty in a world that honors pale angels. But she was a striking young thing with warm dark eyes and features that held the promise of adult beauty. If she let herself grow up.

By some arcane miracle, Dr. Silver happened to be between patients when we arrived, and was willing to give us five minutes. Nurse Irma gave our sports costumes a deserved dirty look as we passed, but left it at that. I suspect we were far from the most shocking thing she'd seen, even that day. The doctor waved us into her office, then sat down, not entirely successfully concealing her pleasure at being able to sit for a moment.

"I'm actually very glad you came by." She pushed her glasses back up on her nose. "I have a few more thoughts on that poor girl."

"Really?"

She nodded. "She didn't just wake up one morning and start doing this. She may have had a history, or—"

"She did."

As I spoke, the doctor and I both looked at Hetty. She shrugged. "The story is the medications, not poor Frances. Anything about her stays between us."

"All right," Dr. Silver said. "If she had a history of this, and had stopped, something must have made her start again."

"'Something'?"

"A concern, a problem in her life, some kind of strain."

I thought of the scores in the trunk, and what Louis had said about her upper range sounding raspy in vocalization. "What about the knowledge that she was harming her voice by trying to sing music she wasn't ready for?"

"I really don't know. You're the singer—would that be a significant disappointment?"

"If I wanted to sing roles I feared I would never be able to sing, absolutely yes."

The doctor looked at me over her glasses. "Then you have your answer." She turned to Hetty, who was holding the box. "Is that what she was using?"

"We think so." Hetty handed it over.

She looked at the bottle, opened it, sniffed at the liquid inside and grimaced. "I can't tell much from this, and, of course, there's no list of ingredients. I can tell you there's little or no alcohol, so that was not a part of it."

"It's made in New York City." I tapped the address on the box.

"Is it, now?" Her eyes narrowed. "I should love to have a word with the maker."

"We may do just that," Hetty said grimly.

"Just remember, even though we believe it's wrong, they have the right to sell whatever they like. Unless it's an abortifacient, it's legal."

I nodded. "That's right. There've been raids."

Dr. Silver's face tightened a little. "Well, those unregulated nostrums *are* terribly dangerous. The problem is that the police sometimes come after people who are offering women safe ways to protect themselves."

We were on exceedingly dangerous ground here, and all three of us knew it.

"At any rate," the doctor said, handing the box back to Hetty, "you can at least make Mrs. Redfern into a public scandal. That's something."

Hetty and I thanked the doctor and, of course, Irma. We left them to their good work.

"So on to the mad scientist's laboratory?" I asked as we walked down the stairs.

"For me, not you." Hetty shook her head. "You can't come with me."

"Are you sure?" I hated the thought of her confronting Mrs. Redfern, or whoever it might really be, alone.

"Suppose our witch doctor recognizes you? It'll ruin my story."

I sighed. She was right, of course. "I guess I am a distraction."

Hetty grinned at me. "Mostly, a good one."

"Take Yardley, then, or Preston."

"It's my story, and I'll do it on my own."

"All right." Not fair to argue that question. "Then stop by my house for a moment before you go home to change."

She was puzzled, but complied. My mind was much more at ease once she had my old stiletto tucked into her bag, and I'm sure hers was, too. Naturally, Hetty was still a bit nervous; the fact that she agreed to call me when she returned to the office told me the truth, even if she'd never acknowledge it. But she also promised to send a boy around with the bulldog edition, so there was no question of confidence.

As it happened, it was an earlier and higher-ranking messenger. Preston appeared with a copy as Tommy and I were relaxing with our books in the drawing room.

"She's done a bang-up job, kids." He spread the article out on the coffee table. "This is exactly what she needs. Morrison will be happy to have his own Nellie Bly."

"I'm glad." I eagerly read her vivid description of a nasty, grubby office where the potion was concocted, and the vile, toadlike man who did the compounding. And nearly fell off the settee when I got to the part where he sold Hetty a "woman's tonic," an offense that had already put him out of business with a little help from her Sunday-school chum the postal inspector. "Amazing."

"Sure enough." Preston gave me a satisfied smile. "Looks like our girl has finally found her spot."

"About time," Toms said. "Hopefully, no more baseball games."

I laughed. "You like baseball games."

"Not when Hetty and Yardley spend the whole time fighting over women's rights."

Preston laughed. "That's about right."

"I'm just glad it all worked out. I wanted to go with her."

Both men glared at me.

"I knew I'd ruin her story."

"Never mind that, kid. You could have been black-mailed. No matter what excuse you offered, there'd always be a question about why you were at such a place asking about such things."

Tommy nodded. "That'd be a good bit more than a breath of scandal, Heller."

"I know. All a lady has is her reputation."

"Overworked turn of phrase because it's true." Preston glared sternly at me. "You can't just run off and do things like anyone else."

I nodded and took my medicine, doing my best to look like a good little girl while I put the marker in my book, and considered the idea.

Blackmail. I have no real secrets, of course. But what if someone did? What, say, if you were trying to pass yourself off as someone you weren't . . . would you perhaps try to buy silence with a jewel or two? Two of the jewels *were* missing.

Tommy and Preston had moved into an amiable argument over some boxing rule, which I only vaguely understood, leaving me free to contemplate for a moment. Would Frances have been willing to surrender some of her stake—and her inheritance—to prevent anyone from finding out who she was?

The truth would not have bothered us. She did a fine-enough job, overacting notwithstanding, and it would have taken more than a coronet in her family tree to convince us to get rid of a Juliet in the midst of a tour. Far too much trouble to find a replacement, though I'd surely have made it very clear what I thought of her lying.

Fear of her family? Perhaps. Saint Aubyn was clearly opposed to her career at the time she left, and there were certainly lurid tales of British aristocrats forcing errant females back to the family fold. Yes, I had a hard time envisioning him as the man to do it, but, of course, he wasn't the head of my family. He might have behaved differently with her, and she might have had an entirely different view of him than I did.

If she were afraid of being found out and dragged back to the drawing room she'd run so far to escape, she might well have tried to pay someone off. But who?

Henry? Doubtful. He'd have to be a very creative and subtle liar to play that game, and from his reaction to the donnybrook over Arden, I didn't think he was.

Arden. Certainly a better possibility.

A paper glider, Tommy's most recent bookmark, landed in my lap.

"Come back here, Heller!" Tommy called with a laugh. "What on earth were you thinking of?"

"Not much." I shrugged. "Just puzzling out a few things."

Both gave me the hard look that I knew meant they neither believed me nor planned to leave me to my thoughts.

"Nothing serious. Truly. Just wishing there were some way I could help Hetty more."

Preston smiled. "She didn't need it."

"True."

"You're just upset about missing out on an adventure," Tommy said with a laugh. "Maybe you wanted to meet that postal inspector."

"Charles Burley?" My turn for a giggle. "She met him at Sunday school. He's nearly seven feet tall and hasn't laughed since he was in short trousers."

"Sounds like the perfect man for you, kid."

"Not on your tintype." I glared at Preston, then decided it was time for a subject change. "So, gentlemen, now that we've done with investigative reporting, perhaps you'd care to investigate some of Mrs. G's strawberry-rhubarb crumble?"

Preston smiled. "That is definitely worthy of further study."

Tommy put the sheets down on top of his book. "I can read later."

"Me too."

Not only was the aforementioned crumble available, so, too, was its maker. Mrs. G told us she was setting up a batch of bread for tomorrow's baking day, and she'd miscalculated the time. I'm quite sure that was the honest truth.

She was not, however, any less pleased to see Preston wandering into the kitchen than he was to see her. Tommy and I exchanged glances as Preston swept over and bowed extravagantly, and the cook's face turned rosy pink beneath her crown of still-golden braids.

"Mr. Dare, really!"

"Mrs. Grazich, it's always delightful to see you."

"I suppose these poor hungry children need some more crumble," she said, looking at Tommy and me before returning to her main interest. "Have you had a proper dinner, Mr. Dare?"

"Proper enough," he assured her. "But no dessert."

"Well, we must remedy that at once." She motioned him to the kitchen table and started fussing over a bowl of crumble.

"Any chance you'd sit with us, Mrs. G?" I asked. "Otherwise, we'll be an awkward three at the table."

She considered for a moment, weighing the protocol violation versus the opportunity to sit with Preston. Thankfully, Preston won. "All right, since we are at the kitchen table, after all, and it's quite late. I haven't had a chance to have dessert, either."

There was a fresh pot of coffee on the stove, and I took over to pour as Mrs. G dished up bowls of crumble and topped them generously with whipped cream. I was amused to see that Preston got more, and more artistically composed, topping than anyone else, though no one need worry about going to bed hungry.

Once we were all settled in, I asked Preston for the latest developments on the wretched Cleveland Spiders, knowing that Mrs. G has a cousin who lives in that city. That was all that was required. Preston happily regaled us with tales of the Spiders, their home city and (carefully edited for maidenly ears) the sports-writing circuit, playing to a highly appreciative audience of one. Mrs. G watched him with sparkling eyes, occasionally asking an encouraging question or offering an apposite comment.

Tommy and I were quite superfluous, except perhaps as chaperones. Although from the worshipful gaze Preston was giving Mrs. G, the only thing she would have to worry about was how she might climb down from the pedestal and get home. She was glowing right back at him, clearly enjoying his stories on their merits, as well as the pleasure of having an appealing man perform just for her.

The crumble and coffee were long gone, and Tommy and I were both starting to get dozy, when Mrs. G noticed the kitchen clock.

"Heavens!" she exclaimed. "Is that really the time?"

"I'm afraid it is," I said. "I'm sorry we've kept you so late."

"I'll happily walk you home, Mrs. Grazich," Preston offered.

"Well, Mr. Dare, that's quite kind, but—"

She was going to say no, and I quickly looked over at Tommy. He had already divined his role. "I'll come along, too. I need to, ah, ask Preston about that . . . thing."

"That's all right, then. Thank you, Mr. Tommy."

Tommy and I kept our smiles very much to ourselves as Mrs. G picked up her wrap and Preston offered his arm.

"Good night, everyone," I said. "I am going to bed. I have a rehearsal tomorrow, and the benefit Saturday night, and I'd do well to sleep."

"Good night, kid." Preston took his focus away from

Mrs. G, for just a moment, and smiled at me, looking less weary and more happy than I've ever seen him. "Don't slam any doors on your way."

Mrs. G looked puzzled, but Tommy knew what he was about and gave me a wise nod.

I nodded. "I've slammed far too many in my day."

"Just leave the right one open. That's all." Preston offered his parting shot and turned back to squiring Mrs. G.

I headed upstairs and brushed out my hair in my quiet room, with much to think about. The right door . . . and the right man on the other side.

Chapter 29

What It Was, and
How It Was Done

Friday morning, I brought the final edition of the *Beacon*, with Hetty's story on the front, below the fold, to the theater, in case I got a chance to finish reading it in the dressing room while waiting for my rehearsal with Marie. Since this was a large and important benefit for the settlement house, we actually rehearsed a day in advance, instead of just showing up and singing like everyone had at the school event.

While it's easier for the stagehands if they do, rehearsals don't absolutely have to go in show order. Since Marie was on a very tight schedule because of her children, the stage manager agreed to let us go a little earlier. Arden Standish grumbled, but gave us his space in the rehearsal, informing the stage manager at a volume clearly intended for us that he would go for a nice walk around the neighborhood. I suspected some smoking might be involved as well, even if it is terrible for the voice.

Our set pieces were the biggest in the show, but worth it: Giulietta's balcony and a wall for me to scale to her window. The climb was perhaps ten feet, just enough to feel a little scary if you look down at the wrong angle while you're singing. When I got to the top, Marie threw open her door and walked out onto the balcony.

The practice went easily enough, and once safely on the ground again, we lingered in the wings to talk for a few moments.

"How is Louis doing on the scores?"

"We should have copies before I leave for the Western tour, and we can start working on it."

She grinned. "Premiere in the fall."

"Yes." I returned the grin. "And Tommy is working on a theater."

"Excellent."

"And he thinks we should do a *carte de visite.*"

"Like that famous painting. I love it."

I sighed.

"Stop. We'll be absolutely lovely."

"That's what Anna said, as she promised to make us nice black velvet doublets."

"It's perfect. What are you complaining about?" She motioned to my breeches, the old dark blue ones again today. "You're out in trousers all the time. Nobody but Paul has seen my legs since I put on long skirts."

"You'll be fine. Anna won't let you look bad."

"I know." She shook her head at me. "So if I can manage it, you certainly can."

"All right."

"Anything else from the duke?"

"You saw the paper." I meant the *Beacon;* the *Illustrated News* and "The Lorgnette" were beneath her notice. Should have been beneath mine.

"Yes. You set up the interview."

"Of course. There's really nothing else. It looks like a sad accident, and he'll have to accept it."

Marie shook her head. "Very sad. But at least they don't have to live with her doing it deliberately."

I nodded. "That will help, I hope."

"It will." A twinkle came into her eyes. "And what about the very attractive His Grace?"

"What about him?"

"Ells, the way he looked at you—he's dead gone on you."

"And he's still who he is, and I'm still who I am."

Marie glared at me. "And it's 1899, *not* 1799."

I sighed. "But not 1999."

"You know what I mean."

"And you know what I mean."

She looked at her watch. "We'll have to settle this later. This discussion is not over, you know."

"I know." We exchanged a quick embrace and she swept out.

Back in the dressing room, I finished the last few paragraphs of the article. Hetty's piece was a classic exposé, and it was having the desired effect: Not only was the mad scientist in a world of legal trouble, but some of our local members of Congress were now talking about regulating patent medicines. Even better, druggists were promising to make sure they knew what they were selling. She was causing the right kind of trouble, and things were going to change for the better. And best of all, it was a perfect Nellie-Bly-style investigation, exactly as Preston had suggested, carving out a good place for Hetty. Morrison would have to let her do more now.

Or at least let her escape from hats.

With a little help from Anna, I got back into my mauve shot-silk day dress much more quickly than I'd have done on my own. I was pinning my new hat, a mauve version of the one Marie had worn a week or so ago, into place as I heard a knock at the door.

Anna looked up nervously. "Surely, none of those awful men today." We'd both been looking forward to being done with the rehearsal and getting out of the theater. She was going home to Louis and her boy; I to a relaxing afternoon and early night at home with Tommy, and perhaps some unfair speculation about Preston and Mrs. G.

"None of them should know to look for me here." I shrugged. "Come in."

No Lothario here. "Is your wretched city trying to kill me?" Saint Aubyn asked by way of greeting.

"And a good day to you, too."

"I'm sorry, Miss Shane. Someone very nearly pushed me in front of a beer wagon just now."

"Really?" I remembered my close escape the day of our tea at the Waldorf. And wondered a bit. "Are you sure you were pushed? Or was it just being in the crush of people here in the Theater District?"

"It certainly felt like someone was trying to push me off the curb," he reflected. "But I suppose it could have been the crush of the crowd. I could be seeing threats where none exist because of all that's happened."

"Perhaps." I wasn't convinced, but I saw no need to add to his burdens.

Saint Aubyn looked around my dressing room. "This is much nicer than your quarters the other evening."

"Well, this is a real theater. As a leading singer, I will always have my own room and plenty of space for Anna to do her work."

"What would Frances have had?"

"As the second lady, she would never share a room like the chorus, but she wouldn't have a dresser, either. Her space at Poli's Wonderland was smaller, and on a lower level, a few doors down from the tenor." The tenor. Arden Standish, complete with imagined passion for Frances and nasty habits. And out for an angry walk nearby when Saint Aubyn almost met his Maker with the help of a beer wagon, just a day after the world found out that the duke was Lady Frances's cousin.

I looked down at my dressing table, with makeup jars, brushes and my little tins of horehound and peppermint lozenges ranged across it, along with a few other things, like the handkerchief I gave Marie, the only prop I needed. All of the items were left out the way they always were for the time that I took over the leading lady's room in a theater. Suddenly, like the turn of a kaleidoscope, the plot came together. I knew what happened, and I knew who. What I didn't know was whether I could prove it.

"What?" Saint Aubyn saw something in my face.

He deserved the truth. "I don't think your cousin's death was an accident."

"You mean . . ." His eyes widened and he waited.

"You know she was using a patent medicine. She would likely have left it, and her prop vial, out on her table. Someone just walked in and poured an additional dose of it into the vial."

"Not just someone."

I shook my head. "I can't prove it yet."

"Tell me."

"I need to figure out how to prove it. Right now, I would just be slandering someone's name with no evidence."

He glared at me. "That's not acceptable, Miss Shane."

"It will have to be." I glared right back. "A barrister should know that. No police officer will make an arrest in a months-old death based on a mere theory with no evidence. I don't have the bottle, and I don't have an admission of guilt."

And I'm the only one who can figure out how to get that. *My company, my Juliet. My responsibility to get justice for her,* I thought.

Saint Aubyn's eyes were sharp and cold on my face. "What are you going to do?"

"The less you know, the better, I'm afraid." I took a breath. I wasn't sure myself. "But, hopefully, there will be good news soon."

"I rather wish I were the sort of old-fashioned ruffian who would force you to tell me." He put a hand on my arm, and I could see him trying to look menacing, and failing both comically and miserably.

"No, you don't." I smiled at him. "You're incapable of threatening a woman. Even a mere theater person such as me."

He shook his head and lightly ran his hand down my arm, sparking more of that weird energy, fingers lingering a moment at the charm bracelet, as he returned the smile. "There is nothing *mere* about you, Miss Shane, and I have nothing but the highest respect for you."

"Oh." Somewhere, as a background theme, mixed in with all those confusing electrical disturbances, I heard Mrs. Corbyn's smoothly evil little voice: *"If he's spending time with you, dear, it's not because he wants to court you."*

"I've surely given you no reason to question that." His eyes held mine, sharp and concerned.

"No, no," I said quickly, reassuringly. "Nothing you've said or done."

"Yet more for the horrid Mrs. Corbyn's account, I suppose."

"What?"

"I can guess." Saint Aubyn scowled. "It probably went something like this." He cocked his head and pitched his voice a bit higher, with almost exactly the same falsely kind tone as Mrs. Corbyn's. "My dear, he can't possibly have honorable intentions toward someone like you."

It's fair to say I am almost never speechless. But I was then.

"What utterly mystifies me is why you would even allow her to speak to you, or God forbid, believe one word she said." He shook his head and spat the next words: "Nasty, grasping fishwife."

My eyes widened.

"I'd say something else, if I weren't in the presence of a lady," Saint Aubyn pronounced very deliberately. "Right, Miss Shane. *A lady,* which is how I think of you."

I nodded.

"And further, there's one thing you need to remember. I am a duke." He smiled, the scary, humorless one that he'd used to back off Grover Duquesne. "I decide what is appropriate for me, not some society matron trying to foist off her vapid daughter."

I just stared. *I'm glad he's on my side,* I thought, not for the first time. But, of course, I had forgotten that Northerners are not Londoners; border lords have always played by their own rules, and Heaven help anyone who tried to tell them what to do. If Henry VIII could not make them bend the knee, Mrs. Corbyn had not a prayer.

"I know the difference between a 'soprano' and a 'soubrette' these days, Miss Shane."

I smiled at the reference to our first meeting. "I probably brought my point home a little too forcefully."

"I probably deserved it. Don't think that because I misjudged you that first day that I would ever make such a mistake now."

"I misjudged you, too." *Do* not *slam the door.*

For a very long second, we looked at each other, and then he finally spoke. "Enough. We can take up my intentions on another day when we are not trying to stop a murderer. Suffice to say, my intentions are indeed entirely honorable."

"Good to know," I managed. He hadn't moved his hand from my wrist. The nerves under my skin danced from his touch, warm where his thumb still rested lightly at the pulse. The sun was shining outside, so I couldn't even blame it on some weird electricity in the atmosphere. I could feel a blush creeping across my cheeks as I returned his gaze, and I took a breath. "I think I might look forward to that day."

"I know I shall."

We just stared at each other again. *I could truly drown in those eyes . . . if he were my man.* So much for married to my art.

He carefully let go of my wrist and gave me a wry smile. "Next time, kindly take my word over that of some greedy, socially mobile *nathrach* of a mother."

I'd heard that word before. "What's that?"

Saint Aubyn shrugged. "Scots Gaelic. Means 'snake.' Not an especially unusual insult in the North Country." .

Unusual enough that I remembered the place I'd heard it before. Backstage in New Haven that last night. The Scottish boy. Or was it a boy? *"Take yer hands off me, ye nathrach."* And Frances had the handprint bruise on her arm. More pieces, very ugly ones, were falling together. "Your cousin, when you knew her, did she sound like you?"

"What do you mean?"

"By the time she worked with us, she spoke almost like an American. Close enough that we believed she was Canadian."

"I suppose she spoke more like a Northerner."

"Which might sound almost Scottish to an American ear?"

"Why?"

"I think she argued with someone that night. And it led them to put an extra dose in her vial."

"The handprint bruise on her arm?"

"Yes. Now I simply need to figure out how to prove it."

"Be careful, Miss Shane."

"As much as I can."

"Surely, a good Irish girl must know a kindly officer of the law."

I smiled a little at that. "At least I know how to find one."

"Good." The cool blue eyes suddenly warmed more than a little. "I should truly hate to see you come to harm."

"All right, now," I said finally, breaking the spell because I must. "Move along. Perhaps you can get a fencing lesson with *Le Comte du Bois*."

He managed a small laugh. "Or Mr. Woods from the Bronx."

"As Toms says, everybody's got a confidence game."

"Not quite everybody, Miss Shane." He bowed to me. "But I take your meaning. I will leave you to your plan. Please be careful. You are dealing with a murderer."

"I will be." I returned his bow. "It would do you no harm to exercise caution as well."

"A beer wagon may not be just a beer wagon?" Saint Aubyn nodded. "It may be wise for us all to stay on our guard."

His eyes held mine a fraction too long, and then he turned and walked away.

Anna shook her head as the door closed. "He's an odd fish, but you've got the hook in his mouth but good."

I looked at her. I doubted my New York–born-and-bred dresser had ever even seen a fishing pole. I hadn't, outside of books. "'Hook in his mouth'?"

"Good figure of speech." She gave me a sheepish smile. The lyricist likes language. "He wants you."

I shrugged. "It's been known to happen."

"Not like the fans and admirers, Miss Ella. I saw how he looked at you and Morrie. This one wants to be the father of your children."

All of the shocking things I'd been thinking the other day, he'd been thinking them, too?

"Something to think about," Anna said, finishing her check of the buttons on my doublet.

A few minutes later, Anna and I were walking out as Arden stepped off the stage from his rehearsal.

We exchanged superficially friendly greetings. I carefully maintained my pleasant demeanor, to avoid giving anything away; Arden spoke with a tiny, deliberate edge in his voice so we knew he was annoyed at having to change his rehearsal time. I ignored that as beneath my notice.

If the stagehands hadn't been putting up the arc lights just as he turned, and he hadn't been at exactly the right angle to the beam, he might well have walked away free. But the light struck the little drop on his watch chain, and when I saw the spark, I knew. Paste doesn't flash like that.

It was just one piece. I imagined he'd sold the other, somewhere. But this one was worth a good sight more. His life. It was the evidence that would prove what he'd done.

Now I just needed a plan.

Chapter 30

In Which We Seek Counsel with the Good Father

After that stunning end to rehearsal, I sent Anna home in a hansom, and had mine drop me at Holy Innocents instead of the town house. The realization that Arden was a blackmailer and a killer made me heartsick enough, never mind the possibility that he might get away to Philadelphia before we could figure out how to prove it. A few minutes with Father Michael might help. Or, at least, his sunny, sensible charm might jolly me out of this terrible, dark mood.

More useful than spiritual consolation, however, might be a recommendation to his "Cousin Andrew the Detective," as he was always known in the family. Cousin Andrew was probably no more open to the unproven theories of ladies than any other man, Irish or not, but a word from his sanctified cousin might help.

"Miss Ella. You are looking both lovely and troubled today," Father Michael said as I stepped out of the cab.

"Troubled, for sure. I should have known you'd see it immediately."

"Come into the parlor and we'll talk. Mrs. O'Bannon

doesn't make nearly as good a tea as Mrs. G, but I doubt that's the point just now."

It only took a few moments for us to get settled, with Mrs. O'Bannon providing mediocre tea and impressive dirty looks. While she treats Tommy like an emissary from the pope, as far as she's concerned, I'm not quite respectable—and I think she fears I will seduce Father Michael if she gives me the least chance. It's not for me to point out the inaccuracy of those concerns. On this particular day, the attitude was especially grating.

"So, Miss Ella," Father Michael said finally, taking a good look at me over his cup. "Does this have to do with your man, the duke?"

"He's not my man." I was willing to tolerate this line of conversation for a few moments before pulling it over to the real matter at hand.

"Not for lack of wanting on either side, I suspect."

I just shook my head. "Neither here nor there, Father."

"Too bad. You may have finally found a man who's almost your equal." He watched me for a moment. "Miss Ella, how is your Gaelic?"

"About as good as your French."

"Fair enough." The priest grinned. "All right, you'll have to take my word for it. Have you ever heard the phrase '*anam cara*'?"

"No."

"Your duke's Scots mother may have taught him this one. It means 'soul friend.' A person, not necessarily a husband or wife, but someone with whom you can share your true self and deepest thoughts and concerns."

I nodded slowly.

"We can live without romantic love, Miss Ella, and many of us choose to, whether for God, or art, or family." He took a sip of his tea. "But we can't live without a good friend."

"Very true."

"Of course, you know Tom is my soul friend and I am his."

He said it matter-of-factly, and I left it there. "Of course."

"Well, I think your duke might make that for you."

"A friend is good," I said slowly.

Father Michael twinkled at me. "Of course, in this case, a husband could be better. He might well prefer to be that."

"*Suffice to say, my intentions are indeed entirely honorable.*" "But what if he does? It doesn't change who or what we are."

"Doesn't it?"

"I'm a singer, Father. Even a clerk expects his wife to give up her work. What would a duke expect?"

"But is a singer *all* you are, or want to be?" Father Michael smiled a little. "And is he so narrow-minded that he would expect you to give up who you are?"

I did not have a good answer for that.

"You have much to think about." He looked down into his tea for a moment. "I know there are many barriers to love when you two are so different. But none to friendship, surely."

"A good insight, Father."

"Does that help a bit with your troubles?"

I sighed. "It would, if it were only a matter of love."

" '*Only* a matter of love'? What's more important?"

"On any other day, Father, nothing. But it's not a matter of love. It's a matter of murder."

He put down his teacup and stared at me. "*Murder?*"

"I am reasonably sure, but cannot yet prove, that someone killed the duke's cousin."

"And you know who."

"I believe I do. I don't know how to flush him out."

Father Michael's usually-rosy face went pale. "Miss Ella, have you done something foolish?"

"No." I scowled. Of course, I'd considered just confronting Arden, but that likely would not have done much good. "I'm hoping your Cousin Andrew the Detective might be of some use."

Father Michael smiled, relieved. "All right. I'll talk to him. You haven't told anyone of your suspicions."

"No. I'm not even sure there's enough evidence to bring in your cousin. But it's probably our only chance to catch the killer before he leaves for Philadelphia."

"So, how do you propose to do that?"

"He's wearing a jewel on his watch fob that I think is from a necklace Frances took from her family."

"Your duke friend can identify it."

"Exactly."

The priest nodded. "And that might just be enough to convince him to give up the rest, you think."

"In Cousin Andrew's hand? Quite possibly."

"So, what do you propose?"

"Perhaps Cousin Andrew could meet me backstage tomorrow night?"

"I'll ask him. In the meantime, why don't you go home and stay safe with Tom."

"Father, there's no danger."

"Miss Ella, you are mixed up in murder. Of course, there's danger." The good priest glared down at me like any other Irishman concerned for the safety of his women. It was likely only the Holy Orders that prevented him from yelling. Tommy would have no such scruples.

"Not much at the moment," I said irritably. "Unless, somehow, my suspect reads minds."

"Be that as it may," the priest began with a glance that was supposed to squash me, and failed miserably, "I am walking you home and handing you over to Tom, who will not let you out of his sight. And then I am going to the police station to talk to Cousin Andrew the Detective."

"That makes sense." I could give him that.

The usually amiable priest shot me one more glare, which I knew was only a shadow of what I would get from Tommy, once he tattled.

Indeed it was. There was a good bit of yelling (mostly from him), a little crying (from me) and plenty of sulking afterward (both).

I had barely hung up my coat and put away my hat when the fireworks began.

"Have you taken leave of your senses?"

Tommy warmed to his theme from there. It is the Irish way; men yell when they are concerned about their women, and we would not feel loved if they didn't. And usually we yell right back. The problem is, an angry and concerned Irishman can yell much longer than a woman can respond in kind. Eventually we just give up and start crying.

Wretched as it is, the crying has the desired effect. It stops the man cold and gives us an excuse to run from the room. This argument unfolded perfectly to pattern. Before it was even fully dark, I had locked myself in my room to cry, and Tommy had holed up in the sitting room across the hall, after yelling that he was still going to be here watching over me, even if I was acting like a baby.

Mrs. G, who has seen the occasional scene before, shepherded Rosa out before the crying started. As for Montezuma, the bird wisely decided to hide in the studio, after squawking at us both.

Well after dark, my temper cooled, and I realized I hadn't lit my Sabbath candles. Which only made me cry again, and harder.

After all of that, it's fair to say that nobody had a restful night. Except possibly Montezuma. Tommy and I didn't really make up until breakfast, when I lobbed a muffin at his head and made him laugh despite himself.

"All right," he said, catching it. "You don't have to waste any more baked goods. I'm good and mad at you, but you're still my little coz."

"I didn't put myself in any danger, Toms. I asked Father Michael to bring in his cousin."

"And now you're going to have some kind of donnybrook backstage tonight." Mama Bridgewater might not be able to set me on fire with her eyes, but Tommy was making a very strong effort at it.

"I don't know any other way to stop Arden. It's not dangerous."

"Anything involving murder is dangerous."

"Do you two compare notes so you can give me the same lines?"

Tommy sighed, refusing to dignify that with a response. "Does your friend the duke know about this?"

"Not much."

"And what do you think he would do?"

"Do British aristocrats yell?"

He smiled. "You may yet get to find out."

I looked down into my coffee.

A muffin bounced by my plate. *"Hey!"*

"'Hay' is for horses."

"Thanks for the grammar lesson."

"You could use a little reminder on deportment, too."

Chapter 31

"O Happy Dagger"

Cousin Andrew the Detective, a short, round-faced redhead, with sparkly eyes much like his reverend relative's, posed as my newest bewitched admirer, appearing at my dressing-room door before performance time with a straggly bouquet to cover his notebook. His rumpled red-brown tweed jacket covered his gun, which I devoutly hoped he would not need.

"I don't mind telling you I don't like your plan, Miss Shane. But I imagine my cousin and the Champ have already read you the riot."

"Quite loudly, as it happens."

He twinkled at me. "Well, I'm going to just sort of hover about the wings and see what I can see. And perhaps have a word with the unfortunate young lady's cousin."

"I expect him backstage any moment."

"Good. I'll leave you to your primping. Just come get me when Mr. Standish is on, so I can search his dressing room."

I didn't see the duke before I went on. I assumed that he'd been buttonholed by Cousin Andrew, and gave it no further thought. Tommy was, of course, also lurking about in the wings, periodically coming into the dressing room to check on me. I couldn't imagine how Arden might miss all of this, and I wondered if they would scare him into doing something intelligent, like hiding the evidence.

As the benefit concert wore on, I was beginning to worry that perhaps I'd been wrong. Or worse, that I was right, and nothing was going to happen. If that damned jewel wasn't in Arden's possession, we'd have no chance of proving anything. All Arden had to do was hide the thing, keep his head and walk away, and he'd be free to torment the good people of Philadelphia with his Radamès. By curtain time, I was starting to think that was exactly what he was going to do.

Arden was the last act before Marie and me, and he was at the top of his form, offering a very acceptable *"Celeste Aida,"* one of those arias I wasn't at all sure he could carry off night after night in Philadelphia. If I was wrong about that, I wondered with a sick feeling in the pit of my stomach, could I have been wrong about the rest of it?

As the tenor sang away, I slipped into the wings. It took longer than I'd expected to find Cousin Andrew, then climb the stairs to the men's dressing rooms. I was keenly aware of the passing of time as I walked him to Arden's door and pointed to the dressing table. I breathed a little prayer of thanks as I saw that the watch chain, with the fatal jewel, was clearly visible. Whatever Deity was listening, it was helpful of Him to leave Arden arrogant and stupid to the end. The detective nodded to me and slipped inside, closing the door.

As he did, I realized Arden was no longer singing.

I turned away to head downstairs to prepare for my entrance, but there he was, standing at the top of the stairs.

"You!" he snarled.

"It's over, Arden. We know."

"It's over for you, too, then." Arden lifted his sword

and lunged for me. There was only one place to go. The stagehands' catwalk, a few steps up from where we were, and far into the flies.

I took off. The catwalk, a little metal bridge with a thin rail on one side, was significantly higher than the balcony, but I didn't have time to be scared. Arden followed me, swinging his sword, the big heavy blade of his character, an Egyptian Captain of the Guard. I heard a couple of slashes and dings as he hit things on his way.

I drew my own sword. I was going to need it.

As I stepped onto the catwalk, there was suddenly a lot of light—and an almighty crash. The scenic drop that hid the bridge from the audience had fallen away. I guessed Arden had slashed the rope with one of those wild sweeps of his sword.

Applause from the audience, which likely thought it was part of the evening's entertainment; and five feet below, a scream from Marie, standing on her balcony, waiting for me. She looked up at us, stunned for a second.

"Go to your room, Madame Marie!" Arden shouted down at her. "You don't belong here."

"I'll decide where I belong, you filthy wretch!" she snapped, casting about for a weapon.

"Stay out of this. It's not your affair. I don't want to harm a mother."

Marie threw her fan, the only thing she had, at his head. "I'll show you for a mother!"

The closed fan sailed near his face and he lost his balance for a second as he dodged it, but that was all. Marie started climbing down from the balcony, clearly planning to get help—or more ammunition.

Arden turned to me with an unpleasant smile and swiped his big sword. "Never mind her. I've always wanted to take you in the final duel."

"The hell you will." I stepped into my fighting stance,

watching Marie reach the wings out of the corner of my eye. At least she was safe. "I'll be happy to defeat you yet again before the police drag you off."

"I'm going to kill you." He moved a little closer with a wild stroke. "Violette would have wanted to be a wife and mother if not for you."

"Not me." I blocked him easily and held my ground. "The music."

"I'll settle for you."

"Not fencing like that, you won't." I backed him off.

As duels go, it was rather awkward. He wasn't especially nimble to begin with, and that big sword (why *will* men always put their faith in large weapons?) just hampered his limited skill. I didn't have to do much beyond maintain balance and block his strikes as his swings grew wilder. Eventually, I hoped, I'd just tire him out and hand him over to the authorities.

"It's all your fault," he hissed. "Filling Violette's head with all that nonsense."

"She had a right to her career, just like you."

"'Women' and 'rights' don't belong in the same sentence," Arden spat, with another swipe of that silly weapon. "She was going to make me a nice little wife, and I was going to get my hands on her nice little fortune."

From his expression, I had no doubt that he'd planned to lay lustful hands on more than Frances's money. My stomach twisted. "You couldn't win her, so you blackmailed her."

"Such a harsh word. I simply tried to persuade her that a match would be best for us both."

"While leaving a handprint bruise on her arm."

"She would not see reason." He took a stab in my direction, but I held my ground. "She should just have married me."

"I doubt her family would have allowed that."

"You mean your duke? You don't really think he's courting *you*?"

I just kept my sword up for the next block, and refused to take the bait.

"Too bad I didn't kill him for you yesterday," Arden went on, advancing a little.

"How's that?" I backed him off with a thrust.

"I was walking back from the smoke shop when I saw him ambling along, all full of himself, like he's better than anyone else—"

"Better than you."

Arden let out a small, bitter laugh. "Is the fair maiden dreaming of our Wicked Duke?"

"None of your damned business." I pushed him back a little more, realizing unhappily that it brought me farther from the other end of the catwalk and escape.

"More like an old maid than a fair maiden."

I ignored that as I fended off another of his graceless strokes. "What did you do?"

"Gave him a nice shove into the street. If I'd just been a little faster, I'd have gotten to see his fancy skull smashed under the wheels."

"Bad luck for you."

"Good luck for you that I was a little too slow that day outside the Waldorf."

"*What?*"

He gave me an evil smile. "That was just for fun. You're just like him. Think you're so much better than the rest of us."

"Better than a murdering blackmailer," I pointed out with a jab.

"Defending your man again?" he asked with that evil leer. "Don't worry, he'll find some other whore."

He came at me with what was supposed to be a kill thrust. I blocked it and made a hard move forward to back him away. It was too much for him. He couldn't reverse direction and hang on to the heavy sword, so something had to go. The sword. He fumbled for it, but it dropped and landed on the stage below with another shattering crash.

"Time to give up, Arden. I'm not going to fight an unarmed man."

"No!" He grabbed my sword blade with both hands and pulled on it, almost throwing me off balance. I had to let go or fall.

But he gained no advantage, losing his balance on the forward motion as he threw my sword down to join his weapon. The sound of it landing reminded me just how high up we were, and what would likely happen to either of us if we fell.

Choking down that happy thought, I quickly regained my balance and waited for whatever came next as he wobbled. God forgive me, I'll admit I thought about just giving him a good kick. Father Michael would not have denied me absolution—but I couldn't do it.

He finally caught the catwalk rail, glaring at me, breathing hard. "I'll kill you with my bare hands if I have to."

"You'd like that, wouldn't you?" I snapped, taking a couple of careful steps back. I doubted I could get all the way across to the stairs on the other side before he reached me. No question I would win in a sword fight, but hand-to-hand combat, two stories up, with a larger man determined to kill me—

"Miss Shane!"

I looked across to the wings to see Saint Aubyn throwing something. I caught it by reflex, and only then happily saw it was a dagger. *That'll even the odds,* I realized. "All right, then."

"That won't save you." Arden took a menacing step toward me, but then accidentally looked down. His knees wobbled and his face went pale, but he clung to his bravado. "You're just a woman, after all. I took care of Violette, and I'll get you, too."

"With poison," I reminded him as I inched toward the far end of the catwalk. "A girl's weapon."

"No poison this time. I'll snap your neck!"

It would have been far more frightening if he'd been able to let go of the rail as he said it.

I took another step back, right into a stroke of luck: a couple of ropes within arm's length. Escape at hand: I could just grab one and swing to safety. As long as I kept my grip. I reached for the closest rope.

He scrabbled toward me, still hanging on to the rail with one hand as he grabbed for me with the other, getting far too close. That was the real danger here: this fool might knock me off balance and kill us both. I jabbed the dagger in his direction. "Back off!"

"Afraid?" He gave a nasty bark of a chuckle. "You were plenty scared when I almost brained you with that sandbag."

"That *was* you." I should have known the night of the girls' school benefit, the way he'd suddenly appeared right after it happened.

He cackled. "It was such fun to see our precious diva jump for her life."

"I'm glad I provided some entertainment." I kept a wry tone as I held the dagger ready, testing the rope with my other hand.

"Oh, the perfect diva. Acting like you're so far above me, when you're really just a little Jewish mongrel from the Lower East Side."

I knew he'd thrown the fighting words because he wanted to rattle me. I met his burning gaze with a cool smile. "I'm Malka O'Shaughnessy's daughter, and proud of it."

"Pride won't save you," he snapped, trying to lunge at

me and not quite managing to let go of the rail. "It didn't save Violette."

"I'll just save myself, thank you." I held him at bay with the dagger in one hand as I pulled the rope close to me. "I'm leaving now."

I stuck the dagger in my belt, then took a good strong grip as he again tried to take a step and fought for balance.

"And, by the way," I said as I took off, "her name was Frances."

Arden roared in fury as the audience applauded. At first, I thought it was for me, but as I flew down, I saw Tommy and Cousin Andrew finally reaching the catwalk.

"You murdering son of a bitch!" Toms snarled as he grabbed Arden, who might well have come out better in the twenty-foot drop.

The rope was longer than I thought, and I'd slid down with a bit more force than I intended, sending me right into the wings, where I still managed a near-perfect landing by Saint Aubyn. He put an unnecessary, but not unwelcome, hand on my waist to steady me.

I explain, if not excuse, what happened next by the fact that I was still thinking like a swashbuckling hero. I kissed him. I just pulled him to me and kissed him right on the lips—and, yes, in answer to Marie's question of a couple weeks ago, it was the first time in my life I'd kissed a man, either on the stage or off. In fairness, it was absolutely not an unwanted advance.

Nor was it any pretended stage embrace. It was more like the flash electrical fire you see when an arc light explodes. He responded with enthusiasm and skill—a good thing, since someone ought to know what they were doing here. I came to my senses as he pulled me closer, and quickly broke away.

"I'm sorry," I started, breathless from the kiss, as well as stunned and horrified at what I'd just done.

Gilbert Saint Aubyn, damn him, just laughed. "Nothing to apologize for, Shane. Although, after that assault on my honor, I'm afraid you'll have to marry me."

I stared at him for a second, and he at me. While it might have started as a joke, it was suddenly a glimpse at an entirely different life than either of us had ever imagined. For at least that second backstage, though, it didn't seem impossible.

Not only did it feel like we were the only people in the world at that moment, we may actually have been alone, between the curtains, with everyone else's attention focused on Arden's apprehension.

Finally I straightened myself and held the dagger out to him, handle first. "Good thing you throw better than you catch, Your Grace."

"I caught rather well just now, actually."

That's a way to put it. My eyes widened, and I couldn't think of a suitable reply.

"Well done, Miss Shane." He took the dagger and slipped it back in its sheath as he grinned at me. Not smiled, grinned, like a little boy who was up to something he shouldn't be. "On all counts."

" 'O happy dagger,' " I managed.

Saint Aubyn nodded at the tomb scene reference and tapped the closed dagger. "Much happier in this sheath."

"Indeed. Nobody dies in the Balcony Scene."

"No." He nodded farther backstage, where Cousin Andrew was dragging a disheveled and dazed Arden Standish away. "But they do get their just desserts."

"Good thing."

He returned my own rather dazed stare for a moment. Then: "I believe your public calls."

I shook my head. "What?"

"*Brava, Diva,*" Saint Aubyn said, echoing the chant from the audience, and sweeping me a bow of his own.

"Right." I took a breath and sorted myself out, then returned Saint Aubyn's bow.

I walked onto the stage to the largest ovation I'd ever received. It was only as I prepared to do my usual encore, and could not remember the opening bars of the piece, that I realized I was shaking and wobbly, and closer to fainting than I'd ever been in my life. From the proximity to my Maker, not the duke, I might add.

Tommy, God love him, swept in from the wings at that second. "Not tonight, folks. The lady's been through enough."

"Marie?" I whispered to him as I took my bow.

"Just fine." He nodded. "Her husband's already taking her home."

"Good." I grabbed his arm, hard. "Then get *me* home, Toms," I pleaded as he wrapped an arm around me. "Now."

"You're fine and safe, Heller. Anyone who wants you will have to come through me."

I don't know how I did it, but I stayed upright and basically calm as Tommy dragged me off the stage and into a waiting hansom. Divas don't faint or cry in public, and indeed I didn't. And Tommy won't tattle about the rest of that night.

Chapter 32

All Things Resolved After the Curtain

By the next day, I was perfectly fine, as far as I was concerned. A small glass of medicinal brandy and a large crying jag were all the healing I required. My doctor, though, pronounced me shaken, if not seriously injured, and ordered me to rest at home for a few days to recover from the shock. I suspected she was really just forcing me to take a break with the next tour coming up fast, and as we know, she had expressed similar concerns before, but you do not argue with Dr. Edith Silver.

So I spent that Sunday ensconced on the chaise in the drawing room, with a pot of Mrs. Grazich's dainty orange-blossom tea, and a pretty lavender afghan thrown over my feet, reading my reviews and entertaining the occasional visitor. I knew, thanks to a quick call from the telephone in the foyer, once again proving Tommy right for installing the newfangled device, that Marie was on her own chaise, with her own tea, chafing at her own set of orders from her doctor. At least she had the pleasure of watching the small Winslows cavort about the room. Montezuma wasn't cavorting, but he was staying quite close to me, perched on a bookshelf behind the chaise as if to watch over me, too.

Aside from the reading, the rest of my pleasure consisted of accepting floral tributes and sending them on to the charity hospital. The Captain of Industry, Teddy Bridgewater, and many others I hadn't thought had the time or inclination to express affection, including the awful Mrs. Corbyn's kindly old father, had sent a variety of flowers, mostly the infamous red roses and lilies of the valley. And the poor mothers in the lying-in ward would no doubt be delighted to see them. I'd kept all the cards, to send thank-you notes later.

Even little Betsy and Jackie Martin appeared at the door late in the morning, bearing a damp clutch of daises that had certainly been pillaged from a corner of the park, and before Rosa could shoo them back to their mother, I invited them in for a few minutes of awestruck chat. The daisies went in a glass on the bookshelf below Montezuma.

Shortly before noon, obscenely early for him, Preston brought the latest batch of newspapers, along with yet another iteration of the riot act. He was on his way to the *Beacon*, so he had a limited amount of time to yell, which was a mercy. Tommy, still good and mad at me, didn't stop him, just sat in his corner and pretended to read. Finally Preston noticed I was perilously close to tears, patted me on the head and ended with: "I was worried about you, kid."

I swallowed hard and nodded. "I'm sorry."

"Try not to scare me, huh? And let him watch out for you." He indicated Tommy, who looked up from his book with a somewhat contrite expression.

Of course, I couldn't stay at odds with him. "All right."

Preston kissed me on the top of the head. "Good girl. Is Mrs. G about?"

I couldn't help but smile at that. "About and fussing over her poor invalid," I growled, indicating the vile tea.

Preston smiled. "Perhaps I'll go distract her for a few moments before I leave for the office."

"If it stops her from making more orange-blossom tea, Godspeed."

"Glad to help."

"I'll bet you are." I couldn't help smiling when he straightened his tie and smoothed his hair as he marched out. I wasn't sure exactly how courtship was conducted among the mature-adult set, but I had the distinct impression we were all about to find out . . . and I was quite sure I could find a suitable song to offer for that particular blissful occasion. Even Tommy was smiling a little, not that he'd let me see it. I hid my grin behind the latest papers.

The headlines described me in such terms as LADY SWASHBUCKLER SAVES THE DAY and DIVA SOLVES MURDER BEFORE CURTAIN CALL, which vastly overstated my detective skills, if not my admittedly impressive swordsmanship. Hetty's version in the *Beacon* was, of course, the best, but we had to see how the others told the story. All were exceedingly complimentary and melodramatic. Even "The Lorgnette" struck a serious note: *Let us offer a prayer of thanks for the safety of our heroic trouser diva, and for the soul of the troubled young man who caused so much harm.* All in all, a good day in the papers.

Tommy, I suspected, would have liked to use some unprintable words. He had barely left my side, sitting across the room and occasionally tossing a newspaper my way, while looking like a thundercloud, except for a friendly greeting he'd given the children—and that one glance at Preston, because, after all, *he* wasn't the one who'd caused all the trouble.

Of course, it was merely the typical Irish male reaction to a loved one's danger. We have seen this before. He was no doubt itching to punch someone, but, of course, there was no one to blame but Arden, and the law had charge of him. Plus, Toms had already helped drag him in. So he sulked and read his book.

I knew how this would end, and I'll warrant you do, too. Eventually he would say something really sharp to me, I would probably cry, and we would make up with a walk to the ice cream parlor. I rather wished we could just skip to the ice cream, since it was late enough in the spring that there just might be my favorite flavor: violet. I was quite sure Dr. Silver would not mind my rising from the chaise for that.

Toms hadn't said anything about my backstage indiscretion with the duke, which, even though he was restricting himself to surly syllables, would not have passed without comment. And after reading the papers, I was reasonably certain that neither he nor anyone else had seen anything. I had no intention of 'fessing up, which left me with the odd feeling that I might have gotten away with it, though I wasn't entirely certain that I wanted that. And the enforced rest gave me far too much time to think.

Worse, what I found myself thinking about was not how utterly unladylike my behavior had been, or even of the potential consequences to my reputation. No, despite being a woman of years and discretion, I found myself remembering the feel of Saint Aubyn's lips on mine, and the unavoidable electricity between us. Preston would smirk and raise a glass, Dr. Silver would probably tell me that's exactly how normal, healthy people react when they're attracted to each other, and Marie would likely remind me that the body will not be denied, but that was slim consolation.

Fortunately, Father Michael appeared in the midafternoon, with an impish smile. "The afflicted doesn't seem to need comforting, but I'm not too sure about you, Tom."

Tommy laughed, the first time since last night. "Well, Father, I'm not fond of people trying to kill me little coz."

I laughed, and so did the priest, at Tommy's burlesqued Irish accent and the reference to me as "little."

"I'm not fond of it, either." He sat down in the chair beside Tommy's. "Cousin Andrew sends his thanks, and word that Arden confessed. He's charged with murder and, of course, attempted murder for Miss Ella. I'm sorry to say I will have a hard time offering a prayer for that young man's soul."

"I'm glad it's not my job," Tommy said, rummaging a plate of cookies off a bookshelf. "I'll call for some proper tea. That orange-blossom stuff she's drinking isn't meant for men."

"Nor me." I sighed. "Mrs. Grazich seems to think I am rehearsing for *The Lady of the Camellias*."

Then Mrs. G, who appeared with pink cheeks and an all-too-easy-to-read smile, remedied the tea situation, at least for the gentlemen. She also brought Father Michael his very own plate of cookies—of course, nicer than ours. We settled in to chew it all over.

"So it was blackmail, then?" Tommy asked.

"Essentially." I nodded. "I'm guessing he saw her with the necklace at some point, perhaps even found it among her things, and decided he deserved some of the pie."

"Nasty," Father Michael put in.

"Nasty, for certain. Because he didn't just want her money. He wanted *her*. Whether for the financial and social benefits of marrying into the aristocracy, or just the fun of forcing her to marry him, and tormenting her for life, I don't know." I put down my teacup. "I suspect both."

The boys nodded grimly. They did, too.

I could not suppress a shudder. With the new insight into relations between the sexes provided by my shocking—and undeniably wonderful—first kiss, I found it utterly sickening to think about even a small intimacy, never mind marriage and what it probably entailed, with a man I did not want.

"Then it was really a broken love affair, too?" asked Father Michael. "That does make people—especially men—do horrible things sometimes."

"That's true, but it wasn't quite the usual romantic rivalry." I added more sugar to the evil orange-blossom brew, which I'd kept because I didn't want to hurt Mrs. G's feelings, took another sip, then shook my head. "He was upset that she wasn't interested in him because she loved something else."

"Some*thing*? Not someone?"

Tommy smiled. "You, of all people, should be familiar with the idea. She felt called to do something other than be a wife and mother."

Father Michael looked a little puzzled. "She was called to the religious life?"

"No, the artist's life," I explained. "I know men would like to believe that all women consider marriage and family their highest calling, but some of us have gifts we need to follow."

"I put it badly, Father," Tommy said. "I only meant that she saw her gift as a calling and wanted to use it."

"Like Miss Ella here does?"

I shrugged. "That's about right. I figure God gave me my gifts for a reason, and I should use them. I wouldn't be shocked if she saw it much the same way."

"She did."

We all turned to the door, where Gilbert Saint Aubyn was standing, holding a bouquet of lilacs, and looking awfully tentative for a duke.

"*Alba gu bràth!*" Montezuma called.

"Good afternoon, Your Grace," I said, doing my best to ignore the blush creeping across my cheeks. "Please join us for tea."

"That's very kind, but if you're busy—"

"Sit down already," Tommy told him, laughing. "It's all family here. Well, except for Father Michael. He's probably not actually related to us, but close enough."

Saint Aubyn smiled. "That sounds almost like something you would hear in a London drawing room, where everyone may be related as well."

"We are more similar than different," Father Michael observed with a significant smile. "I have a hard time convincing my superiors of this, but out on the ground where God's work is done, differences matter very little."

"No one in this house is what one expects, are they?" Saint Aubyn asked me, his eyes lingering perhaps longer on my face than they should.

"You're the one who said we need to adjust expectations for the coming new century."

He gave me the full force of that smile, and handed me the lilacs. "I'm told your admirers always bring roses . . . and I noticed that you seem to wear this color whenever you're out of your boy's outfit."

"Oh." I took a deep breath of the scent, which was, of course, my favorite.

"Someone said you like lilacs, by the dooryard or not."

The Whitman poem. "You are the only one who knows that." *And the only one I've kissed.*

"Good." He smiled, looking almost relieved, and I knew he understood. "I'm glad you like them."

"They're lovely."

"Not all that is lovely here." He permitted himself an appreciative glance at my (what else) lilac-colored tea gown, the standard feminine confection of lace and ribbons and chiffon for resting about the house. I have heard they are also a favorite among ladies planning midday assignations, but it's obviously never been an issue.

"*Alba gu bràth!*" repeated Montezuma, who clearly hadn't been getting enough attention, as he swooped down to the shelf to nibble on the children's daisies.

"Montezuma!" I snapped. "I don't know if it's safe for you to eat those."

Montezuma, his goal accomplished, swept back to his perch. "Love the birdie!"

"Yes," said Saint Aubyn with a laugh, "love the birdie."

I swear they smiled at each other. I just shook my head.

"You look to be recovering well, Miss Shane," the duke began, apparently attempting ordinary conversation, even though his eyes were twinkling with amusement.

"I'm fine." I smiled back at him. "Doctor ordered me to rest my nerves for a day or two. I'm not even sure what that means."

"It means stay out of trouble long enough for us to catch up," Tommy interposed as Father Michael nodded his agreement.

"I second that," Saint Aubyn said, taking the chair beside my chaise. "It is not, of course, my place to advise, but you may wish to stick to singing instead of detective work in the future."

"Amazing. Something on which we all agree," I observed. "Singing is quite enough for me."

"Good." His Grace looked contemplatively at me for a moment, and I had the distinct impression he was deciding to move past the backstage incident. "It might have been quite enough for Frances also."

"How so?"

"I finally read that letter in her things. The one she never sent." He looked down at the flowers for a moment. "She explained why she ran off. It's exactly as you said. She had a gift and wanted to use it, somewhere other than the family drawing room."

" 'Don't hide your light under a bushel.' " Father Michael would have a biblical reference.

"Yes. But not what a gently-brought-up lady is supposed to do." Saint Aubyn nodded to me. "Since you couldn't afford such niceties, you just set out and built a career. And brilliantly. She might have learned a lot from you."

"If she'd let herself." I smiled a little at the memory of her overacting. "She was too busy trying to take the limelight."

He laughed, clearly enjoying the memory of his cousin. "That was our Frances. Always had to be the center of attention."

"She would have grown out of it, if she had the chance. We all do."

He took a breath. "What a waste."

I nodded. A waste in so many ways. If she had been able to look past her disdain for me and ask for help, or if I had been able to look past my dislike for her and ask that next question, she might have come out of this alive, and with a career. The thought of Frances, and any number of others who never got the chance to grow and change, kept us all quiet for a few measures.

"But at least we stopped him." Tommy finally broke the silence. "He won't hurt another woman."

"Do they still hang them here?"

"Usually the electric chair, but the same basic idea," Tommy said, nodding at the priest. "Father Michael's been known to plead for clemency on occasion."

"Only God should take a life." From Father Michael, it sounded like a declaration of principle, not a line from the catechism.

"I agree." Saint Aubyn studied him as if weighing something. And then: "May I ask you to watch the clemency case and contact me when necessary?"

"Uh, absolutely." Father Michael was as surprised as the rest of us.

"Capital punishment, whatever the means, is unworthy of a civilized society. Sooner or later, we will realize that." His gaze turned back to me. "Shattering more expectations, Miss Shane?"

I just shook my head. "I have none left."

Saint Aubyn nodded. "Hopes are better than expectations."

His eyes held mine for much longer than politeness permitted. I wondered what he might be hoping for, and had utterly no idea what I might do about that. *If he were my man . . .*

"We all live on hope," I said finally.

"We surely do." He smiled faintly. "My ship leaves tonight. I wanted to bid you farewell and say thank you."

"You are very welcome."

"You gave me and my family a great gift, Miss Shane. We can remember our Frances happily."

Father Michael nodded to him with a wise smile. "It is sometimes all we get."

Saint Aubyn returned his smile, then turned to me. "I will not forget your bravery and kindness."

"We were all just doing what was right, Your Grace."

"I don't doubt you see it that way." He reached in his waistcoat pocket and came out with a tiny flat box. "I know that respectable ladies are not in the habit of accepting gifts of jewelry, but I'm told that in America a charm for your bracelet is considered a memento of friendship, not an insult."

I took the box. "That, it is."

He watched me closely, his eyes sparkling, as I opened it and pulled out the polished silver oval, decorated with, of all things, two crossed swords. I turned the charm over: *Until we duel again. G.*

"Shiny!" Montezuma observed, like all birds, easily distracted by glittery things.

"It's perfect." I unclasped my bracelet and threaded the new charm onto the end, where it would do nicely until I could rearrange the charms. "Thank you."

"Allow me." He leaned down to clasp the bracelet back on my wrist, and whispered so quickly and carefully that the boys didn't even notice. "I may yet insist you make an honest man of me."

Had I not been an iron-willed lady swashbuckler (according to the *Herald*!), I might well have swooned at the look that accompanied that comment, and the warmth of his fingers lingering on my wrist. As it was, I could feel my eyes widening and the blush deepening as he moved back to his seat.

"It has been a considerable pleasure making your acquaintance, Miss Shane."

"It has been a great pleasure for me as well." I was amazed that I could produce a cool and polite tone.

He was silent for a moment, then finally spoke again. "Does your next tour bring you to London?"

"Several months from now. I have San Francisco, and then the New York premiere of *The Princes in the Tower* first."

He nodded. "No more dying for love?"

"Not anytime soon. I think I'd rather die for England—and Marie's daughter's college fund—for a while."

"You always seem to have a good cause." He gave me a warm smile, then glanced away, almost shyly. "Perhaps you would permit me to write you the occasional letter, if your family approves."

The duke looked to Tommy, very carefully obeying the forms.

My official protector chuckled. "Fine by me. Just no naughty poems, all right?"

Saint Aubyn, smart enough to know a jape when he heard it, shook his head with a wry smile. "Fair enough."

"I will look forward to your letters." I meant it far more than the conventional words suggested.

"And I will look forward to your replies, Miss Shane."

"Since we are going to be correspondents, Your Grace, you may address me as Miss Ella, if you like."

"I'm afraid I really can't."

I dropped my eyes.

"No, I've come to think of you as Shane, as if you were a friend, and I can't revert to such a dainty handle now."

"I see." I looked back at him, to see his eyes searching my face. "That's all right, then, Your Grace."

"But if you are going to permit me to address you as a friend and colleague, you must do me the same honor."

"Yes?" I replied uncertainly, since my etiquette books had given me no indication what one calls a friendly duke. Or a duke friend, or whatnot.

"My colleagues in the Lords call me Leith. It will do, unless I can convince you to call me Gil, as my mother and aunts do."

"If you wish."

"I do, actually."

"All right, then . . . Gil."

"I like the sound of that, Shane."

We sat there for a moment, taking each other in, and then he nodded to me, and looked to Tommy.

"Right, then. Mr. Hurley, when you and your cousin come to London, may I call on you?"

I just stared at Gil, stunned. We all knew what this was. Far more than the careful request to exchange correspondence, this was an absolutely clear indication of intent. It was nothing less than the formal opening of a courtship: *"My intentions are indeed entirely honorable."*

Tommy grinned at me, then nodded gravely. "We would be delighted."

"And you, Shane?" Gil turned to me, his eyes searching my face.

"Delighted, indeed." I let out the breath I didn't know I'd been holding, then smiled at him.

"Glad to hear it." He took my hand then, and very carefully brought it up to his lips. For a second, I could hardly breathe, and I had the distinct impression he was feeling the same thing.

Oh, my. I understood now. The incident backstage had nothing to do with greasepaint and adrenaline, or atmospheric disturbance, and a great deal to do with the two of us. It was the first time in my life I realized that chaperones might be a practical matter and not simply an antiquated form. If Tommy and the good father hadn't been there, someone's virtue could have been in considerable peril . . . and I do not mean mine.

"Until London, then." I finally managed in a tiny thread of voice.

"Till London." Gil's voice was almost as strangled as my own as he gently let go of my hand, his fingers lingering for a few final seconds on mine before he turned and bowed to Tommy and Father Michael.

As he walked out, I ran my fingers over the charm and slowly pulled my breathing back under control. I was sad to see him go, of course, but almost relieved at the idea of being able to resume my normal existence without all of this confusion. *Truly.* I had months between now and London to sort out what all of this meant, and what I intended to do about it.

It was only after he was gone that I realized the lion

guardians of my virtue were snickering like naughty little boys.

"Heller and the duke, sitting in a tree . . ." Tommy had started a singsong, but broke off laughing.

"Would you ever like me to post the banns, Miss Ella?" asked the father.

" 'Heller and the duke, sitting in a tree,' " sang Montezuma, because he had to get in his word.

"Shut up!" I tossed a pillow at the boys, and I was laughing, too. "All's well that ends, gentlemen. And, of course, the great irony here is that the Juliets were never the problem. It was always the tenors."

Tommy laughed. "Maybe we'll just stick to baritones from now on."

"But I love an Irish tenor." Father Michael cleared his throat and started singing: *I've been a wild rover for many a year . . .*

Montezuma, of course, joined in, as Tommy laughed.

"And that, Father, is why you are working for God, and not us." I shook my head, and shot a glare at Montezuma. "Let's just enjoy our tea."

"Love the birdie!"

Epilogue

The Post from London

A packet of mail was waiting in my dressing room on our second night in San Francisco. *Xerxes* was a winner: General Shane leading the troops to excellent reviews and much praise for reviving a bit of Handel history. If I was ridiculously pleased to see the thick cream-colored envelope with the crest and *Leith House* on it, it was nobody's business, but my own. The first letter had arrived weeks before we left the City, and they came regularly. Like the others, tonight's epistle was in bold hand in midnight-blue ink, as always opening almost, but not quite, formally with *My Dear Shane*. It was mostly comprised of the sort of interesting and amusing tales from daily life you'd share with any faraway friend, with none of the sort of sweet talk one might expect from a man who was, after all, planning to formally pay court. But, as always, there was that last paragraph. This time:

> *I find that I am spending an inordinate*
> *amount of time these days trying to determine if*
> *your eyes are greenish blue, or bluish green.*
> *And wishing I might settle the question in per-*

son. I wonder if you may be given to any simi-
lar concerns. Please advise.

> *Yours with much esteem,*
> *G*

My reply, also to pattern, was much the same. Since I
was on tour, I could send him a cheerful and colorful
travel report of my days in San Francisco and vicinity. I
also included greetings from Tommy and Montezuma,
both of whom were greatly enjoying the city: Tommy for
the scenery, Montezuma for the grapes. Entirely friendly
and appropriate, with no hint that I might be looking forward to the said courtship. I could, for goodness' sakes,
have sent almost the same letter to Preston or Hetty, and
indeed many of the same stories were in my latest missives
to them. But I, too, allowed for just a tiny hint of something else at the end:

> *On occasion, I find myself looking out at the*
> *night sky and reflecting that we are both under*
> *the same stars, though very far away. And I*
> *think of your smile, which seems almost like a*
> *gift. I will very much enjoy seeing it when we*
> *play London.*

> *Yours very sincerely,*

> *S*

All absolutely true. And still, none of it yet enough to
make me surrender my sword, the stage or anything else in
the near future.